THE
THUNDER
BIRD

B. M. Bower

1st WORLD
LIBRARY
Literary Society

The Thunder Bird

B. M. Bower

© 1st World Library – Literary Society, 2005
PO Box 2211
Fairfield, IA 52556
www.1stworldlibrary.org
First Edition

LCCN: 2005906457

Softcover ISBN: 1-4218-1515-X
Hardcover ISBN: 1-4218-1415-3
eBook ISBN: 1-4218-1615-6

Purchase *"The Thunder Bird"*
as a traditional bound book at:
www.1stWorldLibrary.org/purchase.asp?ISBN=1-4218-1515-X

1st World Library Literary Society is a nonprofit
organization dedicated to promoting literacy by:

- Creating a free internet library accessible from any
  computer worldwide.
- Hosting writing competitions and offering book
  publishing scholarships.

CONTENTS

CHAPTER ONE

JOHNNY ASSUMES A DEBT OF HONOR

Since Life is no more than a series of achievements and failures, this story is going to begin exactly where the teller of tales usually stops. It is going to begin with Johnny Jewel an accepted lover and with one of his dearest ambitions realized. It is going to begin there because Johnny himself was just beginning to climb, and the top of his desires was still a long way off, and the higher you go the harder is the climbing. Even love does not rest at peace with the slipping on of the engagement ring. I leave it to Life, the supreme judge, to bear me out in the statement that Love must straightway gird himself for a life struggle when he has passed the flowered gateway of a woman's tremulous yes.

To Johnny Jewel the achievement of possessing himself of so coveted a piece of mechanism as an airplane, and of flying it with rapidly increasing skill, began to lose a little of its power to thrill. The getting had filled his thoughts waking and sleeping, had brought him some danger, many thrills, a good deal of reproach and much self-condemnation. Now he had it - that episode was diminishing rapidly in importance as it slid into the past, and Johnny was facing a problem quite as great, was harboring ambitions quite as dazzling, as when he rode a sweaty horse across the barren stretches of the Rolling R Ranch and dreamed the while of soaring far above the barrenness.

Well, he had soared high above many miles of barrenness. That dream could be dreamed no more, since its magic vapors had been dissipated in the bright sun of reality. He could no longer dream of flying, any more than he could build air castles over riding a horse. Neither could he rack his soul with thoughts of Mary V Selmer, wondering whether she would ever get to caring much for a fellow. Mary V had demonstrated with much frankness that she cared. He knew the feel of her arms around his neck, the look of her face close to his own, the sweet thrill of her warm young lips against his. He had bought her a modest little ring, and had watched the shine of it on the third finger of her tanned left hand when she left him - going gloveless that the ring might shine up at her.

The first episode of her life thus happily finished, Johnny was looking with round, boyish, troubled eyes upon the second.

"Long-distance call for you, Mr. Jewel," the clerk announced, when Johnny strolled into the Argonaut hotel in Tucson for his mail. "Just came in. The girl at the switchboard will connect you with the party."

Johnny glanced into his empty key box and went on to the telephone desk. It was Mary V, he guessed. He had promised to call her up, but there hadn't been any news to tell, nothing but the flat monotony of inaction, which meant failure, and Johnny Jewel never liked talking of his failures, even to Mary V.

"Oh, Johnny, is that you? I've been waiting and *waiting*, and I just wondered if you had enlisted and gone off to war without even calling up to say good-by. I've been perfectly *frantic*. There's something -"

"You needn't worry about me enlisting," Johnny broke in, his voice the essence of gloom. "They won't have me."

"Won't *have* - why, Johnny Jewel! How *can* the United States Army be so stupid? Why, I should think they would be glad to get -"

"They don't look at me from your point of view, Mary V." Johnny's lips softened into a smile. She was a great little girl, all right. If it were left to her, the world would get down on its marrow bones and worship Johnny Jewel. "Why? Well, they won't take me and my airplane as a gift. Won't have us around. They'll take me on as a common buck trooper, and that's all. And I can't afford -"

"Well, but Johnny! Don't they know what a perfectly wonderful flyer you are? Why, I should think -"

"They won't have me in aviation at all, even without the plane," said Johnny. "The papers came back to-day. I was turned down - flat on my face! Gol darn 'em, they can do without me now!"

"Well, I should say so!" cried Mary V's thin, indignant voice in his ear. "How perfectly idiotic! I didn't want you to go, anyway. Now you'll come back to the ranch, won't you, Johnny?" The voice had turned wheedling. "We can have the duckiest times, flying around! Dad'll give you a tremendously good -"

"You seem to forget I owe your dad three or four thousand dollars," Johnny cut in. "I'll come back to the ranch when that's paid, and not before."

"Well, but listen, Johnny! Dad doesn't look at it that way at all. He knows you didn't mean to let those horses be stolen. He doesn't feel you owe him anything at all, Johnny. Now we're engaged, he'll give you a good -"

"You don't get me, Mary V. I don't care what your father thinks. It's what I think that counts. This airplane of mine cost your dad a lot of good horses, and I've got to make that good to him. If I can't sell the darned thing and pay him up, I'll have to -"

"I suppose what I think doesn't count anything at all! I say you don't owe dad a cent. Now that you are going to marry me -"

"You talk as if you was an encumbrance your dad had to pay me to take off his hands," blurted Johnny distractedly. "Our being engaged doesn't make any difference -"

"Oh, doesn't it? I'm tremendously glad to know you feel that way about it. Since it doesn't make any difference whatever -"

"Aw, cut it out, Mary V! You know darn well what I meant."

"Why, certainly. You mean that our being engaged doesn't make a particle -"

"Say, *listen* a minute, will you! I'm going to pay your

B. M. Bower

dad for those horses that were run off right under my nose while I was tinkering with this airplane. I don't care what you think, or what old Sudden thinks, or what anybody on earth thinks! I know what I think, and that's a plenty. I'm going to make good before I marry you, or come back to the ranch.

"Why, good golly! Do you think I'm going to be pointed out as a joke on the Rolling R? Do you think I'm going to walk around as a living curiosity, the only thing Sudden Selmer ever got stung on? Oh - h, no! Not little Johnny! They can't say I got into the old man for a bunch of horses and the girl, and that old Sudden had to stand for it! I told your dad I'd pay him back, and I'm going to do it if it takes a lifetime.

"I'm calling that debt three thousand dollars - and I consider at that I'm giving him the worst of it. He's out more than that, I guess - but I'm calling it three thousand. So," he added with an extreme cheerfulness that proved how heavy was his load, "I guess I won't be out to supper, Mary V. It's going to take me a day or two to raise three thousand - unless I can sell the plane. I'm sticking here trying, but there ain't much hope. About three or four a day kid me into giving 'em a trial flight - and to-morrow I'm going to start charging 'em five dollars a throw. I can't burn gas giving away joy rides to fellows that haven't any intention of buying me out. They'll have to dig up the coin, after this - I can let it go on the purchase price if they do buy, you see. That's fair enough -"

"Then you won't even listen to dad's proposition?" Mary V's tone proved how she was clinging to the real issue. "It's a perfectly wonderful one, Johnny, and really, for your own good - and not because we are engaged in the least - you should at least consider it. If you insist on owing him money, why, I suppose you could pay him back a little at a time out of the salary he'll pay you. He will pay you a good enough salary so you can do it nicely -"

Johnny laughed impatiently. "Let your dad jump up my wages to a point where he can pay himself back, you mean," he retorted. "Oh - h, no, Mary V. You can't kid me out of this, so why keep on arguing? You don't seem to take me seriously. You seem to think this is just a whim of mine. Why, good golly! I should think it would be plain enough to you that I've got to do it if I want to hold up my head and look men in the face. It's - why, it's an insult to my self-respect and my honesty to even hint that I could do anything but what I'm going to do. The very fact that your dad ain't going to force the debt makes it all the more necessary that I should pay it.

"Why, good golly, Mary V! I'd feel better toward your father if he had me arrested for being an accomplice with those horse thieves, or slapped an attachment on the plane or something, than wave the whole thing off the way he's doing. It'd show he looked on me as a man, anyway.

"I'll be darned if I appreciate this way he's got of treating it like a spoiled kid's prank. I'm going to make him recognize the fact that I'm a *man*, by golly, and that I look at things like a man. He's got to be proud to have me in the family, before I come into the family. He ain't going to take me in as one more kid to look after. I'll come in as his equal in honesty and business ability, - instead of just a new fad of Mary V's -"

B. M. Bower

"Well, for gracious sake, Johnny! If you feel that way about it, why didn't you say so? You don't seem to care what I think, or how I feel about it. You don't seem to care whether you ever get married or not. And I'm sure I wasn't the one that did the proposing. Why, it will take years and *years* to square up with dad, if you insist on doing it in a regular business way -"

Johnny's harsh laugh stopped her. "You see, you do know where I stand, after all. If I let it slide, the way you want me to, that's exactly what you'd be thinking after awhile - that I never had squared up with your dad. You'd look down on me, and so would your father and your mother. They'd always be afraid I'd do some fool thing and sting your dad again for a few thousand."

"Well, of all the crazy talk! And I've gone to the trouble of coaxing dad to give you a share in the Rolling R instead of putting it in his will for me. And dad's going to do it -"

"Oh, no, he isn't. I don't want any share in the Rolling R. I'd go to jail before I'd take it."

Mary V produced woman's final argument. "If you cared anything at all for me, Johnny, when I ask you to come back and do what dad is willing to have you do, you'd do it. I don't see how you can be stubborn enough to refuse such a perfectly wonderful offer. You wouldn't, if you cared a snap about me. You act just as if you were sorry -"

"Aw, lay off that don't-care stuff!" Johnny growled indignantly. "Caring for you has got nothing to do with it, I tell you. It's just simply a question of what kinda mark I am. You know I care!"

"Well, then, if you do you'll come right over here. If you start now you can be here by sundown, and it's nice and quiet and no wind at all. You've absolutely no excuse, Johnny, and you know it. When dad's willing to forget about those horses -"

"When I come, your dad won't have anything to forget about," Johnny reiterated obstinately. "I do wish you'd look at the thing right!"

Mary V changed her tactics, relying now upon intimidation. "I shall begin to look for you in about an hour," she said sweetly. "I shall keep on looking till you come, or till it gets too dark. If you care anything about me, Johnny, you'll be here. I'll have dinner all ready, so you needn't wait to eat." Then she hung up.

Johnny rattled the hook impatiently, called hello with irritated insistence, and finally succeeded in raising Central's impersonal: "Number, please?" Whereupon he flung himself angrily out of the booth.

"Do you want to pay at this end?" The girl at the desk looked up at him with a gleam of curiosity. Mentally Johnny accused her of "listening in." He snapped an affirmative at her and waited until "long distance" told her the amount.

"Four dollars and eighty-five cents," she announced, giving him a pert little smile. Johnny flipped a small gold piece to the desk and marched off, scorning his fifteen cents change with the air of a millionaire.

Johnny was angry, grieved, disappointed, worried -

and would have been wholly miserable had not his anger so dominated his other emotions that he could continue mentally his argument against the attitude of Mary V and the Rolling R.

They refused to take him seriously, which hurt Johnny's self-esteem terribly. Were he older, were he a property owner, Sudden Selmer would not so lightly wave aside that debt. He would pay Johnny the respect of fighting for his just rights. But no - just because he was barely of age, just because he was Johnny Jewel, they all acted as though - why, darn 'em, they acted as though he was a kid offering to earn money to pay for a broken plate! And Mary V -

Well, Mary V was a great little girl, but she would have to learn some day that Johnny was master. He considered this as good a day as any for the lesson. Better, because he was really upholding his principles by not going to the ranch meekly submissive, because Mary V had announced that she would be looking for him. Johnny winced from the thought of Mary V, out on the porch, watching the sky toward Tucson for the black speck that would be his airplane; listening for the high, strident drone that would herald his coming. She would cry herself to sleep.

But she had deliberately sentenced herself to tears and disappointment, he told himself sternly. She must have known he was in earnest about not coming. She had no right to think she could kid him out of something big and vital to his honor. She ought to know him by this time.

Briefly he considered returning to the hotel and calling up the ranch, just to tell her not to look for him because he was not coming. But the small matter of paying the toll deterred him. It was humiliating to admit, even to himself, that he could not afford another long-distance conversation with Mary V, but he had come to the point in his finances where a two-bit piece looked large as a dollar. He would miss that small gold piece.

Since the government had refused to consider accepting his services and paying him a bonus for his plane, he would have to sell it - if he could.

There it sat, reared up on its two little wheels, its nose poked rakishly out of an old shed that had been remodelled to accommodate it, its tail sticking out at the other side so that it slightly resembled a turtle with its shell not quite covering its extremities. The Mexican boy whom Johnny had hired to watch the plane in his absence lay asleep under one wing. A faint odor of varnish testified to the heat of the day that was waning toward a sultry night.

Without disturbing the boy Johnny rolled a smoke and stood, as he had stood many and many a time, staring at his prize and wondering what to do with it. He had to have money. That was flat, final, admitting no argument. At a reasonable estimate, three thousand dollars were tied up in that machine. He could not afford to sell it for any less. Yet there did not seem to be a man in the country willing to pay three thousand dollars for it. It was a curiosity, a thing to come out and stare at, a thing to admire; but not to buy, even though Johnny had as an added inducement offered to teach the buyer to fly before the purchase price was taken from the bank.

The stalking shadow of a man moving slowly warned

B. M. Bower

Johnny of an approaching visitor. He did not trouble to turn his head; he even moved farther into the shed, to tighten a turnbuckle that was letting a cable sag a little.

"Hello, old top - how they using yuh?" greeted a voice that had in it a familiar, whining note.

Johnny's muscles stiffened. Hostility, suspicion, surprise surged confusingly through his brain. He turned as one who was bracing himself to meet an enemy, with a primitive prickling where the bristles used to rise on the necks of our cavemen ancestors.

CHAPTER TWO

AND THE CAT CAME BACK

"Why, hello, Bland," Johnny exclaimed after the first blank silence. "I thought you was tied up in a sack and throwed into the pond long ago!"

The visitor grinned with a sour droop to his mouth, a droop which Johnny knew of old. "But the cat came back," he followed the simile, blinking at Johnny with his pale, opaque blue eyes. "What yuh doing here? Starting an aviation school?"

"Yeah. Free instruction. Want a lesson?" Johnny retorted, only half the sarcasm intended for Bland; the rest going to the town that had failed to disgorge a buyer for what he had to sell.

"Aw, I suppose you think you could give me lessons, now you've learned to do a little straightaway flying without landing on your tail," Bland fleered, with the impatience of the seasoned flyer for the novice who thinks well of himself and his newly acquired skill. "Say, that was some bump you give yourself on the dome when we lit over there in that sand patch. I tried to tell yuh that sand looked loose -"

"Yes, you did - not! You was scared stiff. Your face

looked like the inside of a raw bacon rind!"

"Sure, I was scared. So would you of been if you'd a known as much about it as I knew. I knew we was due to pile up, when you grabbed the control away from me. You'll make a flyer, all right - and a good one, if yuh last long enough. But you can't learn it all in a day, bo - take it from me. Anyway, I got no kick to make. It was you and the plane that got the bumps. All I done was bite my tongue half off!"

Boy that he was, Johnny laughed over this. The idea of Bland biting his tongue tickled him and served to blur his antagonism for the tricky aviator who had played so large a part in his salvaging of this very airplane.

"Uh course you'll laugh - but you wasn't laughing then. I'll say you wasn't. I thought you was croaked. Cost something to repair the plane, too. I'm saying it did. Had to have a new propeller, and a new crank-case for the motor - cost the old man at the ranch close to three hundred dollars before I turned her over to him, ready to take the air again. That's including what he paid me, of course. But I guess you know what it cost, when he handed you the bill."

This was news to Johnny, news that made his soul squirm. Lying there sick at the Rolling R ranch, he had not known what was taking place. He had found his airplane ready to fly, when he was at last able to walk out to the corrals, but no one seemed to know how much the repairing had cost. Certainly Sudden Selmer himself had suffered a lapse of memory on the subject. All the more reason then why Johnny should repay his debt.

"What I'm wondering about is why you aren't in Los Angeles," he evaded the unpleasant subject awkwardly. "Old Sudden gave you money to go, and dumped you at the depot, didn't he? That's what Mary V told me."

"He did - and I missed my train. And while I was waiting for the next I must 'a' et something poison. I was awful sick. I guess it was ten days or so before I come to enough to know where I was. I've had hard luck, bo - I'll say I have. I was robbed while I was sick, and only for a tambourine queen I got acquainted with, I guess I'd 'a' died. They're treacherous as hell, though. Long as she thought I had money - oh, well, they's no use expecting kindness in this world. Or gratitude. I'm always helpin' folks out and gittin' kicked and cussed for my pay. Lookit the way I lived with snakes and lizards - lived in a cave, like a coyote! - to help you git this plane in shape. You was to take me to Los for pay - but I ain't there yet. I'm stuck here, sick and hungry - I ain't et a mouthful since last night, and then I only had a dish of sour beans that damn' Mex. hussy handed out to me through a window! Me, Bland Halliday, a flyer that has made his hundreds doing exhibition work; that has had his picture on the front page of big city papers, and folks followin' him down the street just to get a look at him! Me - why, a yellow dawg has got the edge on me for luck! I might better be dead -" His loose lips quivered. Tears of self-pity welled up into his pale blue eyes. He turned away and stared across the barren calf lot that Johnny used for a flying field.

Johnny began to have premonitory qualms of a sympathy which he knew was undeserved. Bland Halliday had got a square deal - more than a square deal; for Sudden, Johnny knew, had paid him generously for repairing the plane while Johnny was sick. Bland had undoubtedly squandered the money in one long debauch, and there was no doubt in Johnny's mind of Bland's reason for missing his train. He was a bum by nature and he would double-cross his own mother, Johnny firmly believed. Yet, there was Johnny's boyish sympathy that never failed sundry stray dogs and cats that came in his way. It impelled him now to befriend Bland Halliday.

"Well, since the cat's come back, I suppose it must have its saucer of milk," he grinned, by way of hiding the fact that the lip-quiver had touched him. "I haven't taken any nourishment myself for quite some time. Come on and eat."

He started back toward town, and Bland Halliday followed him like a lonesome pup.

On the way, Johnny took stock of Bland in little quick glances from the corner of his eyes. Bland had been shabby when Johnny discovered him one day on the depot platform of a tiny town farther down the line. He had been shabbier after three weeks in Johnny's camp, working on the airplane in hope of a free trip to the Coast. But his shabbiness now surpassed anything Johnny had known, because Bland had evidently made pitiful attempts to hide it. That, Johnny guessed, was because of the hussy Bland had mentioned.

Bland's shoes were worn through on the sides, and he had blackened his ragged socks to hide the holes. Somewhere he had got a blue serge coat, from which the lining sagged in frayed wrinkles. His pockets were torn down at the corners; buttons were gone, grease spots and beer stains patterned the cloth. Under the coat he wore a pink-and-white silk shirt, much soiled and with the neck frankly open, imitating sport style because of missing buttons. He looked what he was by nature; what he was by training, - a really skilful birdman, - did not show at all.

He begged a smoke from Johnny and slouched along, with an aimless garrulity talking of his hard luck, now curiously shot with hope. Which irritated Johnny vaguely, since instinct told him whence that hope had sprung. Still, sympathy made him kind to Bland just because Bland was so worthless and so miserable.

At a dingy, fly-infested place called "Red's Quick Lunch" whither Johnny, mindful of his low finances, piloted him, Bland ordered largely and complained because his "T bone" was too rare, and afterwards because it was tough. Johnny dined on "coffee and sinkers" so that he could afford Bland's steak and "French fried" and hot biscuits and pie and two cups of coffee. The cat, he told himself grimly, was not content with a saucer of milk. It was on the top shelf of the pantry, lapping all the cream off the pan!

Afterwards he took Bland to the hotel where his room was paid for until the end of the week, led him up there, produced an old suit of clothes that had not seemed to wear a sufficiently prosperous air for the owner of an airplane, and suggestively opened the door to the bathroom.

Bland took the clothes and went in, mumbling a fear that he would do himself mortal injury if he took a bath right after a meal.

"If you die, you'll die clean, anyway," Johnny told him grimly. So Bland took a bath and emerged looking almost respectable.

Johnny had brought his second-best shoes out, and Bland put them on, pursing his loose lips because the shoes were a size too small. But Johnny had thrown Bland's shoes out of the window, so Bland had to bear the pinching.

Johnny sat on the edge of the dresser smoking and fanning the smoke away from his round, meditative eyes while he looked Bland over. Bland caught the look, and in spite of the shoes he grinned amiably.

"I take it back, bo, what I said about gratitude. You got it, after all."

"Huh!" Johnny grunted. "Gratitude, huh?"

"I knowed you wouldn't throw down a friend, old top. I was in the dumps. A feller'll talk most any way when he's feeling the after effects, and is hungry and broke. Now I'm my own man again. What next? Name it, bo - I'm game."

"Next," said Johnny, "is bed, I guess. You're clean, now - you can sleep here."

Bland showed that he could feel the sentiment called compunction.

"Much obliged, bo - but I don't want to crowd you -"

"You won't crowd me," said Johnny drily, "I aim to sleep with the plane." Bland may have read Johnny's reason for sleeping with his airplane, but beyond one quick look he made no sign. "Still nuts over it - I'll say you are," he grunted. "You wait till you've been in the game long as I have, bo."

With a blanket and pillow bought on his way through the town, Johnny disposed himself for the night under the nose of the plane with the wheels of the landing gear at his back. He was not by nature a suspicious young man, but he knew Bland Halliday; and to know Bland was to distrust him.

He felt that he was taking a necessary precaution, now that he knew Bland was in Tucson. With the landing gear behind him, no one could move the airplane in the night without first moving him.

Now that he thought of it, Bland had been left fifty miles farther down the line, to catch his train. Tucson was a perfectly illogical place for him to be in, even for the purpose of carousing. One would certainly expect him to hurry to the city of his desires and take his pleasure there. Johnny decided that Bland must still have an eye on the plane.

That he was secretly envious of Bland as an aviator did not add to his mental comfort. Bland could speak with slighting familiarity of "the game," and assume a boredom not altogether a pose. Bland had drunk deep and satisfyingly of the cup which Johnny, to save his honor, must put away from him after a tantalising sip or two. Not until Bland had said, "Wait till you've been in the game as long as I have," had Johnny realized to the full just what it would mean to him to part with his airplane without being accepted by the government as an aviator.

At the Rolling R, when his conscience debt to Sudden pressed so heavily, he had figured very nicely and had found the answer to his problem without much trouble. To enlist as an aviator with his airplane, or to sell the plane in Tucson, turn the proceeds over to Sudden to pay his debt and enlist as an aviator without the machine, had seemed perfectly simple. Either way would be making good the mistakes of his past and paving the way for future achievements. Parting with the plane had not promised to so wrench the very heart out of him when he fully expected to fly faster and farther in airplanes owned by the government; faster and farther toward the goal of all red-blooded young males: glory or wealth, the hero's wreath of laurel or the smile of dame Fortune.

Mary V stood on the heights waiting for him, as Johnny had planned and dreamed. He would come back to her a captain, maybe - perhaps even a major, in these hot times of swift achievement. They would all be proud to shake his hand, those jeering ones who called him Skyrider for a joke. Captain Jewel would not have sounded bad at all. But -

There is no dodging the finality of Uncle Sam's no. They had not wanted Johnny Jewel to fly for fame and his country's honor. And if he sold his own airplane, how then would he fly? How could he ever hope to be in the game as long as Bland had been? How could he do anything but go back meekly to the Rolling R Ranch and ride bronks for Mary V's father, and be hailed as Skyrider still, who had no more any hope of riding the sky?

Gloom at last plumbed the depths of Johnny's soul, and showed him where grew the root of his unalterable determination to combat Mary V's plan to have him at the ranch. Much as he loved Mary V he would hate going back to the dull routine of ranch life. (And after all, a youth like Johnny loves nothing quite so much as his air castles.) As a rider of bronks he was spoiled, he who had ridden triumphant the high air lanes. He had talked of paying his debt to Sudden, he had talked of his self-respect and his honesty and his pride - but above and beyond them all he was fighting to save his castle in the air. Debt or no debt, he could never go back to the Rolling R and be a rancher. Lying there under his airplane and staring up at the starred purple of the night he knew that he could not go back.

Yet he knew too that once he had sold his airplane he would be almost as helpless financially as Bland Halliday, unless he returned to the only trade he knew, the trade of riding bronks and performing the various other duties that would be his portion at the Rolling R.

Johnny pictured himself back at the Rolling R; pictured himself riding out with the boys at dawn after horses, or sweating in the corrals, spitting dust and profanity through long, hot hours. There was a lure, of course; a picturesque, intangible attraction that calls to the wild blood of youth. But not as calls this other life which he had tasted. There was no gainsaying the fact - ranch life had grown too tame, too stale for Johnny Jewel. And there was no gainsaying that other fact - that Mary V would have to reconcile herself to being an aviator's wife, if she would mate with Johnny.

He went to sleep thinking bitterly that neither he nor Mary V need concern themselves at present over that point. It would be some time before the issue need be faced, judging from Johnny's present prospects.

CHAPTER THREE

JOHNNY WOULD DO STUNTS

Bland woke him, just as day was coming. A new Bland, fresh shaven, - with Johnny's razor, - and with a certain languid animation in his manner that was in sharp contrast to his extreme dejection of the night before.

"Thought I'd come out and see if you was going to make a flight this morning," he said. "It's a good morning for it, bo. How's she working, these days? Old man at the ranch wouldn't let me try her out after I'd fixed her up; said you was too sick to have the motor going. So I couldn't be sure I'd made a good job of it. Give you any trouble?"

Johnny sat up and knuckled his eyes, his mouth wide open in a capital O. It seemed to him that Bland had his nerve, and he guessed shrewdly that the aviator was simply making sure of his breakfast. When cats come back they have a fashion of hanging around the kitchen, he remembered. Oh, well, there was nothing to be gained by being nasty and even Bland's company was better than none.

"Hey, ain't yuh awake yet? I asked yuh how the motor's acting."

"O - o - h, aw-righ!" yawned Johnny, blinking around for his boots. "I ain't been flying much. Just flew over here from the ranch, and a little circle now and then when something come along that looked like money. I wanted to keep her in good shape in case the gover'ment -"

"Trying to sell it back to the gover'ment, huh? I coulda told yuh, bo, they wouldn't take it as a gift. She's a back number now - a has-been, from the gover'ment viewpoint. Why don't you keep it? What yuh want to sell it for, f'r cat's sake? She's a gold mine if you know how to work it, bo - take it from me."

"Well, I wish to thunder you'd show me the gold, then," Johnny retorted crossly, pulling on his boots.

"Lend us a smoke, will yuh, old top? The money's here, all right, if yuh just know how to get it out. And flying for the gover'ment ain't the way. I'll say a man's got to be his own boss if he wants to pull down real money. Long as you're workin' for somebody else, he's getting the velvet. You ain't, believe me. And the gover'ment as a boss -"

"Well, good golly, come to the point!" snapped Johnny. "How can I make money with this plane?" He gave it a disgruntled look, and turned to Bland. "She's a bird of a millionaire's toy, if you ask me," he said. "She's a fiend for gas and oil, and every time you turn 'er around there's some darned thing to be fixed or replaced. I'm about broke, trying to keep her up till I can sell out. It's coffee and sinkers for you, old timer, if you're going to eat on me. Another meal like you had last night, and we'll both have to skip a few in order to buy gas to joy-ride some cheap sport that lets on he's thinking of buying. I suppose your idea is -"

"F'r cat's sake give me a chance to tell yuh! Course you'll go broke trying to support the plane. You're goin' at it backwards. Make the plane support you. That's my idea. And you do it by exhibition flying for money - not sailin' around giving the whole damn country a free treat.

"I know - you think I'm a bum and all that; maybe you think I'm a crook, fer all I know. And you turn up your nose at anything I say. But lemme tell yuh, old top, I ain't a D. and O. because I never made any money flyin'. It's because I blowed what I made. And it's because I made so damn' much it went to my head and made a fool outa me. Listen here, bo: I bought me a Stutz outa what I earned flyin' in one season - and I blowed money right and left and smashed the car and like to of broke my neck, and had to pay damages to the other feller that peeled my roll down to the size of a pencil. The point is, it took *money* to do them things, didn't it? And I made it flyin' my own plane. That's what you want to soak into your system. *I made big money flying.* What I done with the money don't need to worry you - you ain't copyin' me for morals.

"Now what you want to do is learn some stunts, first off. You learn to loop and tail-slide and the fallin' leaf, and to write your name, and them things. It ain't so hard - not for a guy like you that ain't got sense enough to be afraid of nothing. The way you went off in that plane with the girl made my hair stand on end, and that's no kiddin', neither. If you'd had a fear germ in your system you wouldn't 'a' done that. But you done it, and got away with it, is the point. And you been gittin' away with it right along - and you not knowin' your motor any more'n I know ridin' on a horse!"

"Aw, say! That's goin' too far," protested Johnny, but Bland gave him no heed.

"You learn the stunts - early in the morning when there ain't the hull town out to rubber - and then pull off an exhibition or two. Seventy-five dollars is the least you ever need to expect. Don't go in the air for less. From that up - depends on how spectacular you are. The public loves to watch for the death fall. That's what they pay to see - not hopin' you get killed, but not wantin' to miss seeing it in case yuh do. And with this the only airplane around here - why, say, bo, it's a cinch!"

Johnny fanned the smoke away from his face and eyed Bland with lofty tolerance. "And where do you expect to come in? You needn't kid yourself into hoping I'll take you for a self-forgetful martyr person. What's the little joker, Bland?"

Bland turned his pale, opaque stare upon Johnny for a minute. "Aw, for cat's sake, gimme the doubt, bo! I'm human in more ways than tryin' to see how much booze I kin lap up. It's a chance I want to start fresh. This bumming around ain't getting me anything. I'm sick of it. You gotta be learnt to do exhibition stuff, and I'm the guy that can learn yuh. You'll want a mechanician to keep your motor in shape. I can *make* a motor, gimme the tools. You want somebody that knows the game to kinda manage things. You're Skyrider Johnny, same as the boys at the ranch calls yuh. Yon gotta have a flunkey, ain't yuh? I'm willin' to be it. I'll change my name, so nobody needs to know it's Bland Halliday. Or you can gimme a share in the net profits, and I'll keep the name and make it pull things our way. They's no use talking, bo, I've got the goods! The name Bland Halliday is a trademark for flyin' - and never mind if it also stands for damfool. I'll brace up and give yuh the best I got. Honest, that's what I want - a chance to get on my feet again. I'd ruther help you fly your plane than fly one of my own. I'd run amuck agin if I owned anything I could raise money on.

"If you think I tried to do you dirt, back there in the desert, bo, you're wrong. Ab-so-lutely. I thought you was fixing to double-cross me, and git away with the plane and leave me there. It got my goat - I'll say it did - that desert stuff. So I hid the gas, so you couldn't go off and leave me. But that's behind us. You can give me a chance now to straighten up, and I can put you in the way to make big money. You think it over, bo. They's no great hurry, and we can make a flight now and see how she stacks up. Be a sport - go fill up the tank and let's go."

Johnny ground the cigarette stub under his heel in the dirt, shrugged his shoulders with a fine imitation of perfect indifference, and yawned. He would think over Bland's idea. He did not, of course, intend to fall for anything that did not look like good business, and he was not at all anxious to have Bland for a partner. Indeed, having Bland for a partner was about the last thing Johnny would ever expect himself to do. Still, there was no harm in letting Bland down easy. A flight or two, maybe, would give Johnny some good pointers. He had learned much from Bland, in a very short time, he admitted readily to himself. He could learn more, and he could let Bland go over the motor. By that time he would maybe have a buyer. If not, he would have time to decide about exhibition flying.

Johnny did not know that as he went after gas his step was springier than it had been for a long, long while. He did not know why it was that he whistled while he filled the torpedo-shaped tank - indeed, Johnny did not even know that he whistled, nor that it was the first time since he had worked over his plane down at Sinkhole Camp when all his dreams were bright, and bad luck had not knocked at his door. Yet he did whistle while he made ready for flight, and his eyes were big and round and eager, said he moved with the impatient energy of a youth going to his favorite game. These signs Mary V would have recognized immediately; Johnny did not know the signs existed.

Bland helped himself to a pair of new coveralls of Johnny's and tinkered with the motor. Johnny went around the plane, testing cables and trying to conceal even from himself his new hope of keeping it.

"All right, bo," Bland announced at last. "Kick the block away and let's run her out. She sounds pretty fair - better than I expected."

It pleased Johnny that Bland seemed to take it as a matter of course that he should occupy the front seat. The last time they had flown together, Bland had occupied it perforce, with Johnny and two guns behind him. After all, Johnny reflected, he would not have been so suspicious of Bland if Mary V had not influenced him. And every one knows that girls take notions with very little reason for the foundation. Bland was a bum, but the little cuss seemed to want to make good, and a man would be pretty poor stuff that wouldn't help a fellow reform.

With that comfortable readjustment of his mental attitude toward the birdman, Johnny strapped himself in, pulled down his goggles while Bland eased in the motor. He saw Bland glance to right and left with the old vigilance. He felt the testing of controls, the unconscious tensing of nerves for the start. They raced down the calf pasture, nosed upward and went whirring away from a dwindling earth, straight toward the heart of the dawn.

It was like drinking of some heady wine that blurs one's troubles and pushes them far down over the horizon. Johnny forgot that he had problems to solve or worries that nagged at him incessantly. He forgot that Mary V, away off there to the southwest, had probably cried herself to sleep the night before because he had disappointed her. He was flying up and away from all that. He was soaring free as a bird, and the rush of a strong, clean wind was in his face. The roar of the motor was a great, throbbing harmony in his ears. For a little while the world would hold nothing else.

They were climbing, climbing, writing an invisible spiral in the air. Bland half turned his head, and Johnny caught his meaning with telepathic keenness. They were going to loop, and Bland wanted him to yield the control and to watch closely how the thing was done.

They swooped like a hawk that has seen a meadow mouse amongst the grass. They climbed steeply, swung clean over, so that the earth was oddly slipping past far above their heads; swung down, flattened out and flew straight. It was glorious.

A second time Bland looped, and yet again. It was

exactly as Johnny had known it would be. He who had flown so long in his day-dreaming, who had performed wonderful acrobatics in his imagination, felt the sensation old, accustomed, milder even than in his dreams.

Once more, and he did the loop himself, hardly conscious of Bland's presence. Bland turned his head, signalling, and did a flop, righted, and was flying straight in the opposite direction. Again, and flew southeast by the sun. They practised that manoeuver again and again before Johnny felt fairly sure of himself, but once he did it he was one proud young man!

All this while the familiar landmarks were slipping behind them. Tucson was out of sight, had they thought to look for it. And all this while the sturdy motor was humming its song of force triumphant. Subsequently it stuttered faintly in expressing itself. Triumph was there, but it was not so joyously sure of itself. Bland glided, cocking an anxious ear to listen while he slowed the motor. It was there, the stutter - more pronounced than before; and once that pulsing power begins to flag a little and grow uncertain, there is but one thing to do.

They glided another ten miles or so before Bland picked a spot that looked safe for landing. They had one ill-chosen landing still vivid in their memory, and Johnny carried a long, white scar along the side of his head and a tenderness of the scalp to assist him in remembering.

Wherefore they came down circumspectly in a flat little field beside a flat little stream, with a huddle of flat dwellings drawn back shyly behind a thin group of willows. They came down gently, bouncing toward the willows as though they meant to drive up to the very doorway of the nearest hut. As they came on, their great wings out-spread rigidly, the propeller whirring at slackened speed, the motor sputtering unevenly, the doorway spewed forth three fat squaws and some naked papooses who fled shrieking into the brush behind the willows.

CHAPTER FOUR

MARY V TO THE RESCUE

Mary V Selmer was a young woman of quick impulses, a complete disdain for consequences as yet unseen, and a disposition to have her own way, to override obstacles man-made or sent by fate to thwart her desires. Ask any man on the Rolling R Ranch, where Mary V was born; they will bear witness that this is true.

Mary V had fired the first gun in the battle of wills. She had told Johnny Jewel that she would expect him to fly straight to the ranch - if Johnny loved her. Mary V did not mean to seem dictatorial; she merely wanted Johnny to come back to the Rolling R, and she took what seemed to her to be the surest means of bringing him. So, serenely sure of Johnny's love, she had no misgivings when the sun went down and those wonderful, opal tints of the afterglow filled all the sky.

Johnny would be hungry, of course. She wheedled Bedelia, the cook, into letting her keep the veal roast hot in the oven of the gasoline range. She herself spread one of mommie's cherished lunch cloths on Bedelia's little square table in the kitchen alcove, where she and Johnny could be alone while he ate. She dipped generously into the newest preserves and filled a glass dish full for him. She raided the great refrigerator, closing her eyes to the morrow's reckoning. Johnny would be hungry, Johnny was a sort of prodigal, and the fatted calf should be killed figuratively and the ring placed upon his finger.

She told her mommie and her dad that Johnny was coming, and that everything was all right, and Johnny would be sensible and settle down now, because he was not going to enlist after all. She kissed them both and flew back to the kitchen because she had thought of something else that Johnny would like to eat.

This, you must understand, was while Johnny was feeding Bland, - and himself, - in "Red's Quick Lunch", and worrying because Bland tactlessly chose such expensive fare as T-bone steak and French fried. She was out on the porch, watching the sky toward Tucson and looking rather wistful, while Johnny was generously sorting out clothes for Bland and insisting upon the bath and the change before Bland should sleep in Johnny's bed. Mary V, you will observe, had no telepathic sense at all.

She watched while dark came and brought its star canopy, - and did not bring Johnny. Long after she saw the rim of hills draw back into vague shadows, she remained on the porch and listened for the hum of the airplane speeding toward her. He would come, of course; he loved her.

Johnny did love her more than he had ever loved any one in his life, but a man's love is not like a woman's love, they say.

"He must have had some trouble with his motor,"

Mary V observed optimistically to her sleepy parents, when their early bedtime arrived. "I'm going to leave the lights all on, so he'll see where to land. It will be tremendously exciting to hear him come buzzing up in the dark. It'll sound exactly like an air raid - only he won't have any bombs to drop."

"He'll have himself to drop," her mother tactlessly pointed out. "I guess he won't do much flying around in the dark, Mary V. Not if he's got sense enough to come in when it rains. You go to bed, and don't be setting out there in the mosquitoes. They're thick, to-night."

"Well, for gracious sake, mom! It's perfectly easy to fly at night. Over in France they *always* -"

"It's the lightin' I'm talking about," her mother interrupted with that terrible logic that insists upon stating unpleasant truths, "And this ain't France, Mary V. You go on to bed. I'm going to turn out the lights."

"And have him bump right into the house? A person would think you wanted Johnny to smash himself all to pieces again! And it isn't going to cost anything so terrible to leave the lights on for another little minute, mom! A few cents' worth of gas will run the dynamo -"

"For land's sake, Mary V, don't go into a tantrum just at bedtime. Who's talking about cost? Your father can't sleep with all the lights turned on in the house, and neither can I. And it ain't a particle of use for you to sit up and wait for Johnny; he won't come to-night, and you needn't look for him."

Mary V did not want to hear a statement of that kind, even if it were a mere argumentative flourish on the part of a selfish, unsympathetic parent who would jeopardize a person's life rather than annoy herself with a light or two burning. Mary V immediately had what her mother called a tantrum. That is, she began to cry and to declaim unreasonably that no one cared whether Johnny smashed himself all to pieces in the dark - that perhaps certain persons wished that Johnny would fall and be killed, just so they could sleep!

Her mother may have been weak in discipline, but now that Mary V was spoiled to the extent of having tantrums, she proved herself a sensible, level-headed sort of woman. She went away to her bed quite unmoved by the tears and self-pity, and left Mary V alone.

"You turn out all the lights except the porch light, Mary V," Old Sudden himself commanded from his bedroom door. "I guess if he comes, one light will be as good as a dozen. You better do as your mother tells you. The kid's got more sense than to tackle flying from Tucson after sundown. If I thought he didn't have, I'd kick him off the ranch!"

This perfectly heartless statement served to distract Mary V's mind from her mother's lack of feeling. She obediently turned out the lights, - all the lights, since they meant to kill Johnny in cold blood! - and wept anew upon the darkened porch, while swarms of mosquitoes hummed just without the screen, sending a slim scout through now and then to torment Mary V, who spatted her chiffon-covered arms viciously and wished that she were dead, since no one had any feelings or any heart or any conscience on that ranch.

It was midnight before healthy youth demanded sleep and dulled her half-feigned agonies of self-pity. It was morning before she began to feel really uneasy about Johnny. After her tantrum she slept late, so that when she awoke it was past time for Johnny's arrival, supposing he had started at sunrise, which she now admitted to herself was the most sensible time for the flight. Eight o'clock - and he must have started, else he would have called her up on the 'phone and told her he was not coming. For that matter, he would have called up the night before if he had not meant to do as she wanted him to do. Of course, Johnny was awfully stubborn sometimes, and he might have waited until morning, just to worry her. But he would have called up if he hadn't intended to come. A little thing like hanging up her receiver would not bother him, she argued, and a little obstacle like long-distance toll never occurred to Mary V, whose idea of poverty was vague indeed.

He must have started this morning, at the latest. And he should have been here before now. To make sure that he had not come while she slept Mary V went to a window overlooking the open space between the house and corrals. It was empty, but to make doubly sure she asked Bedelia. For answer, Bedelia threatened to quit, declaring shrilly that she would not work where nothing was safe under lock and key, and a girl might work her fingers to the bone putting up jell for spoiled, ungrateful, meddlesome Matties to waste, and so forth and so on.

Mary V wisely withdrew from the kitchen without having her question answered. She asked no more questions of any one. In silk kimono and Indian moccasins, one of her pet incongruities, she forthwith explored the yard down by the corrals which the bunk house had hidden from her view. There was no sign of Johnny Jewel's airplane anywhere. Mary V was thorough, even to the point of looking for tracks of the little wheels, but at last she was convinced, and returned to the porch to digest the ominous fact of Johnny's failure to arrive.

He must have started, - she would not admit the possibility that he had deliberately ignored her ultimatum, - but she would make sure. So she called Tucson on the telephone and was presently in conversation with the clerk at Johnny's hotel.

Hotel clerks are usually quite positive that they know what they are supposed to know about their guests. This clerk interviewed somebody while Mary V held the line, and later returned to assure her that Mr. Jewel had been seen leaving the lobby the night before, and had not returned. A strange young gentleman had occupied Mr. Jewel's room. No, Mr. Jewel had not been seen since last evening. The clerk was positive, but since Mary V's voice was young and feminine, he permitted her to hold the line while he called the night clerk to the 'phone. The result was disheartening. Mr. Jewel had brought in a young man, and later had left the hotel. The young man had gone out very early and neither had returned. Could he do anything else for her?

Mary V thanked him coldly and hung up the receiver, mentally calling the clerk names that were not flattering. Why in the world did he keep harping on that one fact that Johnny had gone out and had not come back? Why didn't he know where Johnny had gone? What, for gracious sake, was a hotel clerk for, if not to tell a person what she wanted to know? The strange young man who had slept in Johnny's room meant nothing at all to Mary V just then.

She had a dislike of creating unnecessary excitement, but it did seem as though something ought to be done about Johnny. All her faith was pinned to the fact that he had let her final word stand uncontradicted; he had not told her he would not come. She went outside and stared for awhile in the direction of Tucson, turning with a little start when her mother spoke just behind her.

"Did Johnny tell you he was coming, Mary V?"

"My goodness, mom! Of *course*, he - well, it was just the same as saying he would. I told him he had to come and I'd expect him, and he didn't say he wouldn't. Why, for gracious sake, do you suppose I went and fixed his din - dinner - ?" Mary V gulped down a sob she had not suspected was present.

"Well, there, now, don't cry about it. You'll have plenty better reasons to cry after you're married to him. Seems to me the boy's changed considerable, if he comes and goes at the crook of your finger, Mary V. Johnny's most as stubborn as you be, if I'm any judge. If I was in your place, Mary V, I'd 'phone and find out if he's started, before I commenced crying because he was late."

"I did 'phone. And he wasn't at the hotel -"

"Land sakes, child, I heard you! You might as well have asked what the weather was like. If I was you I'd ask if his airplane is there. If it is, there's no sense in you straining your eyes looking for it. If it ain't, he's likely on the way somewhere. But from what I heard of your talk last night, and from what I know about Johnny -"

"For pity's *sake*, mom! If you listened in -"

"There now, Mary V, you shouldn't object to your own mother overhearing anything you've got to say. And if you expect me to clap my hands over my cars and start on a long lope across the desert the minute you begin to 'phone -"

Mary V laughed and gave her mother a bear-hug. Mommie was a plump matron, and the idea of her loping across the desert with her hands over her ears was funny. "You do have tremendously sensible ideas, mommie, though you simply do not understand Johnny as I do. I am perfectly positive that he would not disappoint me. However, I'll just make sure when he started. I'm so afraid of some horrible accident -"

"Well, you 'phone first, before you begin to borrow trouble," her mother advised her shrewdly. "I know if you had laid down the law to me the way you did to Johnny, I'd stay away if it was the last thing I did on earth. And Johnny -"

Mary V called Tucson again, and mommie subsided so as not to interrupt. There was a delay while the hotel clerk obligingly sent a boy over to where Johnny kept his airplane. While she waited for his ring, Mary V went restlessly out to watch the sky toward Tucson. Half an hour slipped away. Mary V was just declaring pettishly that she could walk to Tucson and find out, while she waited for that idiotic clerk, when he called her. Mary V listened, hung up the receiver with trembling fingers, and went to find her mother in the kitchen.

"Mommie, the plane is gone, and they are almost sure he went last night, because he was seen going that way after he left the hotel. So he did start, just as I told him to do - and something awful has happened to him - and where's dad?"

Mary V's father, whom men for some unaccountable reason called "Sudden" when he was not present, crawled out from under the rear end of his battered touring car when Mary V's moccasins and the fluttering hem of blue kimono moved within his range of vision. Sudden's face was smudged with black grease and the dust of the desert, and in his hand was a crescent wrench worn shiny where it had nipped nuts and bolts.

"You musta done some fancy driving the other day," he greeted his anxious-faced daughter. "Didn't you know you was sliding a wheel every time you threw on the brake? Wonder to me is you didn't skid off a grade somewhere!" He hitched himself into a new and uncomfortable pose and set the wrench on a nut, screwing his well-fed face into an agonized grimace while he put his full strength into the turn. "If I could find a man that I'd trust my life with on these roads, I'd have me a chauffeur," he grumbled for the millionth time. "That reformed blacksmith musta welded these nuts on to the bolts," he added, and muttered something savage when the wrench slipped and he barked a knuckle. "Well, what yuh want? Go ahead and have it, or do it - only don't stand watching me when I'm trying to -" He gritted his teeth, threw the wrench away and picked up another. "Go ask your mother," he exclaimed. "Tell her I'll let you if she will."

At another time Mary V would have deeply resented the implication that she never approached her dad save when she wanted something; or more likely she would have stated her want before her dad had time to speak. Just now she was hopefully watching a buzzard that sailed on outstretched, rigid wings, high in the sky. It seemed to be circling toward the ranch, and it looked like an airplane flying very high. Mary V's heart forgot to beat while she watched it. But the buzzard sighted something, flapped its wings and went off in another direction, and the girl winced as though some one had dropped a leaden weight on her chest.

"Dad!" The voice did not sound like Mary V's, and her father ducked his head out where he could look up at her with startled attention. "We must have the car - and all the boys - and get out and find Johnny. He - he started in his airplane, to come to the ranch. And they haven't seen him since last night, and - and you know what happened at Sinkhole!"

Sudden got heavily to his feet and stood looking down at her, his whimsical mouth slack with dismay. But he pulled himself together and took the dominant, cool initiative which was so much a part of his nature.

"You say he started last night. How do you know?"

"The hotel clerk - I 'phoned - oh, don't start cross-questioning, dad! I *know*! His plane is gone, and - he should have been here last night! He was alone, and - oh, get the boys and start them out! There isn't a minute - he may be dead somewhere - or hurt -"

"Now, now, we'll only bungle things by getting excited, Mary V. I'll send the cook after the boys while I fix this brake and fill up the gas tank. You go get some clothes on, and tell your mother to get the emergency box ready, in case he's hurt. And if you can be calm enough, you 'phone to Tucson to the sheriff, and tell him to send out a party from that end, and work this way. Tell them to scatter out, but keep the general airline to the ranch. We'll start in from here. And for Lord's sake, baby, don't look like that! We'll find him - and the chances are he's all right; maybe landed for some little repair or something. Now hurry along, if you expect to go with me, because I won't wait a minute."

Mary V looked at her dad, standing there grease-smudged and calm and capable, and half the terror went out of her eyes to leave room for hope. Her dad had such a way of gathering up the threads of logic and drawing them firmly into coherent action - just as a skilled driver would take the slack reins of a runaway team and pull them down to a steady pace. It seemed to her that Johnny Jewel was half found before ever her dad laid down the wrench and began unscrewing the cap of the gas tank.

Like a fluttering bluebird she flew back to the house to do his bidding. Excited she was, and worried, and more than ever inclined to exclamation points and unfinished sentences; but she was no longer panic-stricken. She was the Mary V who would move heaven and earth and slosh all the water out of our five oceans in her headlong determination to do what she had set out to do.

In two minutes she had her mother and Bedelia rushing

B. M. Bower

around like scared hens, trying to collect the things she wanted to take for Johnny's comfort and welfare. In three she was bullying the long-distance operator. In five she was laying down the law to the sheriff, just as though he were one of her father's cowpunchers.

"Get all the men you can," she commanded, when she had reached the details, "and scatter them like a round-up. You know how, of course. And keep them within sight of each other, and make them keep watch in every hollow and wash and high brush - because an airplane might not show up very plainly if it's all smashed. And 'phone to all the places down this way, and make all the men you can get out and help. It's tremendously important that you find Mr. Jewel immediately, because he may be badly hurt. My father will give a thousand dollars to the man who finds him. You tell that to every one, Mr. Sheriff, will you, please? And say that the Rolling R will pay well for the time of those who aren't lucky enough to win the reward. We will pay every man twenty-five dollars that goes out. And have an automobile follow you, with a doctor in it, to take care of John - Mr. Jewel, when he is found. We will start all our riders out from here, and ride until we meet you. Now hurry! Don't stop for a lot of red tape and orders and things - get right out on the trail. And don't forget the thousand dollars reward." Just when the sheriff was saying "Aw right - goo'by," Mary V thought of something else.

"Be sure and have every man carry an extra canteen for Mr. Jewel. Injured men are always tremendously thirsty. And don't forget that every man will get twenty-five dollars, and the man that finds him -"

The sheriff had hung up, which was rude of him. Mary

V had several other little suggestions to make - but men never do want to be told anything, especially by a woman. Mary V was glad she had not been permitted to say that the sheriff would of course receive an especially attractive reward. He could go without, now, just for his smartness.

The Rolling R boys, hastily summoned by the cook who had galloped off without removing his flour-sack apron, came racing in and saddled fresh mounts. In a surprisingly short time they were filling canteens and gathering in a restive circle around the big touring car where the boss sat behind the wheel, and Mary V, fidgeting on the seat beside him, was telling them all for gracious sake to hurry up and get started, and not fool around until dark.

Bill Hayden got his orders, leaning down from his horse so that Mary V's impatient young voice should not submerge her father's in Bill's big, sun-peeled ears. "All right - better scatter out right now, soon as we git past the fence. You foller along about in the middle." He wheeled and was gone, overtaking the boys who were already starting for the gate, which little Curley held open until the last man should pass.

Sudden stepped on the starter, the big car began to gurgle. The search was on. A hundred men were presently combing the desert land and looking for an airplane that had not flown that way - just because Johnny Jewel was true to his supreme purpose in life. And just because Johnny's whole heart and soul were set upon repaying a conscience debt to Mary V's father, Mary V herself was innocently saddling his conscience with a still greater debt. For that is the way

Fate loves to set us playing at cross-purposes with each other.

CHAPTER FIVE

GODS OR SOMETHING

"Well, here we are," Johnny announced with more cheerfulness than the occasion warranted. "Now what?"

Bland was staring slack-jawed after the squaws. "Wasn't them Injuns?" he wanted to know, and his voice showed some anxiety. "We want to get outa here, bo, while the gittin's good. You bring any guns?" His pale eyes turned to Johnny's face. "I'll bet they've gone after the rest of the bunch, and we don't want to be here when they git back. I'll say we don't!"

Johnny laughed at him while he climbed down. "We made a dandy landing anyway," he said. "What ails that darned motor? She didn't do that yesterday."

Bland grunted and straddled out over the edge of the cockpit, keeping an eye slanted toward the brush fringe. What Johnny did not know about motors would at any other time have stirred him to acrimonious eloquence. Just now, however, a deeper problem filled his mind. Could he locate the fault and correct it before that brush-fringe belched forth painted warriors bent on massacre? He pushed up his goggles and stepped forward to the motor.

"I put in new spark plugs just the other day," Johnny volunteered helpfully. "Maybe a connection worked loose - or something." He got up on the side opposite Bland, meaning to help, but Bland would have none of his assistance.

"Say, f'r cat's sake, keep a watch out for Injuns and leave me alone! I can locate the trouble all right, if I don't have to hang on to my skelp with both hands. You got a gun?"

"Yeah. Back in Tucson I have," Johnny suppressed a grin. Bland's ignorance, his childlike helplessness away from a town tickled him. "But that's all right, Bland. We'll make 'em think we're gods or something. They might make you a chief, Bland - if they don't take a notion to offer you up as a burnt offering to some other god that's got it in for yuh."

Bland, testing the spark plugs hastily, one after the other, dropped the screwdriver. "Aw, f'r cat's sake, lay off that stuff," he remonstrated nervously. "Fat chance we got of godding over Injuns this close to a town! They're wise to white men. Quit your kiddin', bo, and keep a watch out." And he added glumly, "Spark plugs is O.K. Maybe it's the timer. I'll have to trace it up. Quit turning your back on that brush! You want us both to git killed? Hand me out that small wrench."

"Say, I know what ailed them squaws, Bland. Gods is right. You know what they thought? They took us for their Thunder Bird lighting. I'll bet they're making medicine right now, trying to appease the Bird's wrath. And say, listen here, Bland. If they do come at us, all we've got to do is start up and buzz at 'em. There ain't an Injun on earth could face that."

Bland lifted a pasty face from his work. "Fat chance," he lamented. "You'd oughta brought your gun. Back there at Sinkhole you was damn generous with the artillery - there where you had no use for it. Now you fly into Injun country without so much as a sharp idea. Bo, you give me a pain!"

Johnny spied an Indian peering fearfully out from the branches of a willow. He ducked behind the motor and hissed the news to Bland. Bland nearly fell from his perch.

"Gawd!" he gasped, clinging to a strut while he stared fascinatedly in the direction Johnny had indicated. "Git in, bo, and we'll beat it. She may have power enough to hop us outa this death trap. We can come down somewheres else." He clawed back and climbed in feverishly.

Johnny emitted a convulsive snort. "Death trap" sounded very funny, applied to this particular bit of harmless landscape. Behind him, Bland was imploring him to hurry, and Johnny climbed in.

"You let me pilot the thing," he ordered. "I know Injuns. I still have hopes of saving our lives, Bland. We'll scare 'em to death. We'll be their Thunder Bird for 'em. Now lemme tell yuh, before we start - oh, we're safe for the present. They'll stutter some before they attack us in here - say, good golly, Bland! Is that your teeth chattering? Hold your jaws still, can't yuh, while I tell yuh what we'll do?"

"F'r cat's sake, hurry! I seen another one peekin' around the corner of the house!"

B. M. Bower

"Now listen, Bland. The Navajos have got a Thunder Bird mixed up in their religion, and I guess maybe these Injuns will have, too. If so, we are reasonably safe. They must not know we're plain human - we've got to be gods come down to earth, and this is the Thunder Bird. Or another kind of bird. We'll make 'em think that. They don't sabe flying machines - see? And we'll find out where they're all at, and fly low over their heads to convince them that didn't see us come down. It'll scare 'em, and work on their superstition, so when we come down again to locate that motor trouble, they'll stand in awe of us long enough to give us time to get in shape. You leave the soaring to me, Bland. I'll pull us through all right. Think she'll lift us off the ground?"

"She's *gotta* lift us!" Bland chattered. "She's runnin' better since we landed. And say, bo, don't go any closer to them -"

Johnny told him to shut up; he was running things. Whereupon he circled and taxied back down the field, thankful that the soil was sun-baked and hard. The motor ran smoothly again - a fact which Bland was too scared to notice. He gasped when Johnny turned back toward the huts, but beyond a protesting look over his shoulder he gave no sign of dissent.

They started to climb, got fifty feet from the ground and the motor began to spit and pop again. Then it stalled completely, and they came down and went bouncing over the uneven surface and stopped again, a rod or so nearer the willows than before.

Several scuttling figures left that particular hiding place like rabbits scared out of a covert, and Bland took heart again. A few minutes he spent crouched down in the cockpit, watching the willows, and when nothing happened he ventured forth, armed with pliers and wrench, and went at the motor.

"Sounds to me like poor contact," he diagnosed the trouble. "Like the breaker-points are roughened, maybe. You'll have to work the gawd stuff, bo, and work it right. Because if I start tearing into the hull ignition system, we ain't going to be able to hop outa here at a minute's notice, nor even start the motor and buzz at 'em."

"Fly at it," said Johnny, eyeing the huts speculatively. He was hungry, and certain odors floated to his nostrils. Something left cooking over a fire was beginning to scorch, if his nose told the truth, and it seemed a shame to let food burn when his stomach clamored to be filled.

With Bland watching him nervously, he crossed the little open space and entered the hut nearest, presently emerging with two flat cakes in his hand. Another hut yielded a pot of stew which he thought it wise not to analyze too closely. It was this which had begun to burn, but it was still fairly palatable. So, with a can of water from a muddy spring, they breakfasted, their hunger charitably covering much distrust and dulling for the time even Bland's fear of the place.

The sun, shining its Arizona fiercest though the season was early fall, brought a cooked-varnish smell from the wings. There was no shade save the scant shadow which the scraggly willows and brush cast over the edge of the parched field, and of that Bland refused to avail himself. He would rather roast, he said.

B. M. Bower

Johnny conscientiously carried the kettle back to the hut, then set to work helping Bland. Which help consisted mainly of turning the propeller whenever Bland wanted to start the motor; a heartbreaking task in that broiling heat, especially since the motor half the time would not start at all. Crimson, the perspiration streaming down his cheeks like tears, Johnny swung on that propeller until Bland's grating voice singing out "Contact!" stirred murder within his soul and he balked with the motor and crawled under a wing.

"Yon can start her yourself if you want to start," he growled when Bland expostulated. "I've turned that darned propeller enough to fly from here to New York. Why don't you get in and locate the trouble?"

"There ain't any trouble - not according to the look of things. Acts like water in the gas, or something. F'r cat's sake, don't lay down on the job now, bo! We gotta beat it outa here."

"I'm ready to go any time you are," Johnny retorted, mopping neck and chest while he lay sprawled on his back. "But I'd rather stay here till Christmas than get sun-struck trying to start, I'm all in."

Bland could not budge him and swore voluminously while he worked over the motor. Finally he too gave up and crawled under a wing where the heat was not quite so unendurable, and tried to think of something he had not done but which he might do to correct the motor trouble. No Indians having been sighted since their second landing, he could push his fear of them into the back of his mind until a dark face peered out at him again.

Miles away to the west men were sweating while they rode, searching for this very airplane that sat so placidly in the midst of an Indian corn field. Farther away the news went humming along the wires, of a young aviator lost with his airplane on the desert. The fame of that young aviator was growing apace while he lay there, casually wishing there was a telephone handy so he could call up Mary V and tell her he had a plan which might make him big money without his having to sell his plane.

Not once did it occur to him that any one would be especially concerned over his absence. Not once did he look upon this mishap as anything more serious than an unpleasant incident in the life of a flyer. He went to sleep, lying there under a wing of his plane, and presently Bland himself drifted off into dreams that would have been much less agreeable had he known that a full two dozen Indians had crawled into the willows and were peering timorously out at them.

It was past noon when Bland awoke. Johnny was still sound asleep, snoring a little now and then. Bland grumbled more profanity, sent a questing glance toward the willows and saw nothing to alarm him, crawled out into the searing sunlight and tried to work. But the motor was so hot he could not touch it anywhere. His pliers and wrenches were too hot to hold, and his face felt scorched where the sun fell upon it. So Bland crawled back again and cursed the land that knew such heat, and himself for being in it, and presently slept again.

Hunger woke Johnny at last, and he straight-way woke Bland, politely intimating that it was about time he got busy and did something. Johnny did not propose to settle down for life in that neighborhood, he pointed out. There must be something they could do, if the darned engine wasn't broken anywhere.

Bland, too miserable to argue, sat up and pushed greasy fingers through his lank hair. Having remained alive and unharmed for so long in that neighborhood, his faith in Johnny's knowledge of Indians waxed stronger. He began to think less of his danger and more about the motor.

The thing mystified him, who could tear a motor apart and put it together again. What he felt he ought to do was impossible for lack of the proper tools, Johnny's emergency kit being quite as useless for any real emergency as such kits usually are. Merely as an experiment he removed the needle valve and washed several specks of dirt off it with gasoline. Without hesitation the motor started, and Bland cursed himself quite sincerely for not having sooner thought of the simple expedient. He must be getting feeble-minded, he said, while he adjusted the mixture and made ready to fly.

Once more they taxied down the denuded corn field, turned and ascended buoyantly, boring into the hot breeze that rose as the shadows lengthened into late afternoon. They circled, climbing steadily. Then pop - pop-pop-pop - pop, the motor began to stutter. The earth lifted to them as if pulled up by a string. They could see more huts and tiny figures running like disturbed ants. The field where they had spent most of the day broadened beneath them, like a brown blanket spread to receive them.

They came down with a jolt that bent the axle of the

landing gear, sent them bounding into the air, and all but wrecked them. They went ducking and wobbling up to the willow fringe and swung off just in time to escape plunging into a deep little creek. As they stopped they heard a great crackling of brush and glimpsed many forms fleeing wildly, but they were too engrossed in their own trouble to be greatly impressed. One wing had barely escaped damage with the tilting of the machine, and the near-catastrophe chilled them both with the memory of a certain other forced landing which had not ended so harmlessly. They climbed down soberly and inspected the landing gear.

"Well, that can be fixed," Bland stated in the tone of one who is grateful that worse has not befallen. "I'll say it was a close shave, though, bo."

"I'll try and straighten the axle, while you see what ails that cussed motor. Good golly! We'll be here all night at this rate. And if we keep on hopping over this field like a lame crow, we'll be plumb outa gas. For a mechanic that can *make* a motor, Bland, you sure ain't making much of a showing!"

"Aw, f'r cat's sake, lay off the crabbing! Gimme the tools and I'll rip your damn motor apart so quick it'll make your head swim! I'll say I've tied into a sweet mess of trouble when I tied up with you. I mighta knowed I'd git the worst of it. Look at what I was handed the other time I throwed in with you! Got stuck in a cave and had to live like a darned animal, and double-crossed when I'd helped you outa the hole you was in. And now you wish this job on to me and begin to lay the blame on me when this mess of junk fails to act like a motor. Come off down here with a monkey wrench and a can opener and expect me to rebuild a motor that oughta been junked ten year ago!"

"Aw, shut up!" snapped Johnny, and stalked off to find something they could eat. "Monkey wrench and can opener are about as many tools as you know how to use - unless maybe it's a corkscrew."

He went on, muttering because he had ever let himself be imposed upon by Bland Halliday. Muttering too because he had started out that morning to do stunts, instead of trying to find a buyer for the machine as he had first planned. Now the prospect of getting back to Tucson that night looked very remote indeed. And the winning of a fortune doing exhibition work looked even more remote. "Unless we take up a collection amongst the Injuns cached out in the brush," he grinned ruefully to himself. "We're liable to take up a collection all right, if we have to sleep here - but it won't be money."

CHAPTER SIX

FAME WAITS UPON JOHNNY

That day was a terrible one for Mary V. The big car went lurching here and there over roads that never expected an automobile to travel them, and Mary V watched and hoped and would not give up when even her dad showed signs of yielding to heat and discouragement.

Before noon they had met the sheriff and some of his men, and had compared notes and given what information they could. The sheriff, in a desert-scarred Ford loaded mostly with water and some emergency rations, had managed to scatter his men and yet keep in fairly close touch with them, and he seemed very sure that the search had been thorough as far as they had gone. Young Jewel, he asserted, had not so much as dropped a handkerchief on the ground they had covered, or his men would certainly have found it.

This, while it served as a temporary relief from the dread of hearing the worst, merely postponed the full knowledge of a disaster which Mary V could not bear to contemplate. They drove to a rendezvous previously agreed upon with Bill Hayden and gleaned what news the boys had to tell. Which was no news at all. Their search had been as barren of results as the sheriff's, and

B. M. Bower

Mary V's eyes, when they turned from face to face, were hard to meet. Little Curley, who had been Johnny Jewel's especial admirer and champion when that youth was spending his days more or less tumultuously at the Rolling R Ranch, was seen to draw his shirt sleeve hastily across his eyes after he had confronted Mary V for a minute's questioning.

She watched with painful interest a car that came bouncing toward them over the rough trail they had taken. When it arrived their fears might become a terrible certainty. Two men occupied the dusty roadster, and neither was Johnny, and their haste implied great urgency. Mary V weakened to the point of covering her face with her hands as they drew near. But they were merely reporters anxious for news.

That afternoon other reporters appeared, and the next day an enterprising motion-picture concern had a camera man on the job. The mystery of the vanished airplane grew with the passing hours. The desert fairly swarmed with men, and theories were thick as lizards. On the second night beacon fires were burning on every hilltop, and water was being hauled in barrels to certain rest stations where the searchers could come and recuperate. Old Sudden achieved some front-page fame himself as a stalwart Napoleon of the desert - which he profanely resented, by the way.

On the third day Mary V was ordered to stay at home. There were reasons which her father did not care to dwell upon, which made it extremely undesirable that the girl should be present when her lover was discovered. And, since the search had narrowed to a point where discovery was practically certain within a few hours, Sudden was not to be cajoled or bullied.

Mary V was lying on the porch, wondering dully when the nightmare would end and she would wake up and find life just as it had always been, with Johnny alive and full of fun and ready to argue with her over every little thing. It seemed grotesquely impossible that her own innocent command that he come to her should result in all this horror.

Upheld at first by a frenzied hope that they should find him, she now dreaded the finding, and refused to reckon the time since she had last heard his voice over the telephone. Hurt and without water or food on the desert in all that heat - she set her teeth to stifle a groan. A little while ago when he had been so sure that he could enlist as a flyer, she had shrunk from the thought of his going to war. Before that, when he had lain unconscious for so many days there in the bedroom behind her; when a trained nurse had stood guard and would not let Mary V so much as look at Johnny, and the doctor had spoken glibly of hope, when his eyes told her how little hope there was, she had suffered terribly. She had thought that she had touched the depths of worry over Johnny - and she had not begun to know the meaning of the word.

She lay a small, huddled heap of heartache, shrinking from her own thoughts, shrinking from the sight of every one, dazed with terror of what she might hear if any one spoke. Into this nightmare jingled the telephone bell. Mary V gave a faint scream and put her hands over her ears.

"There, there, baby - I'll answer it," her mother's voice came soothingly, and Mary V shrank farther down in the hammock cushions.

"Oh - why - land alive! Just a minute - hold the line," she heard her mother say in a strange, flustered voice. Then she called, "Mary V - I guess you better come and -"

"Oh, I - *can't*, mommie! I'll go crazy if I have to hear -"

"There, there, baby, it's something you want to hear!"

Mary V's knees shook under her as she went to the telephone. Her voice was pinched and feeble when she tried to call the stereotyped hello.

"Oh, hello, Mary V. That you? I just got in, and I thought I'd better call up. I hear they're out looking for me -"

Mary V's eyes turned glassy. She made a faint sound and drooped forward until her forehead rested on the table. The receiver slid soundlessly into her lap and lay there while Johnny Jewel rattled on hurriedly.

"- And so after that happened, we were held up till dark getting the landing gear straightened out. And of course we couldn't fly very well after dark. And then next morning, after Bland had cleaned out the carburetor - say, it was straight mud in there and the screen was packed solid, so of course she didn't get gas half the time, and that's what ailed her - and when we did start, or was going to start, we found out there wasn't enough gas in the tank to take us home. So I had to catch an Injun and make him take a note to the nearest station for gas, and wait till he got back with some. I'd have sent word on to you, but I was in such a darned hurry I forgot - and the Injuns were all scared stiff, and it was only by making them understand I wanted water for the Bird, and nothing else would do."

"Mary V's fainted," mommie interrupted him then. "I guess it was too sudden, hearing you on the wire when she thought you was dead. You better wait and call up after awhile when her mind's more settled. She's had an awful hard time. I'm real glad you're all right, Johnny, but I've got to take care of Mary V now."

Johnny's eyes were very wide open when he came out of the telephone booth in the hotel lobby. That Mary V should faint when she heard his voice sounded rather incredible, but it seemed to confirm the strange intent looks and the flustered manners of every one around that hotel. People seemed to be flocking in from the street and from other parts of the hotel, and that they were gathering to gaze upon him, Johnny Jewel, came with a shock.

Three reporters came at him so impetuously that the foremost man skidded on the polished floor and all but fell. Bland was plucking at his elbow and whispering, "You let me handle the publicity, bo!" The clerk was staring at him, both palms planted firmly on the desk, and men were pushing up and craning for a look at him. Johnny whirled suddenly and retreated to the telephone booth, shutting the door tightly behind him. It was the first time in his life that he had run from any one.

To gain time, he called up the Rolling R Ranch again and managed to get Bedelia, the cook, on the 'phone. Bedelia was perfectly willing to tell all she knew, and she appeared to know a great deal. Johnny held the receiver to his ear until his elbow cramped, and said "uh-huh" once in a while, and wondered how much Bedelia was exaggerating the truth. As a matter of fact Bedelia was giving him a conservative history of the past three days and, indirectly, she was explaining the crowd in the lobby behind him.

Telephone booths are not any too comfortable on a hot day, and Johnny emerged rather limp and sober.

He edged in to where Bland was gesticulating in the center of a group that seemed to be drinking in his words eagerly.

"I'm going on to the ranch, Bland," he said shortly. "Jar loose here and come help get the machine ready."

"In a minute, bo. As I was saying -"

"Ah - I hear you had quite an adventure, Mr. Jewel, down among the Indians with your airplane. Now, just where -"

"I'm in a hurry," Johnny hedged. "I don't know anything about any adventure. We had a little carburetor trouble, and had to wait for gas before we could get back. That's all." He grabbed Bland firmly by one arm and hustled him outside, where men were seemingly waiting far his appearance.

"Oh, Mr. Jewel! I wish you'd tell me -"

"I'm in a hurry! Good golly, folks seem to think talking is all there is to do in this world! Come on, Bland." He hurried on, his mind absorbed in grasping the full significance of Bedelia's excited report of events at the Rolling R and this curious crowd that gaped at him.

The thought of Mary V lying unconscious, stricken by the sound of his voice over the telephone, nagged at him persistently and unpleasantly. He had not told Bedelia that he was coming, and now he feared that his unheralded appearance might be another shock to Mary V; but he would not take the time to go back and warn her, for all that. Instead, he walked a little faster to where his plane was waiting.

"I think you're making a bad play, bo - duckin' out when all them newspaper guys are hot after dope on us," Bland expostulated while he drilled along beside his boss. "I give 'em some scarehead stuff, but they'd lap up a lot more. We can get a lot of valuable publicity right now if we play 'em right. I give 'em that gawd stuff for a start-off, and I made -"

"Shut up and save your breath," snapped Johnny. "I'm not chasing up any newspaper notoriety now."

"Well, it'd be better business if yah did, bo - I'll say it would. Why, it's free advertising we couldn't have pulled off on a bet, if we'd tried to frame it. Absolutely not. Well, mebby your duckin' out right now is a good play, too. It'll keep 'em chasin' yuh for more - and I'll say that's about the only way to handle them smart guys. Oncet you chase them, the stuff's off. You can bust your spine in four different places and wreck your machine, and mebby get a four- or five-line notice down in a corner next the dentist ads. It's worse, too, since the war begun. There ain't no more chance, hardly, of getting front-page publicity. Say, a couple of 'em took your picture. D' yuh know that?"

"No, and I don't care," Johnny retorted.

Just now nothing mattered save getting to the Rolling R as soon as possible and stopping that idiotic search for him. He hustled Bland around to such good purpose that by the time the reporters had trailed him to the hangar he was already in his seat and was barking "Contact!" at Bland, who was unhappily turning the propeller at stated intervals and wondering when he would ever again have a square meal, and hoping that no misfortune would delay their arrival at the Rolling R, where he remembered hungrily certain past achievements of the cook.

"Going back to your Indian tribe?" one smiling, sandy-haired fellow called out to Johnny.

"No. I'm going to the Rolling R!" Johnny retorted unguardedly. "Ready, Bland? Contact!"

The motor started, and Bland pulled down his cap. "His best girl lives at the Rolling R. He's goin' to see her," he informed the sandy-haired man as he passed him. "They're engaged." He climbed up and took his place, tickled at the chance to hand out more "dope." The sandy-haired one seemed tickled, too, until he saw that his ears had not been the only ones to drink in Bland's words.

They moved hastily aside as the big plane swung round and went down the field like a running plover. They watched it swing and come back, taking the air easily, thrumming its high, triumphant note. They tilted heads backward and followed it as Johnny circled, getting his altitude. They squinted into the sun to see the plane head straight away toward the Rolling R, its little wheels looking very much like the tucked-up feet of some gigantic bird, until it had dwindled to the rigid, dragon-fly outline.

"He's got nerve, that kid!" the sandy-haired one declared to his fellows. "Didn't care a whoop for publicity - did you fellows get that? I'd been wondering if it wasn't some frame-up, but it's on the level. That boy couldn't frame anything."

"Not with those eyes," a sallow companion agreed. "I seem to know that other bird. He's a crook, if I know faces."

"He's just the mechanic. He don't count. But that kid - say, I like that kid!" And he added enthusiastically, "Great story, that stuff the mechanic doped out for us. We'd never have pulled it out of the kid."

"I wish I could remember that bird. I ought to know him. Leaves a bad taste in my memory, somehow. You're right - it's some story."

CHAPTER SEVEN

MERELY TWO POINTS OF VIEW

Mary V wadded a soft cushion under the nape of her neck, looked again at Johnny sprawled in her dad's pet chair and smoking a cigarette after a very ample meal that had been served him half-way between dinner and supper, and stifled a sigh. Johnny was alive and well and full of enthusiasm as ever. He had just finished telling her all the wonderful things he could do and would do with his airplane, and the earnings he had hopefully mentioned ran into thousands of dollars, and left a nice marrying balance after her father's debt was paid. Yet Mary V felt a heaviness in her heart, and though she listened to all the wonderful things Johnny meant to do, she could not feel that they were really possible.

Something else troubled Mary V, but just now, with Johnny there before her almost like one risen from the grave, she dreaded to recognize the thing that shadowed the back of her mind. Johnny turned his head and looked at her, and she forced a smile that held so little joy that even Johnny was perturbed.

"What's the matter? Don't you believe I can do it?" he challenged her instantly. "There's no reason why I can't. It's being done all the time. Other flyers make as much money as your dad makes here on the ranch. And - you know yourself, Mary V, I couldn't settle down and be just a rider again. Fighting bronks is too tame, now - too slow. I'll have to make a flyer of you, Mary V, and then you'll know -"

Mary V suddenly buried her face in a cushion. Johnny heard a smothered sob and got up, looking very much astonished and perturbed. With a glance over his shoulder to make sure no one saw him, ho put an arm awkwardly around her shaking shoulders.

"If you don't want to fly, you needn't," he reassured her. "I didn't mean you had to. I only meant -"

"It - it isn't that at all," Mary V managed to enunciate more or less clearly. "But we've been simply crazy, worrying about you and thinking all kinds of horrible things, and -"

"Well, but I'm all right, you see, so you don't need to worry any more. I was all right all the time, if you had only known it. You don't want to let that give you a prejudice against flying. It's just as safe as riding bronks."

"It - it isn't the safeness." Mary V choked back a sob and wiped her eyes. "But you don't seem to take it seriously at all!"

"Now, you know I do! It's the most serious thing in my whole life - except you, of course. And you know -"

"I don't mean that!" Mary Y gave a small stamp with her slipper toe on the porch floor, thereby proving how swiftly her resilient young self was coming back to a

B. M. Bower

normal condition after the strain of the past forty-eight hours. "You ought to know what I mean."

Johnny sat down again and looked at her with his eyebrows pulled together. Mary V had always been more or less puzzling in her swift changes of mood, wherefore this sudden change in her did not greatly surprise him.

"Well, what do you mean, then?" he asked patiently. "Seems to me I've been taking everything too seriously to suit you, till just this minute. I've been pretty serious, let me tell you, about making good, and now I can see my way clear for the first time since all those horses were run off right under my nose, while I was busy with my airplane, getting it in shape to fly. You've been after me all the time because I couldn't let things slide. Don't you think, Mary V, you're kinda changeable?"

Mary V gave him a quick, intent look and bit her lower lip. "I only wish I could change you a little bit," she retorted. "I don't want to be disagreeable, Johnny, after you were given up for lost and everything, and then turned out to be all right. But that's just the trouble! You -"

"The trouble is that I wasn't killed? Good golly!"

"No, I don't mean that at all. But we thought you were, and everybody in the country was simply frantic, and you weren't even -"

"Huh!" Johnny got up, plainly hesitating between dignified retreat and another profitless argument with Mary V. Another, because his acquaintance with her had been one long series of arguments, it seemed to him; and profitless, because Mary V simply would not be logical, or ever stick to one contention, but instead would change her attack in the most bewildering manner.

"I'm very sorry," he said stiffly, "that the whole country was frantic without due cause. But I never asked them to take it upon themselves to get all fussed up because I happened to be late for my meals. I was foolish enough to take it for granted that a man has a right to go about his business without asking permission of the general public. I didn't know the public had my welfare on its mind like that. I'll have to call a meeting after this, I reckon, and put it to vote whether I can please go up in my little airplane. Or maybe the public will pass the hat around and buy a string to tie on to me, so I can't get too far away. Then they can take turns holding the string and pull me down when they think I've been up long enough! Darned boobs - what did they want to get up searching parties for? Couldn't they find anything else to do, for gosh sake?"

"Why, Johnny Jewel!" Righteous indignation brought Mary V to her feet, trembling a little but with the undaunted spirit of her fighting forebears shining in her eyes. "Johnny Jewel, you silly, ungrateful boy! What if you had been hurt somewhere? You'd have been glad enough then for the public to take some interest in you, I guess!"

"Well, but I wasn't hurt," Johnny reiterated with his mouth set stubbornly. "They had to go and worry the life outa you, Mary V - that's what I'm kicking about. They -"

Mary V gazed at him strangely. "But you see, Johnny, it was I who worried the life out of them! When you didn't come, I got dad started, and then I 'phoned the sheriff and offered a reward and big pay and every- thing, to get men out. All the sheriff's men will get twenty-five dollars a day, Johnny, for hunting you. And there was a reward and everything. So don't blame the public for taking an interest in whether you were killed or not. Blame me, Johnny - and dad, and the boys that have been riding day and night to find you."

Johnny reddened. "Well, I appreciate it, of course, Mary V - but I don't see why you should think -"

"Because, Johnny, you didn't come the next morning after I told you to come. And the hotel clerk found your plane was gone, so -"

"But I never said I'd come. I told you I wouldn't come to the ranch till I had the money to square up with your dad. I meant it - just that. You must have known I wasn't talking just to be using the telephone."

"But you knew I expected you just the same. And how could I know - how could I *dream*, Johnny, that instead of coming or letting me know, or anything, you would take up with that perfectly horrible Bland Halliday again, and go off in the opposite direction, and be gone three whole days without a word? I'm sure I wouldn't have believed it possible you'd do a thing like that, Johnny. I - I can't believe it now. It - it seems almost worse than if you had started for the ranch and -"

"Got killed on the way, I suppose! I like that. I must say, I like that, Mary V! You'd rather have me with my neck broken than not doing exactly as you say. Is that it?"

Mary V set her teeth together until she had herself under control, which, had you known the girl, would have meant a great deal. For Mary V was not much given to guarding her tongue.

"Johnny, tell me this: After knowing Bland Halliday as you do, and after knowing what I think of him, and what he tried to do down there at Sinkhole when he was going to steal your airplane and fly off with it, *why* have you taken up with him again, without one word to me about it? And why didn't you take the time and the trouble to call me up and say what you were going to do, when you knew that I'd be looking for you? I hate to say it, Johnny, but it does look as though you didn't care one bit about me or what I'd think, or anything. You've just gone crazy on the subject of flying, and that Bland Halliday is just working you, Johnny, for an easy mark. You think it's pride that's holding you back from taking dad's offer and staying here and settling down. But it isn't that at all, Johnny. It's just plain conceit and swell-headedness, and I hate to tell you this, but it's the truth.

"That airplane has simply gone to your head and you can't look at anything sensibly any more. If you could, you'd have *kicked* that miserable Bland Halliday when he came sneaking around - wanting money and a square meal, and you needn't deny it, Johnny. But no, instead of taking the chance that's given you to make good, you turn up your nose at it because it isn't spectacular enough to keep you in the limelight as the original Boy Wonder! And you - you take that crook, that tramp, that - that *bum* as a partner, and imagine you're going to do wonderful things and get rich and

B. M. Bower

everything! And you won't do anything except give that tramp a chance to steal you blind!"

"I didn't say I'd taken Bland as a partner. But I may do it, at that - if my judgment approves of the deal."

"Your judgment! Johnny Jewel, you haven't got any more judgment than a cat!"

This was putting it rather strongly, since Mary V had fully intended to guard her tongue, being careful not to antagonize him. That heady young man now stood glaring at her in a thoroughly antagonistic manner. Speech trembled on his lips that would not formulate the scathing rebuke surging within his mind. He had been called conceited, swell-headed, inconsiderate of others, and now this final insult was heaped upon the full measure of his wrongs, just when he had a clear vision of future achievements that should have dazzled any young woman whose life was to be linked with his. But Mary V, he reminded himself, could not look beyond her own little desires and whims. Because she had tried to lay down the law for him and he had failed to obey, she refused to see that he was playing for big stakes and that he could not be expected to throw everything up just because she had been worried over him for a couple of days. The mere fact that he had not been lost on the desert, as every one supposed he was, could not affect his plans for the future, though Mary V seemed to think that it should.

"Well, since that is the way you feel toward me, I may as well drift," he made belated retort in a tone of suppressed wrath. "I guess it would have been better if I'd stayed away, I'll remember -"

"For gracious *sake*, what does make you so horrid?" Mary V now had one arm crooked around his neck, which he stiffened stubbornly. With her other hand she was tweaking his ears rather painfully. "You're going to stay right here and behave yourself till dad comes, and you're going to have a talk with him about your affairs before you go doing anything silly. You know perfectly well that my father's advice is worth something. Everybody in the country thinks he has a wonderful brain when it comes to business or anything like that. He can tell you what you ought to do, Johnny, if you'll only be sensible and listen to him."

"What do I want to listen to him for?" Johnny's eyes looked down at her with no softening of his anger. "Good golly! Do you think your dad's got the only brain in the world? How do men run their affairs, and get rich, that never heard of him, do you suppose? I don't want to mock your dad - he's all right in his own field, and a smart man and all that. But he don't know the flying game, and his advice wouldn't be worth the breath he'd use giving it. Perhaps I am conceited and swell-headed and a few other things, but I am perfectly willing to take a chance on my own judgment for awhile yet, anyway. When I do need advice, I'll know where to go."

"To Bland Halliday, I suppose!" Mary V took away her arm and stood back from him. "You'd take a tramp's advice before you would my father's, would you?" She pressed her lips together, seeming to hold back with difficulty a storm of reproaches.

"I would, where flying is concerned." Johnny's lips spelled anger to match her own. "He knows the game, and your father doesn't. And just because Bland's

B. M. Bower

playing hard luck is no reason why you need call him names. Give the devil his due, anyway."

"I just perfectly ache to do it!" cried Mary V. "He wouldn't be talking you into all kinds of crazy things -"

"Crazy because they don't happen to appeal to you," Johnny flung back. "Oh, well, what's the use of talking? You don't seem to get the right angle on things, is all." He busied himself with a cigarette, his face, that had been so boyishly eager while he told her his plan, gone gloomy with the self-pity of one who feels himself misunderstood.

Mary V had gone back to her hammock and was lying with one arm thrown up across the cushion, her face concealed behind it. She, too, felt miserably misunderstood. Flighty she was, spoiled and impulsive, but beneath it all she had her father's practical strain of hard sense. Mary V had grown older in the past three days. She had faced some bitter possibilities and had done a good deal of sober thinking. She felt now that Johnny was carried away by the fascination of flying, and that Bland's companionship was the worst thing in the world for him. She was hurt at Johnny's lack of consideration for her, at his complete absorption in himself and his own plans. She wanted him to "settle down," and be content with loving her and with being loved - to be satisfied with prosperity that carried no element of danger.

Moreover, that he had not troubled to send her any message but had deliberately gone flying off in the opposite direction with Bland, regardless of what she might think or suffer, filled her with something more bitter than mere girlish resentment. Johnny was like one under a spell, hypnotized by his own air castles and believing them very real.

Mary V had no faith in his dreams, and not even to please Johnny would she pretend that she had. She had nothing but impatience for his plans, nothing but disgust for his partner, nothing but disappointment from his visit. She moved her arm so that she could look at him, and wondered why it should give her no pleasure to see him standing there unharmed, sturdy, alive to his finger tips - him whom she had but a little while ago believed dead. Johnny, I must confess, was cot a cheerful object. He was scowling, with his face turned so that Mary V saw only his sullen profile; with his mouth pinched in at the corners and his chin set in the lines of stubbornness.

As if he felt her eyes upon him, Johnny turned and sent her a look not calculated to be conciliating. If Mary V wanted to sulk, he'd give her a chance. He certainly could not throw up all his plans just on her whim.

"I guess I'll go down and help Bland," he said in the repressed tone of anger forcing itself to be civil. "We ought to be getting back to-night." He opened the screen door, gave her another look, and went off toward the corral, sulks written all over him.

Mary V waited until she was sure he did not mean to turn back, then went off to her room, shut the door with a force that vibrated the whole house, and turned the key in the lock.

B. M. Bower

CHAPTER EIGHT

SUDDEN MUST DO SOMETHING

"I been thinking, bo, what we better do." Bland climbed down from the motor and approached Johnny eagerly, casting suspicious glances here and there lest eavesdroppers be near. That air of secrecy was a habit with Bland, yet it never quite failed to impress Johnny and lend weight to Bland's utterances. Now, having been put on the defensive by Mary V, he was more than ever inclined to listen.

"Shoot," he said glumly, and sent a resentful glance back at the house. At least, Bland showed some interest in his welfare, he thought, and regretted that it had not occurred to him to tell Mary V that and see how she would take it.

"Well, bo, all this limelight stuff is playing right into your mitt. I didn't spill who I was to them news hounds, and I don't have to. I let you take all the foreground. I was the mechanic - see? So it's you that will have to put this over; and put it over strong, I say.

"Now first off you want some catchy name for the plane, and you've got it ready-made. All yuh need is paint to put it on with. Across the top of the wings you want to paint THE THUNDER BIRD - just like that.

Get the idea? And we'll go back to Tucson and clean up a piece of money. While you work into the exhibition stuff we can take up passengers and make good money. Ten minutes of joyride, at ten dollars per joy - you mind the mob that follered us to the hotel just for a look-in? Say one in ten takes a ride, look at the clean-up! You take 'em yourself, bo - do the flunkey work and look wise. I never mentioned the joyridin' at first, because I look on that as side money, and exhibition flyers don't do nothing like that. They think it cheapens 'em, and it does. But right now it means quick money, see. With all this publicity, and the Injun name - say, it's a cinch, bo! They'll fall over theirselves to git a ride.

"My idea is to get the name painted on right now, before we go back. Then we'll circle over town and do a few flops and show our sign. So right away the name'll stick in their minds and make good advertising. Then when we land, the mob'll be there - I'll say they will! And they'll take a ride, too. I wonder is there any lampblack on the place?"

Johnny smoked a cigarette and studied the proposition. It looked feasible. Moreover, it promised ready money, and ready money was Johnny's greatest, most imme-diate need. Not a little of his captiousness with Mary V was caused by his secret worry over his empty pockets. He grinned ruefully when the thought struck him that, if the bald truth were known, he himself did not have much more than the price of one joyride in his own machine! He had been seriously considering asking Curley for a loan when that staunch little friend returned from the search, but it galled his pride to borrow money from any one. Bland's idea began to look not only feasible but brilliant. It would establish at once his independence and furnish concrete proof to Mary V that his determination to fly was based on sound business principles. Supposing he only took up four or five passengers a day, he would make more money than he could earn in two weeks at any other occupation.

Bland seemed to read this thought. "You can count on an average of ten a day, bo - that's a hundred dollars. Sometimes, like on Sundays, it would run to two and three hundred bones. I guess that will let you throw your feet under the table regular - what?"

"What about you?" Johnny asked, looking up at him studiedly.

"Me? I'll tell yuh, bo. You give me the second ten bucks you take in. You keep the rest until the tenth passenger, and give me that, and then the fifteenth. And you pay all expenses. That's fair enough, ain't it? I'll make good money when you make better. Any exhibition work, you give me half, because it'll really be me that's pulling off the stunts. The public needn't be wise to that. You as Skyrider Johnny, see. I'm just anybody, for the present."

"Why all this modesty to-day? When you first wanted to go in with me, I couldn't call you no violet, Bland. You said then that your name was worth a lot."

Bland's loose lips parted in a crafty grin. "It is worth a lot, bo - to keep it under cover right now. One of them newspaper guys reminded me of somebody. I don't think he remembered me - but it wouldn't do us no good now to joggle his memory, bo. I ain't saying he's got anything on me - only -"

"Only he has," Johnny rounded out the sentence dryly. "All right. I'm willing to play that way till I find out more about you. We'll try your scheme out. It can't do any hurt."

He went off to the shed where all sorts of things were stored, looking for lamp black. And Bland, seeing ready money just ahead, overlooked Johnny's blunt distrust of him, and pulled the corners of his mouth out of their habitual whining droop and whistled to himself while he tinkered with the motor.

Johnny was up on a stepladder laboriously painting the R on THUNDER when old Sudden drove into the yard with half the Rolling R boys packed into the big car. They had heard the strident humming of the plane when Johnny made his homing flight, and craning necks backward, had seen him winging away to the Rolling R. They had guessed very close to the truth, and for them the search ended right there. So, after signalling the other searchers, many of the boys had ridden back in the car, leaving patient, obliging little Curley to bring home their horses.

Bud and Aleck, who had ridden uncomplainingly from dawn to dark, looking for Johnny's remains, straightway pulled him, paint-pot and all, from the stepladder and began to maul him affectionately and call him various names to hide their joy and relief. Which Johnny accepted philosophically and with less gratitude than he should have shown.

"What yo' all doin', up there?" Bud wanted to know when the first excitement had subsided. "Writin' poetry for friend Venus to read? I'll bet that there's where Skyrider has been all this while! I'll bet he's been

B. M. Bower

visitin' with Venus and brandin' stars with the Rollin' R whilst we been ridin' the tails off our hawses huntin' his mangled ree-mains. Ain't that right, Eyebrow?"

Bland grinned sourly. "Us, we been gawdin' amongst the Injuns," he stated loftily. "We sure had some time. I'll say we did! Say, we're goin' to be ready to do business now pretty quick. Don't you birds want to fly? Just a little ways - to see how it feels?"

Halfway up the stepladder Johnny stopped. "What's the matter with you, Bland?" he asked sharply. "You crazy?"

"We're out to do business. That's right, boys. Now's your time to fly. All it takes is a little nerve - and ten dollars."

"Shut up!" growled Johnny. "Don't be a darned boob."

The boys looked at one another uncertainly. It might be some obscure joke of Bland's, and they were wary.

"Fly where?" Bud guardedly sought information.

"Anywheres. Just a circle or two, to show yuh how this ranch looks to a chicken hawk, and down again," Bland persisted, in spite of Johnny.

"Yeah - it's that *down again* I wouldn't much hanker for," Aleck put in. "I seen how you and Skyrider come down, once."

"That there was him learnin' not to pick nice, deep, soft sand for a landin'," Bland explained equably, glancing up to where Johnny was painting a somewhat wobbly

B. "He ain't done it lately, bo."

"Lemme up there, Skyrider, and see what it is yo'all are paintin' on," Bud pleaded. "If it's po'try, maybe I can sing it."

Johnny relaxed into a grin, but he did not answer the jibe. He was disgusted with Bland for having such bad taste as to drum up trade here on the ranch, among the boys who had ridden hard and long, believing him in dire need. He hoped the boys would not guess that Bland was in earnest; a poor, cheap joke is sometimes better than tactless sincerity. He was even ashamed now of the name he was painting on the wings. That, too, seemed cheap and pointless. He felt nauseated with Bland Halliday and his petty grafting.

A little more and he would have told Bland so and sent him about his business. At that moment of revulsion against Bland he was almost in the mood to give up the whole scheme and do as Mary V wished him to do: settle down there at the ranch and work out his debt where he had made it. Looking down into the grimy, friendly faces of those who had braved desert wind and sun for him, the sallow, shifty-eyed face of Bland Halliday seemed to epitomize the sordid avariciousness of the man and made him wonder if any measure of success would atone for the forced intimacy with the fellow. Mary V, had she known his mood then, might have won her way with him and altered immeasurably the future.

But Mary V knew only that he was staying down there with that unbearable Bland Halliday, fussing around his horrid old airplane instead of coming to the house and telling her he was sorry. Besides, there was her dad, who had gone to all that trouble and expense for him, not so much as getting a word of thanks or appreciation from Johnny. Instead of coming right away to see her dad, he was down there fooling with the boys. What, for gracious sake, ailed Johnny lately? He ought to have a good talking to, she decided. Perhaps her dad could talk some sense into him - she was sure that she couldn't.

So she stopped her dad when he was on the point of going down where Johnny was, and she told him what perfectly crazy ideas Johnny had, and how he had refused to listen to a word she said, but instead had taken up with Bland Halliday again. And wouldn't dad please talk to Johnny?

"He keeps harping on owing you for those horses he lost," she said impatiently. "I've told him and told him that you don't care and would never hold it against him, but he won't listen. He keeps on talking about paying it back, and making good before we can be married and all that. And he simply will not consent to come and make good on the ranch, and pay you out of his salary, if he feels he must pay.

"He says ranching is too tame for him - dad, think of that! Too tame, when he knows very well it would mean - But he doesn't seem to care whether we're together or not. He says he can make a fortune flying, and he said he might go in partnership with Bland Halliday. He says we can't think of being married until he has paid you - and he imagines he can earn the money with that airplane! And I know perfectly well he can't, because if he does make a cent Bland Halliday will cheat him out of it. And dad -" Mary V's voice trembled " - he went off that morning with that fellow, exactly in the opposite direction from the ranch! He never intended to come, and he didn't care enough to tell me, even. He just went as if nothing in the world mattered! And we were all hunting -"

"Well, if you look at it that way it's easy enough to handle him," Sudden observed. "I've been thinking myself the young imp showed mighty little thought for you. Of course you don't want to marry a fellow like that."

"Why, I do too! What, for gracious sake, ever put that idea into your head? But I don't want him to act like a perfectly crazy lunatic. I wish you'd speak to him. He won't listen to me - we just quarrel when I try to reason with him."

Sudden smoothed down his face with his hand. "I expect you do, all right. The dove of peace is going to find mighty poor roosting on your roof, babe, if I'm any judge."

"I suppose you mean I'm quarrelsome, but you simply don't understand. It was Johnny who quarrelled with me because I wanted him to have some sense. I wish you'd speak to him, dad."

"Oh, I'll speak to him," her dad promised grimly.

Still, he did not immediately proceed to speak. Instead, he drove the car down to the garage and put it away, passing rather close to the airplane without giving much attention to Johnny. His casual wave of a hand could have meant almost anything, and Johnny felt a small tremor of apprehension. When he was merely one of the men on the payroll he had stood just a bit in awe of old Sudden, and he could not all at once throw off the feeling, even though Sudden had willingly enough acknowledged him as a prospective son-in-law. He allowed a blob of black paint to place a period where no period should be while he stared after Sudden's bulky form in the dust-covered car.

Sudden busied himself in the garage, turning up grease cups and going over certain squeaky spots with the oil can while he studied the problem before him. He had once before likened Johnny Jewel to a thoroughbred colt that must be given its head lest its temper be spoiled for all time. Just now the human colt seemed inclined to bolt where the bolting threatened disaster to Mary V. The question of using the curb or giving a free rein was a nice one; and the old car was given an astonishing amount of oil before Sudden wiped his hands on a bit of waste with the air of a man who had just made an important decision.

"If you've got time," he said to Johnny, when he approached the group at the plane, "I'd like to have a little talk with you. No hurry, though. Glad to see you got back all right. You had the whole country guessing for a while."

Johnny scowled, for the subject was becoming extremely unpleasant. "I'm sorry - but I don't see what I can do about it, unless I go off and smash things up to carry out the program as expected," he retorted, and it did not occur to him that the words sounded particularly ungracious. The thing was on his nerves so much that it seemed to him even Sudden was taunting him with the trouble he had caused.

"No, the show's over now, and the audience has gone

home. No use playing to an empty house," Sudden drawled.

Johnny looked at him quickly, suspiciously. He had an overwhelming wish to know just exactly what Sudden meant. He climbed down and took the ladder back to the shed near by.

"I'm ready for the talk, Mr. Selmer," he said when he came back. Whatever Sudden had in his mind, Johnny wanted it in plain speech. A white line was showing around his mouth - a line brought there by the feeling that his affairs had reached a crisis. One way or the other his future would be decided in the next few minutes.

He followed Sudden to the house and into the office room fronting the corrals and yards. Sudden sat down before his desk and Johnny took the chair opposite him, his spirits still weighted by the impending crisis. He tried to read in Sudden's face what attitude he might expect, but Sudden was wearing what his friends called his poker expression, which was no expression at all. His very impassiveness warned and steadied Johnny.

CHAPTER NINE

GIVING THE COLT HIS HEAD

"You and Mary V are engaged to be married," Sudden began abruptly. "Have you any particular time set for it, or any plans made?"

Johnny faced him steadily and explained just what his plans were. That Mary V had undoubtedly forestalled him in the telling made no difference to Johnny. Since Sudden had asked him, he should have it straight from headquarters. We all know what Johnny told him; we have heard him state his views on the subject.

"H-mm. And how long do you expect it will take to pay me for the horses?"

Johnny hesitated before he plunged - but when he did he went deep enough in all conscience. "With any kind of luck I expect to be square with you in a year at the latest."

"A year. H-mm! Will you sign a note for that three thousand, with interest at seven per cent., and give your flying machine as security?"

"I will, provided I can pay it any time within the year," Johnny answered, trying to read the poker face and failing as many a man had failed.

Sudden nodded, pulled a book of note blanks from a drawer and calmly drew up a note for three thousand dollars, payable "on or before" one year from date, with interest at seven per cent. per annum, with a bill of sale of Johnny's airplane attached and taking effect automatically upon default of payment of the note.

Johnny read the document slowly, pursing his lips. It was what he had proclaimed to Mary V that he wished to do, but seeing it there in black and white made the debt look bigger, the year shorter, the penalty of failure more severe. It seemed uncompromisingly legal, binding as the death seal placed upon all life. He looked at Mary V's father, and it seemed that he, too, was stern and uncompromising as the agreement he had drawn. Johnny's shoulders went back automatically. He reached across the desk for a pen.

"There will have to be witnesses," said Sudden, and opened a door and called for his wife and Bedelia. Until they came Johnny sat staring at the bill of sale as though he meant to commit it to memory. "One military type tractor biplane . . . ownership vested in me . . . without process of law . . ." He felt a weight in his chest, as though already the document had gone into effect.

When he had signed his name and watched Bedelia's moist hand, reddened from dishwater, laboriously constructing her signature while she breathed hard over the task, the plane seemed irrevocably lost. Mommie, leaning close to his shoulder so that a wisp of her hair tickled his cheek while she wrote, gave him a little cheer by her nearness and her unspoken friendliness.

She signed "Mary Amanda Selmer" very precisely, with old-fashioned curls at the end of each word. Then, quite unexpectedly, she slipped an arm around Johnny's neck and kissed him on his tanned cheek where a four-day's growth of beard was no more than a brown fuzz scarcely discernible to the naked eye. She gave his shoulder two little affectionate pats that said plainly, "There, there, don't you worry one bit," and went away without a word. Johnny gulped and winked hard, and wished that Mary V was more like her mother, and hoped that Sudden was not looking at him.

Sudden was folding the paper very carefully and slipping it into an envelope, on the face of which he wrote "John Ivan Jewel, $3000. Secured note, due -" whenever the date said. When he finally looked up at John Ivan Jewel, that young man was rolling a cigarette with a fine assumption of indifference, as though giving a three-thousand-dollar note payable in one year and secured with all he owned in the world save his clothes was a mere bagatelle; an unimportant detail of the day's business.

Sudden smoothed his face down with the palm of his hand, as he sometimes did when Mary V demanded that she be taken seriously, and spoke calmly, with neither pity, blame, nor approval in his voice.

"I have held you accountable for the horses stolen through your neglect while you were in charge of Sinkhole range and therefore responsible for their safety within a reasonable limit. The expenses of your sickness after your fall with your flying machine, I will take care of myself. You were at that time trying to find Mary V, which naturally I appreciated. More than that, I make it a rule to pay the expenses of any man hurt in my employ.

"The expense I have been under in hiring men, letting my own work go to the devil, and so forth, while we thought you were lost, I shall not expect you to pay. As I understand the matter, you had no intention of coming to the ranch and had not said that you were coming. The expense of looking for you really ought to come out of Mary V - and serve her right for having so much faith in you. I am lucky in one sense - I shan't have to pay the thousand-dollar reward the kid so generously offered in my name for your recovery. The bonus she offered that sheriff's posse will mighty near eat up that new automobile she's been wanting, though. Maybe next time -"

"I'll buy Mary V an automobile if she wants one - when I get the note paid," Johnny stated boyishly, to show his disapproval of Sudden's hardness.

Sudden once more passed his palm thoughtfully over the lower half of his face. "Mary V ought to appreciate that," he said dryly, and Johnny flushed.

"Anyway, it ain't right to make her suffer for being worried about me. That was my fault, in a way. If you'll tell me how much you're out - ?"

"That's all right. It's on me, for falling so easy for one of Mary V's spasms. I was led to believe you had actually started for the ranch - in which case I was justified in supposing you had come to grief some-where en route. We'll let it go." He cleared his throat, glanced at Johnny from under his eyebrows, took a cigar out of a drawer, and bit off the end.

"Now under the circumstances, I think I have a right to know how you expect to pay that note. I realize that if I leave the flying machine in your hands it's going to depreciate in value, and the chances are it'll go smash and I'll be out my security. Don't you think you had better run it under a shed somewhere and go to work? Of course it's nothing to me, so long as I get my money, just how you earn it. Working for me you couldn't earn any three thousand dollars in a year - you ain't worth it to anybody. You're too much a kid. You ain't grown up yet, and I couldn't depend on you like I can on Bill. But I could strain a point, and pay you a thousand dollars a year, and split the debt into three or four yearly payments. In four years," he pointed out relentlessly, "you might come clear - with hard work and good luck."

"On the other hand, when Mary V marries with our consent she gets a third interest in the Rolling R. Her husband will naturally fall into a pretty good layout. So you might fix it with the kid to jump down the four years some. That's between you and -"

"That's an insult! I'll pay you, and it won't be any Rolling R money that does it, either. When I marry Mary V or any other girl it's my money that will support her. I may be a kid, all right - but I ain't that kind of a hound. I don't know the law on such things, but there ain't anything in that Bill of Sale that says I've got to stand my plane in your cow shed till I've paid the note, and I won't do it. The plane ain't yours till I don't pay. Seems to me you better wait till the note's due before you begin to worry, Mr. Selmer. And I'll set your mind at rest on one point, anyway. The plane may go to smash, as you say, but if I don't smash with it, I'll pay you that three thousand. And you don't have to strain any point, either, to give me a job. When I want to work for you I'll sure tell you so. In the meantime, I don't know as it's very businesslike for you to go prying into my plans. You've accepted my note, and you've got your security, and what the hell more do you want?"

Sudden was very much occupied with his cigar just then, and he did not answer the challenge. Moreover, he was having some difficulty with his poker face, which showed odd twitchings around his mouth. But Johnny did not wait for a reply. He was started now, and he went on hotly, relieving his mind of a good many other little grievances.

"You don't go around asking other men how they expect to meet their obligations a year from now, do you? Then why should you think you've got a right to butt in on my private business, I'd like to know? Put my plane in your cow shed and go to work for you! Huh! I've caused you trouble and expense enough, I should think, without saddling myself on you like that. I appreciate all you have done - but I absolutely will not get under your wing and let you pet and humor me along like you do Mary V. Why, good golly! You've spoiled and humored her now until I can't do a thing with her! Why, she harps on my staying here at the ranch - under dad's wing, of course! - instead of getting out and making something of myself. You didn't fool around and let somebody else shoulder your responsibilities, did you? You didn't let somebody plan for you and dictate to you and do all your thinking - no, you bet your life you didn't! And nobody's going to do it for me, either. If I haven't got brains enough and guts enough to make good for myself, I'll blow the top of my head off and be done with it."

He rose and pushed his chair back with a kick that sent it skating against the wall. His stormy blue eyes snapped at Sudden as though he would force some display of emotion into that smooth, impassive, well-fed countenance, the very sight of which lashed his indignation into a kind of fury.

"If you really think I don't amount to any more than to hang around here for you to support, why the devil don't you kick me out and tell Mary V not to marry me? You must think you're going to have a fine boob in the family! And it's to show you - it's - why the hell don't you - what I can't stand for," he blurted desperately, "is your insinuating right to my face that I'd want to marry Mary V to get a third interest in the Rolling R. I want to tell you right now, Mr. Selmer, you couldn't give me any third interest nor any one millionth interest. If I thought Mary V had put you up to that I'd absolutely - but she didn't. She knows where I stand. I've told her straight out. Mary V's got more sense - she knows me   better   than   you   do.   She knows -"

"There's another thing I neglected to mention," Sudden drawled, blowing smoke with maddening placidity under the tirade. "It's none of my business how you hook up with that tramp flyer out there - but you understand, of course, that flying machine is tied up in a hard knot by this note. I couldn't accept any division of interest in it, you know. You have given it as security, affirming it to be your own property. So whatever kind of deal you make with him or any one else, the flying machine must be kept clear. Selling it or borrowing money on it - anything of that kind would be a penal offence. You probably understand this - but if so, telling you can do no harm; and if you didn't know it, it may prevent you from making a mistake."

"I guess you needn't lay awake nights over my going to the pen," Johnny replied loftily. "I believe our business is finished for the present - so good day to you, Mr. Selmer."

"Good day, Mr. Jewel. I wish you good luck," Sudden made formal reply, and watched Johnny's stiff neck and arrogant shoulders with much secret amusement. "Oh - Mary V's out on the front porch, I believe!"

Johnny turned and glared at him, and stalked off. He had meant to find Mary V and tell her what had happened, and say good-by. But old Sudden had spoiled all that. A donkey engine would have stalled trying to pull Johnny around to the front porch, after that bald hint.

As it happened, Mary V was not taking any chances. She was not on the front porch, but down at the airplane, snubbing Bland most unmercifully and waiting for Johnny. When he appeared she was up in the front seat working the controls and pretending that she was speeding through the air while thousands gaped at her from below.

"I'm doing a make-believe nose dive, Skyrider," she chirped down at him, looking over the edge through Johnny's goggles, and hoping that he would accept her play as a tacit reconciliation, so that they could start all over again without any fussing. No doubt dad had fixed things up with Johnny and everything would be perfectly all right. "Look out below."

B. M. Bower

"You better do a nose dive outa there," Johnny told her with terrific bluntness. "I'm in a hurry. I want to make Tucson yet this afternoon."

Mary V's mouth fell open in sheer amazement.

"Johnny Jewel! Do you mean to tell me you're going to leave? And I was just waiting a chance to ask you if you won't give me a ride! I'm just dying to fly, Johnny."

Johnny looked at her. He turned and looked back at the house. He looked at the boys and at Bland. He took a deep breath, like a man making ready to dive from some sheer height into very deep water. "All right, stay where you are - but leave those controls alone. Want to show the boys a new stunt, Bland? We'll take Miss Selmer up, and you ride here on the wing. You can lay down close to the fuselage and hang on to a brace. They've been doubting your nerve, I hear." He climbed in, pulling off his cap for Mary V to wear. "Reach down there on the right-hand side, Mary V, and get me those extra goggles. All right - come on, Bland, let's show 'em something."

Bland hesitated, plainly reluctant to try the stunt Johnny had suggested. But Johnny was urgent. "Aw, come on! What's the matter with you? They do it all the time, over in France! Turn her over. All ready? Retard - contact!"

Bland cranked the motor, but it was plain that his mind was working furiously with some hard problem. Should he refuse to ride on a wing and let Johnny fly off without him? All Bland's hatred of the wilderness, his distrust of men who wore spurs and big hats as part of their daily costume, shrieked no. Where the plane went he should go. Should he consent to ride flat on his stomach on a wing, with the wind sweeping exhaust fumes in his face and the earth a dwindling panorama of monotonous gray landscape far beneath him? His nerves twittered uneasily at the suggestion.

But when the motor was going and the plane quivering and kicking back a trail of dust, and Johnny had his goggles down and was looking at him expectantly, Bland chose the lesser woe and laid himself alongside the fuselage with his head tucked under a wire brace, his hands gripping brace and wing edge, his toes hooked, and his cheek pressed against the sleek covering. He grinned wanly at the boys who watched him, and sent one fervent request up to Johnny.

"F'r cat's sake, bo, don't stay up long - and keep her balanced!"

"Hang on!" Johnny shouted in reply.

The plane veered round, ran down the smooth space alongside the corrals, lifted, and went climbing up toward the lowering sun. Then it wheeled slowly in a wide arc, still climbing steadily, swung farther around, pointed its nose toward Tucson, and went booming away, straight as a laden bee flies to its hive.

B. M. Bower

CHAPTER TEN

LOCHINVAR UP TO DATE

In the Tucson calf pasture adjoining the shed now vested with the dignity of a hangar, the Thunder Bird came to a gentle stand. Bland slid limply down and leaned against the plane, looking rather sick. Mary V pushed up her goggles and looked around curiously, for once finding nothing to say. Johnny unfastened his safety belt and straddled out.

He had done it - the crazy thing he had been tempted to do. That is, he had done so much of it. Unconsciously he repeated to Mary V what he had said to Bland down in the Indiana corn patch.

"Well, here we are."

Mary V unfastened herself from the seat, twisted around and stared at Johnny, still finding nothing to say. A strange experience for Mary V, I assure you.

"Well," said Johnny again, "here we are." His eyes met Mary V's with a certain shyness, a wistfulness and a daring quite unusual. "Get out. I'll help you down."

"Get - out?" Mary V caught her breath. "But we must go back, Johnny! I - I never meant for you to bring me away up here. Why, I only meant a little ride -"

"Now we're here," said Johnny, "we might as well go on with it - get married. That," he blurted desperately, "is why I brought you over here. We'll get married, Mary V, and stop all this fussing about when and how and all that. When it's done it'll be done, and I can go ahead the way I've planned, and have the worry off my mind. There's time yet to get a license if we hurry."

Bland muttered something under his breath and went away to the calf shed and reclined against it disgustedly, too sick from the exhaust in his face all the way to speak his mind.

"But Johnny!" Mary V was gasping. "Why, I'm not ready or anything!"

"You can get ready afterwards. There's just one thing I ought to tell you, Mary V. If you do marry me, you can't take anything from your dad. I can't buy you a new automobile for a while yet, but I'll do the best I can. The point is, your dad is not going to support you or do a thing for you. If you're willing to get along for a while on what I can earn, all right. I guess you won't starve, at that."

"Well, but you said you wouldn't get married, Johnny, until you'd paid -"

"I changed my mind. The best way is to settle the marrying part now. I'll do the paying fast enough. Are you coming?"

Mary V climbed meekly out and permitted her abductor to lift her to the ground, and to kiss her twice before he let her go. Events were moving so swiftly that Mary V was a bit dazed, and she did not argue the point, even when she remembered that a white middy suit was not her idea of the way a bride should be dressed. The very boldness of Johnny's proposition, its reckless disregard of the future, swept her along with him down the sandy side street which already held curious stragglers coming to see what new sensation the airplane could furnish. These they passed without speaking, hurrying along, with Bland, like a footsore dog, trailing dejectedly after.

They passed the hotel and made straight for the county clerk's office, too absorbed in their mission to observe that their passing had brought the three newspaper men from the hotel lobby. Bland fell into step with one of these and gave the news. The three scented a good story and hastened their steps.

In the county clerk's office were two strangers who glanced significantly at each other when Johnny entered the room with Mary V close behind him and with Bland and the three reporters following like a bodyguard.

"Here they are," said a short, fat man whom Mary V recognized vaguely as the sheriff. He gave a little, satisfied, nickering kind of chuckle, and the sound of it irritated Johnny exceedingly. "Old man's a good guesser - or else he knows these young ones pretty well. Ha-ha. Well, son, you can get any kind of license here yuh want, except a marriage license." Place a chuckle at the end of every sentence, and you will wonder with me what held Johnny Jewel from doing murder.

"And who the heck are you?" Johnny inquired with a deadly sort of calm. "You ain't half as funny as you look. Get out." With a jab of his elbow he pushed the sheriff and his chuckle away, guessing that the man with an indoor complexion and a pen behind his ear was the clerk. Him he addressed with businesslike bluntness. He wanted a marriage license, and he could see no reason why he should not have it. The man with the chuckle he chose to ignore, instinct telling him that haste was needful.

The clerk was a slow man who deliberated upon each sentence, each signature. Eager prospective bridegrooms could neither hurry him nor flurry him. He took the pen from behind his ear as a small concession to Johnny's demand, but he made no motion toward using it.

"Are you sure this is the couple?" he cautiously inquired of the sheriff.

"Sure, I am. I knew this kid of Selmer's - have known her by sight ever since she could walk. It's the couple, all right. The girl's eighteen on the twenty-fourth day of next January, at five o'clock in the morning. If you like, Robbins, I'll call up Selmer. I guess I'd better, anyway. He may want to talk to these kids himself."

The clerk put his pen behind his ear again and turned apologetically to Johnny. "We'd better wait," he said mildly. "If the young lady's age is questioned, I have no right -" He waved his hand vaguely.

"You bet it's questioned," chuckled the sheriff. "Her dad 'phoned the office and told us to watch out for 'em. Made their getaway in that flying machine there's been such a hullabaloo about. He had a hunch they'd make for here." He turned to Johnny with a grin. "Pretty cute, young man - but the old man's cuter. Every town within flying distance has been notified to look out for you and stop you. Your wings," he added, "is clipped."

Johnny opened his mouth for bitter retort, but thought better of it. Nothing could be gained by arguing with the law. He whirled instead on Bland and the three reporters, standing just within the open door.

"What the hell are you doing here?" he demanded hotly. "Who asked you to tag around after me? Get out!" Whereupon he bundled Bland out without ceremony or gentleness, and the three scribes with him; slammed the door shut and turned the key which the clerk had left in the lock. "Now," he stated truculently, "I want that marriage license and I want it quick!"

The sheriff was humped over the telephone waiting for his connection. He cocked an eye toward Johnny, looked at his colleague, and jerked his head sidewise. The man immediately stepped up alongside the irate one and tapped him on the arm.

"No rough stuff, see. We can arrest -"

"Don't you *dare* arrest Johnny!" Mary Y cried indignantly. "What has he done, for gracious sake? Is it a crime for people to get married? Johnny and I have been engaged for a long, long while. A month, at least! - and dad knows it, and has thought it was perfectly all right. I told him just this afternoon that I intended to marry Johnny. He has no right to tell everybody in the country that I am not old enough.

Why didn't he tell me, if he thought I should wait until after my birthday?"

"If that's my father you're talking to," she attacked the sheriff who was attempting to carry on a conversation and listen to Mary V also, "I'd just like to say a few things to him myself!"

The sheriff waved her off and spoke into the mouthpiece. "Your girl, here, says she wants to say a few things . . . What's that? . . . Oh. All right, Mr. Selmer, you're the doctor."

He turned to Mary V with that exasperating chuckle of his. "Your father says he'd rather not talk to you. He says you can't get married, because you're under age, and you can't marry without his consent. So if I was you I'd just wait like a good girl and not make any trouble. Your father is coming after you, and in the meantime I'll take charge of you myself."

"You will like hell," gritted Johnny, and hit the sheriff on the jaw, sending him full tilt against the clerk, who fell over a chair so that the two sprawled on the floor.

For that, the third man, who was a deputy sheriff as it happened, grappled with Johnny from behind, and slipped a pair of handcuffs on his wrists. The deadly finality of the smooth steel against his skin froze Johnny into a semblance of calm. He stood white and very still until the deputy took him away down a corridor into another building and up a steep flight of dirty stairs to a barren, sweltering little room under the roof.

Baffled, stunned with the humiliation of his plight, he

had not even spoken a good-by to Mary V, who had looked upon him strangely when he stood manacled before her.

"Now you've made a nice mess of things!" she had exclaimed, half crying. And Johnny had inwardly agreed with her more sweepingly than Mary V suspected. A nice mess he had made of things, truly! Everything was a muddle, and like the fool he was, he went right on muddling things worse. Even Mary V could see it, he told himself bitterly, and forgot that Mary V had said other things, - tender, pitying things, - before they had led him away from her.

He had no delusions regarding the seriousness of his plight. Assaulting an officer was a madness he should have avoided above all else, and because he had yielded to that madness he expected to pay more dearly than he was paying old Sudden for his folly of the early summer. It seemed to him that the rest of his life would be spent in paying for his own blunders. It was like a nightmare that held him struggling futilely to attain some vital object; for how could he ever hope to achieve great things if he were forever atoning for past mistakes?

Now, instead of earning money wherewith to pay his debt to Sudden, he would be sweltering indefinitely in jail. And when they did finally turn him loose, Mary V would be ashamed of her jailbird sweetheart, and his airplane would be - where?

He thought of Bland, having things his own way with the plane. Dissipated, dishonest, with an instinct for petty graft - Johnny would be helpless, caged there under the roof of their jail while Bland made free with his property. It did not occur to him that that he could call the law to his aid and have the airplane stored safe from Bland's pilfering fingers. That little gleam of brightness could not penetrate his gloom; for, once Johnny's indomitable optimism failed him, he fell deep indeed into the black pit of despair.

Strangely, the failure of his impromptu elopement troubled him the least of all. It had been a crazy idea, born of Mary V's presence in the airplane and his angry impulse to spite old Sudden. He had known all along that it was a crazy idea, and that it was likely to breed complications and jeopardize his dearest ambition, though he had never dreamed just what form the complications would take. Even when he landed it was mostly his stubbornness that had sent him on after the marriage license. He simply would not consider taking Mary V back to the ranch. It was much easier for him to face the future with a wife and ten dollars and a mortgaged airplane than to face Sudden's impassive face and maddening sarcasm.

Darkness settled muggily upon him, but he did not move from the cot where he had flung himself when the door closed behind his jailer. He still felt the smooth hardness of the handcuffs, though they had been removed before he was left there alone.

He did not sleep that night. He lay face down and thought and thought, until his brain whirled, and his emotions dulled to an apathetic hopelessness. That he was tired with a long day's unpleasant occurrences failed to bring forgetfulness of his plight. Until the morning crept grayly in through his barred window he lay awake, and then slid swiftly down into slumber so deep that it held no dreams to soothe or to torment with

B. M. Bower

their semblance of reality.

Two hours later the jailer tried to shake him awake so that he could have his breakfast and the morning paper, but Johnny swore incoherently and turned over with his face to the wall.

CHAPTER ELEVEN

JOHNNY WILL NOT BE A NICE BOY

The jailer reappeared later, and finding Johnny sitting on the edge of the cot with his tousled head between his two palms, scowling moodily at his feet, advised him not unkindly to buck up.

Without moving, Johnny told him to get somewhere out of there.

"Your girl's father is here and wants to talk to you," the jailer informed him, overlooking the snub.

"Tell him to go to hell," Johnny expanded his invitation. "If you bring him up here I'll kick him down-stairs. And that goes, too. Now, get out of here before I -"

"Aw, say, you ain't in any position to get flossy. Look where you are," the jailer reminded him good-naturedly as he closed the door.

He must have repeated Johnny's words verbatim, for Sudden did not insist upon the interview, and no one else came near him. At noon the jailer brought him a note from Mary V, along with his lunch, but Johnny had no heart for either. He had just finished reading the front-page account of his exploits, and his mood was blacker than ever.

No man likes to see his private affairs garbled and exaggerated and dished to the public with the sauce of a heartless reporter's wit. The headlines themselves struck his young dignity a deadly blow:

BIRDMAN FURNISHES NEW SENSATION!

Modern Lochinvar Lands in Jail!

Thunder Bird Carries Maiden Off.

Telephone Halts Flight in County Clerk's Office, Where Couple is Arrested. Abductor Attacks Sheriff Viciously. Is Manacled in Presence of Hysterical Young Heiress Who Faints as Her Lover is Over-powered. Irate Father Hurries to the Scene.

After keeping the country in a turmoil of excitement over his disappearance in an airplane, the Skyrider, young Jewel, flies boldly to Rolling R ranch and abducts beautiful Mary V Selmer, only daughter of the rich rancher who led the search for the missing birdman.

Romance is not dead, though airplanes have taken the place of horses when young Lochinvar goes boldly out to steal himself a bride. Modern inventions cannot cool the hot blood of youth, as young Jewel has once more proven. This sensational young man, apparently not content with the uproar of the country for the past three days, when he was believed to be lost on the desert with his airplane, attempts one adventure too many.

When he brazenly carried off his sweetheart in his airplane he forgot to first cut the telephone wire. That oversight cost him dear, for now he languishes in jail, while the young lady, who is under age, is being held by the sheriff -

It was sickening, because in a measure it was true, though he had never thought of emulating Lochinvar or any one else. He had neither thought nor cared about the public and what it would think, and the blatant way in which he had been made to entertain the country at large humiliated him beyond words.

He picked up the square, white envelope tightly sealed and addressed in Mary V's straight, uncompromising chirography, turned it over, reconsidered opening it, and flipped it upon the cot.

"There was an answer expected," the jailer lingered to hint broadly. "The young lady is waiting, and she seemed right anxious."

But Johnny merely walked to the barred window and stared across at the blank wall of another building fifteen feet away, and in a moment the jailer went away and left him alone, which was what Johnny wanted most.

After a while he opened Mary V's letter and read it, scowling and biting his lips. Mary V, it would seem, had read all that the papers had to say, and was considerably upset by the facetious tone of most of the articles.

". . . and I think it's perfectly terrible, the way everybody stares and whispers and grins. What in the world made you act the way you did and get arrested. And those were reporters that you shoved out of the office, too, and that is why they wrote about us in such a horrid way. And I shall never be able to live it down. I shall be considered hysterical and always fainting, which is not true and a perfect libel which they ought to be sent to jail for printing. I shall probably have that horrid Lochinvar piece recited at me the rest of my life, Johnny, and I should think you would be willing to apologize to the sheriff and be nice now and make them let you off easy. And dad blames me for eloping with you and thinks we had it planned before he got home yesterday, and he says there was no excuse and it showed a lack of confidence in his judgment. He says you are a d. fool and take yourself too seriously, and it is a pity you couldn't have some sense knocked into you. But you must not mind him now because he is angry and will get over it. But Johnny, please do be a good boy now and don't make us any more trouble. I am sure I never dreamed what you had in mind, but I would have married you since we started to, but now it is perfectly odious to have it turn out such a fizzle, with you in jail and I being preached at every waking moment by dad and mommie. If you had only kept your temper and waited until dad and mommie got here, I am sure we would be married by now, because I could have made them give their consent and be present at the Wedding and everything go off pleasantly instead of such a horrid mess as this is.

"I want you to promise me now that you will be good, and I will make dad get the judge to let you off. Won't you please see dad and be nice to him? His calling you a d. fool does not mean anything. That is dad's way when he is peeved, and the jailer says you told him dad could go to h. That is why he said it and not on general principles, because he does really like you, Johnny. Of course we could see you anyway, because you couldn't help yourself, but dad won't do it unless you are willing to be good. So please, dear, won't you let us come up and talk nicely together? I am sure the sheriff bears no ill will though his jaw is swelled a little but not much. So we can get you out of this scrape if you will meet us halfway and be a nice sensible boy. Please, Johnny.

"Your loving Mary V."

Johnny read that last paragraph three times, and gave a snort with each reading. If being let off easy involved the intercession of Mary V's father, Johnny would prefer imprisonment for life. At least, that is what he told himself. And if being a nice sensible boy meant that he was to apologize to the sheriff and say pretty please to Sudden, the chance of Johnny's ever being nice and sensible was extremely remote. His loving Mary V had said too much - a common mistake. What she should have done was confine her letter to a ten-word message, and tear the message up. A fellow in Johnny's frame of mind were better left alone for a while.

He sulked until he was taken down into the police court, where his crime was duly presented to the judge and his sentence duly pronounced. Knowing nothing whatever of the seamy side of life, as it is seen inside those dismal houses with barred windows, Johnny thought he was being treated with much severity. As a matter of fact, his offence was being almost forgiven, and the six days' sentence was merely a bit of discipline applied by the judge because Johnny sulked and scowled and scarcely deigned to answer when he was spoken to.

The judge had a boy of his own, and it seemed to him that Johnny needed time to think, and to recover from his sulks. Six days, in his opinion, would be about right. The first two would be spent in revilings; the third and fourth in realizing that he had only himself to blame for his predicament, and the fifth and sixth days would stretch themselves out like months and he would come out a considerably chastened young man.

Another thing Johnny did not know was that, thanks to Mary V's father, he was not herded with the other prisoners, where the air was bad and the company was worse. He went back to his room under the roof, where the jailer presently visited him and brought fruit and magazines and a great box of candy, sent by Mary V with a doleful little note of good-by as tragic as though he were going to be hanged.

Johnny was sulkier than ever, but his stomach ached from fasting. He ate the fruit and the candy and gloomed in comparative comfort for the rest of that day.

The next day, when the jailer invited him down into the jail yard for a half hour or so, Johnny experienced a fresh shock. Somewhere, high in the air, he heard the droning hum of his airplane. Bland was not neglecting the opportunity Johnny had inadvertently given him, then.

Johnny craned his neck, but he could not see the plane in the patch of sky visible from the yard. He listened, and fancied the sound was diminishing with the distance. Bland was probably leaving the country, though Johnny could not quite understand how Bland had managed to get the funds for a trip. Perhaps he had taken up a passenger or two - or if not that, Bland undoubtedly had ways of raising money unknown to the honest.

Oh, well, what did it matter? What did anything matter? All the world was against John Ivan Jewel, and one treachery more or less could not alter greatly the black total. Not one friendly face had he seen in the police court - since he did not call the reporters friendly. Mary V had not been there, as he had half expected; nor Sudden, as he had feared. The sheriff had not been friendly, in spite of his chuckle. Bland had not shown up - the pop-eyed little sneak! - probably because he had already planned this treachery.

He went back to his lonely room too utterly depressed to think. Apathetically he read the paper which his jailer brought him along with the tobacco which Johnny had sent for. Smoke was a dreary comfort - the paper was not. The reporters had lost interest in him. Whereas two columns had been given to his personal affairs the day before, his troubles to-day had been dismissed with a couple of paragraphs. They told him, however, that the "irate father" had taken the weeping maiden out of town and left the "truculent young birdman pining in captivity." It was a sordid end to a most romantic exploit, declared the paper. And in that Johnny agreed. He could not quite visualize Mary V as a weeping maiden, unless she had wept tears of anger. But the fact that her irate father had taken her away without a word to him seemed to Johnny a silent notice served upon him that he was to be banished definitely and forever from her life. So be it, he told himself proudly. They need not think that he would ever attempt to break down the barrier again. He would bide his time. And perhaps some day -

There hope crept in, - a faint, weary-winged, bedraggled hope, it is true, - to comfort him a little. He was not down and out - yet! He could still show them that he had the stuff in him to make good.

He went to the window and listened eagerly. Once more he heard the high, strident droning of the Thunder Bird. He watched, pressing his forehead against the bars. The sound increased steadily, and Johnny, gripping the bars until his fingers cramped afterwards, felt a suffocating beat in his throat. A great revulsion seized him, an overwhelming desire to master a situation that had so far mastered him. What were six days - five days now? Why, already one day had gone, and the Thunder Bird was still in town.

Johnny let go the bars and returned to his cot. The brief spasm of hope had passed. What good would it do him if Bland carried passengers from morning until night, every day of the six? Bland couldn't save a cent. The more he made, the more he would spend. He would simply go on a spree and perhaps wreck the plane before Johnny was free to hold him in check.

Once more the motor's thrumming pulled him to the window. Again he craned and listened, and this time he saw it, flying low so that the landing gear showed plainly and he could even see Bland in the rear seat. He knew him by the drooping shoulders, the set of his head, by that indefinable something which identifies a man to his acquaintances at a distance. In the front seat was a stranger.

He could see the swirl of the propeller, like fine, circular lines drawn in the air. The exhaust trailed a ribbon of bluish white behind the tail. And that indescribable thrumming vibrated through the air and tore the very soul of him with yearning.

There it went, his airplane, that he loved more than he had ever loved anything in his life. There it went, boring through the air, all aquiver with life, a sentient, live thing to be worshipped; a thing to fight for, a thing to cling to as he clung to life itself. And here was he, locked into a hot, bare little room, fed as one feeds a caged beast. Disgraced, abandoned, impotent.

It was in that hour that Johnny found deeper depths of despair than he had dreamed of before. Bedraggled hope limped away, crushed and battered anew by this fresh tragedy.

CHAPTER TWELVE

THE THUNDER BIRD TAKES WING

The days dragged interminably, but they passed somehow, and one morning Johnny was free to go where he would. Where he would go he believed was a matter of little interest to him, but without waiting for his brain to decide, his feet took him down the sandy side street to the calf shed that had held his treasure. He did not expect to see it there. For three days he had not heard the unmistakable hum of its motor, though his ears were always strained to catch the sound that would tell him Bland had not gone. Some stubborn streak in him would not permit him to ask the jailer whether the airplane was still in town. Or perhaps he dreaded to hear that it was gone.

His glance went dismally over the bare stretches he had used for his field. The wind had levelled the loose dirt over the tracks, so that the field looked long deserted and added its mite to his depressed mood. He hesitated, almost minded to turn back. What was the use of tormenting himself further? But then it occurred to him that his whole world lay as forlornly empty before him as this field and hangar, and that one place was like another to him, who had lost his hold on everything worth while. He had a vague notion to invoke the aid of the law to hold Bland and the plane, wherever he might be located, but he was not feeling particularly friendly toward the law just now, and the idea remained nebulous and remote. He went on because there was really nothing to turn back for.

His dull apathy of despair received something in the nature of a shock when he walked around the corner and almost butted into Bland, who had just finished tightening a turnbuckle and stepped back to walk around the end of a wing. Bland's pale, unpleasant eyes watered with welcome - which was even more surprising to Johnny than his actual presence there.

"Why, hello, old top! They told me you'd be let out t'day, but I didn't know just when. You're looking peaked. Didn't they feed yuh good?"

Johnny did not answer. He went up and ran his fingers caressingly along the polished propeller blade that slanted toward him; he fingered the cables and touched the smooth curve of the wing as if he needed more evidence than his eyes could furnish that the Thunder Bird was there, where he had not dared hope he would find it. Bland came up with an eager, apologetic air and stood beside him. He was like a dog that waits to be sure of his mastery mood before he makes any wild demonstrations of joy at the end of a forced separation.

"I been overhauling the motor, bo, and I got her all tuned up and in fine shape for you. She's ready to take the long trail any old time. I flew her for a couple of days, bo; took up passengers fast as they could climb in and out. I knew you said you was about broke, so I went ahead and took in some coin. I'll say I did. Three hundred bones the first day, - how's that? There was a gang around here all day. I didn't get a chance to eat, even. Second day I made a hundred and ninety, and got a flat tire, so I quit. Next day I took in a hundred and thirty. Then I put her in here and went to work on the motor. I figured, the way they had throwed it into you, you'd probably want to beat it soon as you got out, and I was afraid to overwork the motor and maybe have to wait while I sent to Los Angeles for new parts. It was time to quit while the quittin' was good, bo. Here's your money - all except what I spent for gas and oil and a few tools and one thing and another. I kept out my share, and I ain't chargin' you for flying. That goes in the bargain, that I'll fly in an emergency like that. So this is yours." Then he had to add an I-told-you-so sentence. "Goes to prove I was right, don't it? Didn't I say there was big money in flyin'?"

He held out a roll of bills tied with a string; a roll big as Johnny's wrist. Johnny looked at it, looked into Eland's lean, grimy face queerly. "Good golly!" he said in a hushed tone, and that was the first normal, Johnny-Jewel phrase he had spoken for six days.

"Well, there's plenty to see yuh through, if you want to try the Coast," Bland urged, watching Johnny's face avidly. "Way they done yuh dirt here, bo, I couldn't git out quick enough, if it was me. I'll say I couldn't. And out there's where the real money is. Here, I've taken everybody up that's got the nerve and the ten dollars. In Los Angeles you can be taking in money like that every day. F'r cat's sake, bo, let's git outa this. They ain't handed you nothin' but the worst of it."

He had changed his point of view considerably since he painted the picture of easy wealth in Tucson, to be won on the strength of the newspaper publicity Johnny had acquired. He had seen something in Johnny's face that encouraged him to suggest Los Angeles once more as the ultimate goal of all true aviators. Johnny had nothing to hold him, now that Mary V had broken with him - as Bland understood the separation. With Mary V's influence strong upon Johnny's decisions, Bland had bided his time; but there was nothing now to hold him, everything to urge him away from the place. And Bland pined for the gay cafes on Spring Street. (They are not so gay nowadays, but that is beside the point, for Bland remembered them as being gay, and for their gayety he pined.)

Johnny resorted to his old subterfuge of rolling and smoking a cigarette very deliberately while he made up his mind what to do. And Bland watched his face as a hungry dog watches for flung scraps of food.

"Aw, come on, bo! F'r cat's sake let's get to a regular town where we got a chance to make real money! Why - think of it! We can start now, and with luck we can sleep in Los Angeles to-night. And it won't be hot like it is here, and you can git a decent meal and see a decent show while you put yourself outside it. And," he added artfully, giving the propeller a pull, "the Thunder Bird is achin' to fly. Look underneath, bo. I've got her name painted on the under side, too, so she'll holler her name like a honkin' goose as she flies. And you don't want her to go squawking Thunder Bird to these damn' hicks, I guess, and keep 'em rememberin' that you spent six days -"

"That'll be about all," Johnny cut him short. "No, I don't want anything more of this darn country. I'm willing to fly to Los Angeles or Miles City, Montana - just so we get outa here. Come on, if you're ready. We'll make a bee line for the Coast. We'd better take grub and water in case of accidents. You know what happened to the poor devils that lost this plane in the first place, before I got it."

Bland's jaw went slack. Los Angeles, that had seemed so near, wavered and receded like a fading mirage. What had happened to those who had abandoned the plane where Johnny had found it was a horror Bland disliked to contemplate; a horror of thirst and crazed wanderings over hot Band and through parched greasewood, with lizards and snakes for company.

"There can't be any accidents, bo," he said uneasily. "I've went over the motor careful, and we oughta make it with about two stops for gas and oil. If I thought we'd git caught out -"

Johnny threw away his cigarette stub and straightened his shoulders. "Well, we're going to try it," he stated definitely. "You needn't think I'm anxious to get caught out in that damned desert - I know what it's like, a heap better than you do, Bland. There's ways to commit suicide that's quicker and easier than running around in circles on the desert without water. I aim to play safe. You go down town and buy an extra water bag and some grub. And when we start we'll follow the railroad. Beat it - and say! Don't go and load up with sandwiches like a town hick. Get half a dozen small cans of beans, and some salt and pancake flour and matches and a small frying pan and bucket and a hunk of bacon and some coffee. And say!" he called as Bland was hurrying off, "don't forget that water bag!"

Bland nodded to show that he heard, and struck a trot down the street. And Johnny, while he occupied himself with going over the plane and making sure that the gas tank was full and there was plenty of oil, almost whistled until the thought of Mary V pulled his lips down at the corners. He wanted to call up the ranch and see if she were there, and tell her where he was going, but that seemed foolish, after a week of silence from her. He shrank from the possibility of being told that Mary V wished to have nothing to do with him. So pride stiffened his determination to go on and let them think what they pleased of him.

Bland came back with a furtive look in his pale-blue eyes. Johnny gave him a keenly appraising glance, edged close and sniffed, and decided that he was too suspicious and that Bland's sneaking look was merely an outcropping of his nature and had nothing to do with prohibition. Bland had the supplies in a gunny sack and made haste to stow them away to the best advantage.

Bland carried a guilty conscience. The hotel clerk had hailed him as he passed and had inquired for Johnny. "Long distance" had a call for him, and had insisted that Johnny be found at once and put in connection with the "party" who wished to talk with him. Bland had promised to find Johnny and tell him, and had hurried on. A block farther down the street a messenger boy had hailed him and asked him if he knew where Johnny Jewel was. "Long distance" was calling and had orders to search the town and get Johnny on the 'phone at once. The call had come in just after Johnny had left the jail, and no one seemed to know where he had gone.

"It's his girl - the one he tried to elope with," the boy had informed Bland with that uncanny knowledge of state secrets which messenger boys are prone to display. "She'll tear the telephone out by the roots if we don't get him. Is he over to the flying-machine shed?"

Bland lied, and promised again that he would try and find Johnny and tell him to hurry to a telephone. Bland had shaved seconds off every minute thereafter, getting through with his errand and back to the hangar. He had expected to be followed out there, and he was in a secret agony of haste which he betrayed in every move he made.

But Johnny was himself in a hurry to be gone, and excitement over the adventure and a troubled sense of running away occupied his mind so that he gave little heed to Bland. He climbed in, and Bland raised his two arms to the propeller blade and waited with visible impatience for the word. He had that word. And Bland, who had glanced over his shoulder and glimpsed some one coming, - some one who much resembled a messenger boy, - turned the motor over with one mighty pull, and made the cockpit in two jumps and a straddle.

"We're off, bo! Give it to 'er!" he shouted, in a tone quite foreign to his usual languid whine, and fastened his safety belt.

Johnny settled himself, felt out his controls, gave her more gas. A uniformed young fellow, running toward them, shouted something, but Johnny gave no heed. Uniforms did not appeal to him, anyway. He scowled at this one and went taxieing down the field, spurned the earth, and whirred off into the air.

"We want to climb to about ten thousand," Bland shouted over his shoulder, "and f'r cat's sake, don't let's lose sight of the railroad."

Rapidly the earth dropped away. The town shrunk to a handful of toy houses flung carelessly down upon a dingy gray carpet, with a yellow seam stretched across - which was the railroad - and yellow gashes here and there. The toy houses dwindled to mere dots on a relief map of gray with green splotches here and there for groves and orchards not yet denuded of leaves. Their ears were filled with the pulsing roar of the motor, their faces tingled with the keen wind of their passing through the higher spaces.

Away down below, where the dust they had kicked up had not yet settled, the messenger boy stood open-mouthed, with his cap tilted precariously on the bulge of his head, a damp lock of hair straggling down into his right eyebrow, while he craned his neck to stare after the dwindling speck.

He waited, leaning against the shady side of the shed with his feet crossed; but the Thunder Bird did not circle back and prepare to descend the invisible spiral it had climbed so ardently. Two cigarettes he smoked leisurely, now and then tilting back his head and squinting into the silent blue depth above. He drew out his book and looked at the slip saying that Johnny Jewel was being called by the Rolling R Ranch on long-distance telephone. He squinted again at the sky, cocked his ear like a spaniel and got no faint humming, replaced the slip in his book and the book in his torn-down pocket, and presently meandered back to town.

Away off to the west, so high that it looked a mere speck floating swiftly, the Thunder Bird went roaring, steadily boring its way to journey's end. And a little

B. M. Bower

farther to the south, Mary V was making life unpleasant for the telephone operator and for her mother who preached patience and courtesy to those who toil, and for her dad who had ventured to inquire what she wanted to dog that young imp for, anyway, and why didn't she try waiting until he showed interest enough in somebody besides himself to call her up? And where was her pride, anyway?

Then, after what seemed to Mary V sufficient time to call Johnny from the farthest corner of the universe, the telephone jangled. The operator told her, with what Mary V called a perfectly intolerable tone of spite, that her "party" could not be located for her at present, as he had left town.

"And I hope to goodness he stays!" gritted Mary V, slamming the receiver on its hook. "With dad acting the way he did and treating Johnny like a *dog*, and with Johnny acting worse than dad does and treating me as if I were to blame for everything, I just wish men had never been born. I don't see what use they are in the world, except to drive a person raving distracted. Now, dad, just see what you have done!" She confronted Sudden like a small fury. "You wanted to teach Johnny a lesson, and you refused to let me see him while he was in jail, just because he told you to go somewhere. And you know perfectly well that you swore worse about him. And he did not plan to elope. He - he just did it because I was right there and - handy. And now see what you've done! You wouldn't let me go to him, and now he's out, and he has left town, and nobody knows where he is! I should think, for a parent who is responsible to heaven for his offspring's happiness, you'd be ashamed of yourself. You let me be engaged to him, and now you've gone and balled things up until

I wish I were dead!"

About that time Johnny turned his head and stared wistfully down at the gray expanse sliding away beneath him. Off there to the left was the Rolling R Ranch - and Mary V. He wondered dully if it would hurt her, this abrupt ending of their dreams. Or had she ever really cared?

Bland, sitting in front with his guilty secret, felt the swing Johnny was unconsciously giving to the plane, and set his control against it. The Thunder Bird veered, hesitated, and came back to the course. Johnny took a long breath and turned his eyes to the front again. The past was past - the future lay all before him. He set his teeth together and drove the Thunder Bird straight into the west.

B. M. Bower

CHAPTER THIRTEEN

TEE HEGIRA OF JOHN IVAN JEWEL

Fiction would give to the venture a hairbreadth escape or two and many insurmountable obstacles which would, of course, be triumphantly surmounted by the hero. But fact will have it otherwise, and the chronicler of events must not be blamed if the hegira of John Ivan Jewel lacked excitement.

The Thunder Bird flew high, with a steady air current behind which gave the plane more speed than Johnny had hoped for, and brought them close to Yuma before the gas gauge began to worry him. They descended cautiously, circled over the town like a wild duck over a pond, choosing their landing. They alighted without mishap and Johnny hired a decent-looking Mexican to watch the plane and protect it from curious meddlers while he and Bland went into town and ate their fill, and bought gas and oil to be delivered immediately. Before the town had fairly awakened to the fact that an airplane had descended in its immediate vicinity, they were off again, climbing once more to the high air lanes that made smoother going.

The motor worked smoothly, the hand of the tacho-meter wavering around twelve hundred, and the altometer registering nine thousand feet, save when they dipped and lifted to the uneven currents over the mountains. The Thunder Bird seemed alive, glorying in her native element. The earth slid away like a map unrolled endlessly beneath them. Desert and little towns on the railroad like broken beads strung loosely on a taut wire. Salton Sea was cool and tempting, though the air shimmered all around it with heat. They flew the full length of it and on up the valley. Then they climbed higher and so breasted the currents flowing over the San Jacintos. And over a little town set in level country they wheeled, descending and searching for a field. Again they landed and filled their gas tank and went on. Always it was the distance ahead that called them. Always they grudged the minutes lost, as though they were racing against time and the stakes were high.

After the last stop, exaltation seized Johnny and lifted him high above the sordid things of earth. Trouble dropped away from him; rather, it was left behind as he flew toward the sunset, He lost the sense of weight that clogs the bodies of human creatures plodding over the earth's uneven surface and became as an eagle, soaring high on wings that never tired. Never before had he remained so long in flight, wherefore he had never attained so completely that birdlike feeling of mastery in the air. Falling seemed impossible; as easily could his senses have visualized falling through the earth in the old days of crawling. There was no earth. There was only a sliding relief map far below to guide him in his triumphant flight. Tucson, the Rolling R - they were clouds that hovered far back on the horizon of his mind. Mary V was a dim vision that came and went but never quite took definite form. The roar of the motor he had long ceased to hear. Godlike he floated with wings outspread, straight into the sunset.

The sliding map below took on strange, beautiful colors of purple and gold and rose, with sometimes a wonderful blending of all. Before him the sky was a gorgeous, piled radiance. The earth colors changed, softened, deepened to a mysterious shadowy expanse, with here and there a brightness where the sun touched a hilltop.

"We better drop a little," Bland shouted. "I gotta keep my bearings!"

Swiftly the vague outlines sharpened. Groves and groves and groves appeared beneath them. And small islands of twinkling stars, set in patterns and squares, with here and there a splotch of brightness. And single stars that had somehow strayed and lay twinkling, lost in the great squares of dark green.

"We gotta make it before dark," Bland yelled. "I been away a year. I need daylight -"

They gave her more gas, and Johnny became conscious of the motor's voice. Eighty miles she was doing now, on a gentle incline that lifted the earth a little nearer. The glory before them was deepening to ruby red that glowed and darkened. Beneath the heaped radiance lay a sea of stars - and beyond, a smooth floor of polished purple.

"There's Los Angeles - and over beyond is the ocean!" called Bland, turning his head a little.

Johnny sucked in his breath and nodded, forgetting that Bland could not see the motion.

"Gimme the control - I gotta pick out a landing ! I'll

head for Inglewood. They's a big field -"

Inglewood meant nothing at all to Johnny, even had he heard the name distinctly, which he did not. It cost him an effort to yield the control, but he pulled hands and feet away and sat passive, breathing quickly, gazing down at the wonders spread beneath him. For this was his first amazed sight of Los Angeles, though he had twice passed through the city in a train that clung to dingy streets and left him an impression of grime and lumbering trucks and clanging street cars and more grime, and Chinese signs painted on shacks, and slinking figures.

But this was a magic city spread beneath him. It glowed and twinkled behind the thin veil of dusk. There seemed no end to the lights which overflowed the lower slopes of the cupped hills at their right and hesitated on the very brink of the purpling ocean before them.

Bland shut off the motor and they glided, the plane silent as a great bat. The city disclosed houses, and streets down which lighted cars seemed to be standing still, so much greater was the speed of the Thunder Bird. They passed the thickest sprinkle of lights and headed for dark slopes midway between the indrawing hills. Many pairs of bright lights crawled along a narrow black pathway. Now the ocean was nearer, so that Johnny could see a fringe of white along its edge where waves lapped up to the lights.

They swooped, flattened out, and glided again while Bland picked up certain landmarks. The motor spoke, its voice increased while they banked in a circle and swooped again. Now a long bare stretch lay just ahead.

The motor stopped, and they volplaned steeply; flattened, dipped a little, skimmed close to earth, touched, lifted again.

"F'r cat's sake, what they went and done to this field?" Bland's whining voice complained, and he swung the Thunder Bird away from a long windrow of dried vines, just in time to avoid entangling the wheels. They settled, ran along uneven surface for a space. A small loose pile lay just ahead, and Bland veered sharply away. Another pile to the left caught the wheels just as the tail was settling. The Thunder Bird jerked, staggered drunkenly, wheeled over the pile and then, with a gentle determination quite unexpected in so docile a bird, turned itself up on its nose and with a splintering crash of the propeller tilted on over until it lay flat on its back. Which was a silly ending to so glorious a flight.

Johnny, hanging upside down with the strap strained tight across his loins, with Bland dangling before him, felt even sillier than the Thunder Bird looked. He freed himself after the first paralyzing shock of surprise, dropped on all fours upon the upper wing covering, and crawled out between the front braces. A minute later Bland followed, looking extremely foolish.

"That's a hell of a way to land!" Johnny snorted. "What kinda pilot are you, for gosh sake?"

"Aw, how was I to know they'd went and planted this field to beans? I been away a year, almost. It was a good field when I was here before. Come on and let's turn her back, bo, before all the cylinders is full of oil." Then Bland added with a surprising optimism in one so given to complaining, "We're here, and we ain't hurt, and Los Angeles is just back there a ways. I'm satisfied."

"Yes, and we shelled the beans - that's something more," Johnny sarcastically added to the sum of their blessings.

With some labor they turned the Thunder Bird right side up. It was too dark to estimate the damage, and Bland suggested that they catch a street car and ride into town. He did not inform Johnny then how far they must walk before they would be within catching distance, and Johnny started off willingly enough, after Bland had convinced him that the Thunder Bird would be perfectly safe until morning. It was a quiet neighborhood, he declared, and no one would be likely to come near the place. If they did, they could not fly off with the Thunder Bird unless they happened to be carrying an extra propeller around with them. This, Johnny suspected, was Bland's best attempt at irony.

They walked and they walked, at first along a rough country road that seemed real boulevard to Johnny, who was accustomed to the trails of Arizona. Later they emerged upon asphalt, and trudged along the edge of that for a time, moving aside as swift bars of light bathed them briefly, with the swish of speeding automobiles brushing close. Johnny's head was roaring with the remembered beat of the Thunder Bird's motor. In the silence between automobiles it deafened him so that Bland's drawling voice came to him dully, the words muffled.

"We'll have to get us a car," Bland repeated three times before Johnny understood.

"Oh. I thought you meant we're getting close to a car," Johnny grumbled. "How much farther we got to walk, for gosh sake?"

"About a mile now, bo. It's only -"

"A mile! Good golly! I thought we was flying to Los Angeles! You never said we had to walk half the way from Tucson. What in thunder made you fly forty miles beyond the darned place! Just so you'd have a chance to wreck the plane? A hell of a pilot you are!"

Bland protested, trailing a step behind Johnny, whose stride had lengthened with the bad news. Did Johnny think, f'r cat's sake, he could light in front of the Alexandria and call a bell-hop to take the plane? Did he think they could put the darn thing in an auto park? What about telephone wires and electric light wires and trolley wires? Bland would like to know. Leave it to Johnny, the crowd would now be roped off the spot and the cops fighting to make a gangway for the ambulance, and women would edge up and faint at the ghastly sight. Leave it to Johnny -

"Leave it to me," Johnny cut in acrimoniously, "and we'd have landed right side up, anyway. I wouldn't have lit in the middle of a mess of beans. Beans! Good gosh! For half a cent I'd go back and make camp there. That's what we ought to do, anyway, instead of walking all night, getting to town. We've got grub enough - and there's *beans*!"

"Aw, now, bo, have a heart! You wait till I lead you into the Frolic, and you won't say beans no more. You wait till you git your knees pushed under the mahogany and the head waiter scatters the glasses around your plate, and you lamp the dames -"

He stopped abruptly, his jaw going slack with dismay. "Only we ain't got the scenery for no such place as the Frolic," he mourned. "Lookin' the way we do, we'd be eyed suspicious if we went to grab a tray in Boos Brothers! Some Main Street waffle joint is about our number, unless -"

"A waffle joint sounds good to me," Johnny said. "I didn't come out here to spend money. I'm here to make it."

"That's all right, bo. I ain't going to hit any flowery path either. But listen, old top. We've had a hard day, and before that a bunch of 'em. We've earned one good meal, ain't we? That ain't going to hurt nobody, bo. Just to celebrate our arrival and git the taste of the desert out of our mouths. I'll say we've earned it. And it needn't cost so much. And listen here, bo. I know a place on Main where we can rent the scenery. Lots of fellers do that, and nobody the wiser. I don't mean open-face coats, neither. Just some good clothes that have got class will do fine. And we can git a shave there, and go to the Frolic and have some regular chow, bo, and listen to the tra-la-la girlies warble whilst we eat. Come on. Be a regular guy for oncet!"

"Do regular guys wear borrowed clothes? Not where I come from, they don't."

"Aw, them hicks! Well, you can buy what you want, if that suits you better. I'll take you to a place that keeps open evenings. There'll be time enough. The Frolic don't hardly git woke up till ten or 'leven, anyway."

"At that it will be closed for the night before we arrive," Johnny stated morosely. "It's a wonder to me you let the ocean stop you, Bland.

"Why didn't you go on and light in Japan? We could have caught a boat back then, instead of walking."

Once more Bland protested and explained and defended himself. But Johnny had already drifted off into troubled meditation rendered somewhat vague and inconsequential by his rapid changes of financial condition, moods, environment - the brief ecstasy of his triumphant flight that had so ridiculous a climax. Small wonder that Bland's whining voice failed to register anything but a dreary monotone of meaning-less words in Johnny's ears. Small wonder that Johnny's thoughts dwelt upon little worries that could have no possible bearing upon the big things he meant to do.

How much would a new propeller cost? Would all the barber shops be closed when they reached town? He needed a haircut and a hot bath before he would feel fit to walk the streets. Should he take at once the position he meant to maintain, and stop at the best hotel in town, as an aviator who owned the plane he flew and had a roll of money in his pocket might be expected to do? Or should he go to some cheap rooming house and save a few dollars, and sink into obscurity among the city's strange thousands?

He remembered the headlines concerning him - front-page headlines that crowded Europe's war into second place! He had not seen anything much about himself lately, though the jailer had brought him a paper every morning. Certainly his misfortune had not been given the prominence accorded to his disappearance. If he should go to some good hotel and register as John Ivan Jewel, Tucson, Arizona, the reporters might remember the name. Probably they would, and his arrival would be announced -

What would they think, if he walked in just as he was; leather coat, aviator's cap with the ear-tabs flapping, corduroy breeches tucked into riding boots that needed a shine and the heels straightened? Would they put him out, or would they think he was so rich and famous he didn't give a darn?

He wondered what Mary V would think, if she knew that he was here in Los Angeles. Would she care whether she ever saw him again? Or could girls forget a fellow all at once? Were they still engaged, so long as she did not return his ring? He wished he knew what was the rule in cases like this. Then it struck him that Mary V could not return the ring now if she wanted to. She would not know where to send it. She might have sent it to him while he was in jail - but probably she feared that the reporters might hear about it. How much would a propeller cost, any way? There would probably be more than that broken - the Thunder Bird had turned over with quite a jolt.

No, certainly he should not spend money on high-priced hotels until he had things moving again. There would be no more money coming in until the plane was repaired - darn it, there was always that big hump in the trail; always something in the way, something to postpone his grasping at success! Now he'd have to sleep in some hot, frowsy little room for about four bits, instead of luxuriating in a suite as he would like to do.

B. M. Bower

They reached the little suburban village and the street car. Johnny had an impulse to stop there for the night and leave the city to a more propitious time, but Bland was already licking lips in anticipation of the joys of Spring Street, and made such vehement protest that Johnny yielded. If he stayed in Inglewood Bland would go on without him, and Johnny did not want that, for Bland might not come back. And whatever his mental and moral shortcomings, Bland was somebody whom Johnny knew; if not a friend, yet a familiar personality in a city filled with strangers.

Perhaps it was the night that veiled the city's big human workaday side and showed only the cold, blue-white residence streets palm-shaded and remote, and the inhospitable closed stores and shops of the business district, that gave Johnny a lost, lonesome feeling of utter homelessness. For the matter of that, Johnny could not remember when he was not homeless - but he did not often feel depressed by the fact. He followed Bland down the car steps at Fifth Street, walked with him past a delicatessen store whence apartment dwellers were trickling, their hands full of small paper bags and packages. They looked pale and sickly and harassed to Johnny, to whom desert-browned faces were a standard by which he measured all others.

A barber shop reminded him of grime and untrimmed hair, and he halted so abruptly that Bland forged several paces ahead before he missed him. He turned back grumbling, just as Johnny went in at the door, and followed grudgingly. He had wanted a glass of beer first of all, but yielded the point and took his shave resignedly.

Johnny spent a full hour in that shop, and when he

emerged he was worth the second glance he got from the girls hurrying homeward. Tubbed, shaven, trimmed, a fresh shine on boots that still showed the marks of spurs worn from dawn to dark when those boots were new, he towered above Bland Halliday, who looked dingier and more down-at-heel than ever by contrast. It would take more than shaven jowls to make a gentleman of Bland.

They went on to Broadway, crossed it precariously, and reached the pavement by what Johnny considered a hair's-breadth of safety as a big car slid past his heels. They passed lighted plate-glass windows wherein silver and gold gleamed richly. Then Bland unwittingly pushed Johnny Jewel from the edge of obscurity into the bright light of notoriety again.

Bland said, "I know a joint where we can git a good room for fifty cents - and no questions asked, bo."

They happened at that moment to be nearing the immaculate white-gloved doorman who stands ward over the entrance to the Alexandria. Johnny looked at him, saw what exclusive hostelry was named upon his cap band, and stopped. "You can go to your joint where they don't ask questions," he said somewhat loftily to Bland. "I'll stop here where they don't have to."

Bland gasped, but Johnny was already turning in past the immaculate white-gloved one who bowed as Johnny brushed him by. Bland had only time enough to mutter, "I'll wait here till you register," before Johnny disappeared into the subdued elegance where Bland would not venture. "Till they throw yuh out, you boob , " Bland amended his parting sentence. "Stoppin' at the Alexandria - hnm!"

Johnny, secure in his fresh cleanness and his ignorance of the traditions of the place, strode through the onyx-pillared lobby peopled with well-fed, modish human beings who conversed in modulated voices or bustled in and out, engrossed with affairs which might or might not be of national importance. At the desk a perfectly groomed, worldly wise aristocrat proffered a pen well inked and gave Johnny what Bland would have termed the double O.

Before he had finished pressing blotter upon "John Ivan Jewel, Tucson, Arizona", his brain had registered certain details and his smile had attained a certain quality of deference.

"We are glad to have you with us, Mr. Jewel. Ah - a room and bath, say on the sixth floor? Ah - did you have a good flight, Mr. Jewel?"

Oh, the adaptability of American youth! "Made it in seven hours continuous flight," Johnny informed him carelessly. "Nothing to it. Yes, the sixth floor will be all right. Didn't bring any baggage - didn't want to load the plane down."

And that clerk, to whom baggageless guests are ever objects of suspicion, smiled understandingly and called his favorite boy, and when Johnny's back was turned, immediately whispered the news that that Arizona flyer who had been so much in the public eye lately, was a guest of the hotel, having flown over in five hours.

CHAPTER FOURTEEN

FATE MEETS JOHNNY SMILING

Johnny inspected his room and bath on the sixth floor and straightway began to worry about the bill. The shaded reading lamp by the bed impressed him mightily, as did the smoking set on its own little mahogany stand, and the coat-hangers in the closet. Johnny was accustomed to stopping in hotels where the furnishings were all but nailed down, and the little conveniences were conspicuously absent. This, he decided, was a regular place; a home for millionaires. He doubted very much whether the Thunder Bird was worth the furniture in this one room, and wondered at his own temerity in making free with it. To brace his courage he must untie the roll of money Bland had given him in Tucson and count the bank notes twice.

"By golly, I can stand one night here, any way," he reassured himself finally, and took a long breath.

Just then a bell boy tapped discreetly on the door, and when Johnny opened it he slipped in with a pitcher of ice water, which he carried to a table with the air of a loyal henchman serving his king, which means that he was thinking of tips. In the exuberance of his fresh sensation of affluence and his gratitude for the service, Johnny pulled off a five-dollar bill and gave it to the boy. The bell boy said, "Thank you, sir," and added breathlessly, "Gee, I wish I was an aviator, Mr. Jewel!"

Sir and Mister all in one breath, and to be called an aviator besides had a perceptible effect upon Johnny. He swaggered across the room that had a moment ago awed him to the point of wanting to walk on his toes. Of course he was an aviator! Hadn't he been flying in his own plane? What more did it take, for gosh sake? A pilot's license was a mere detail, alongside the night he had made that day. He should say he was an aviator!

The 'phone tinkled. A man from the *Times* wanted to talk with him, it seemed. Johnny gruffly told him over the house 'phone that he didn't care to be interviewed. "You boys get too fresh," he censured. "You don't stick to facts. You're going to get in trouble if you don't let up on me. I hate this publicity stuff, anyway. I wish you'd go off somewhere and die quietly and leave me alone."

"Well, just let me come up and explain," the reporter urged. "All I want is a story of your flight across country. You're mistaken if you think I'm guilty of -"

"Oh, well, if that's all you want. But I'm just about off reporters for life. You'll have to do some apologizing, believe me!"

Johnny was sprawled on the nice, white bed, with his boot heels cocked up on the expensive mahogany footboard. He had the two big, puffy pillows wadded under his head and the reading lamp lighted and throwing a rosy shadow on his tanned countenance. The smoking set was pulled close and he was reaching for a match when the reporter knocked.

"Come in," he called boredly, and fanned the smoke from before his face that he might look upon this unwelcome visitor who was going to apologize for the sins of his colleagues in Arizona.

The reporter, once he was inside, did not look apologetic, nor did he resemble a reporter, as Johnny knew them. He was a slim young man, tall enough to wear his clothes like the Apollos you see pictured in tailors' advertisements. Indeed, he much resembled those young men. He wore light gray, with the coat buttoned at the bottom and loose over his manly chest. He also wore a gray hat tilted over one temple in the approved style for illustrated catalogues. He had gray gloves crumpled in one hand and a cane in the other, and he stood with his immaculately shod feet slightly apart, gently swung the cane, and regarded Johnny with a faint smile of extreme boredom.

Johnny bore the scrutiny in silence, stifling the impulse to rise and offer Apollo a chair. Instead, he turned lazily and knocked the ash collar off his cigarette, and afterward thumped the top pillow before he resettled himself.

"Won't cost anything to sit down," he observed amiably. "Well, where's that apology?"

The slim young man laughed to himself, deposited his cane and gloves on a chair, moved his feet slightly farther apart and produced a small pad. "For the sins I may commit, I humbly apologize. Whatever it was your sagebrush scribes perpetrated I didn't write it, therefore we should not quarrel. A few details on your trip to-day will be of interest, Mr. Jewel."

Johnny grinned. "There ain't any details. We just flew till we got here, and then we lit."

"We?" The gray-clad one lifted a finely formed eyebrow.

"My mechanic and me."

"Ah." The fellow made a mark or two with his pencil and waited for more - until he perceived that more would not be forthcoming.

"And now that you have lit, what do you expect to do, may I ask?"

"Oh-h -" Johnny covered a wide yawn with his palm, "make money. What else is there to do?"

"Go broke," the reporter suggested, smiling again - with less boredom, by the way.

"Old stuff," Johnny grunted. "I aim to be different."

The fashion plate laughed almost humanly. "If half they said of you is true, you've nothing to complain about. By the way - how much of it was true? I mean how you salvaged the plane from Mexico and used it to catch horse thieves, and the Indian god stuff, and the Lochinvar -"

Johnny sat up belligerently. "Say! What are you looking for? Trouble?"

"Merely verifying rumors. A very natural professional

caution, I assure you."

"Caution! Hnh! Funny way you've got of being cautious, old-timer. I'd call it a fine way of heading down-stairs without waiting for the elevator."

"I understand - perfectly. So you have no settled plans for the future, I take it? Just ready for whatever turns up that looks promising?"

Johnny grunted and looked at his watch. Hunger, which he had forgotten in the novelty of his surroundings, began to manifest itself again. He got up and gleaned his aviator's helmet from a branch of the mahogany hatrack and looked at it dubiously, wishing that it was his Big Four Stetson instead.

"What I'm ready for right now is chuck," he said pointedly. "I ain't fortune teller enough to give you any line on my future. I wish to heck I could. I'm out here to make good at flying. Money - that's what I want. Lots of it. But right now I want a square meal more than anything. So I'm afraid -"

"All right, Jewel. I cease to be a news hound and become your host, with your permission. Let me take you to a regular place, will you? I haven't had dinner yet myself."

"You ain't? Good golly! What you been doing all day?"

The reporter who had ceased to be a reporter checked a smile while he picked up gloves and cane and opened the door.

B. M. Bower

"Say! If I told you all I've been doing, old man, you'd think flying from Tucson is a snap! It's a merry life we newspaper men lead. Not."

They were at the elevator before it occurred to Johnny that he was deviating considerably from his intended line of conduct. He remembered that Bland had promised to wait for him outside the door. He was not at all certain that Bland would do so in the face of temptations, - such as hunger and thirst, - but it seemed a shabby trick to play him nevertheless. Instinct warned him that Bland could not be included in the invitation. Bland was indefinably but inexorably out of it. This fellow - and there Johnny remembered that he did not know the name of his host, and that he had but a moment ago all but threatened to throw him down six flights of winding stairs built all of steel or marble or some hard fireproof substance that would make painful tobogganing. He eyed askance the nameless one and was impressed anew by the absolute correctness of his attire. He wondered that the fellow was not ashamed to be seen in public with him.

"My name, by the way, is Lowell. Cliff Lowell." This was in the elevator. "The desk clerk will tell you as much as any one need know about me, if you feel the need of credentials." The elevator halted, and the human automaton who operated it slid open the door. "I don't often yield to these sudden impulses myself. But life is a bore - and you are different. I somehow feel as if we are going to hit it off all right together. At any rate, I am willing to gamble on the acquaintance for one evening. I take it you are in the same boat - eh?"

"Sure," said Johnny, flattered without in the least

knowing what it was that warmed him toward Cliff Lowell so suddenly. "I suppose I ought to - my mechanic was to wait outside for me -"

Cliff Lowell lifted an eyebrow and smiled a little smile. "You must have a very well-trained mechanic if he really would wait outside at this time in the evening." He bowed and lifted his hat to an impressive old lady in some glittery, lacy kind of gown, and Johnny bowed also and blushed because a girl just beyond the old lady gave him a slant-eyed glance and the shadow of a smile. Ten steps farther a fierce looking man with a wide, white frontage and a high silk hat slowed his pace and cried, "Why, hello, Cliff!" in a manner not at all fierce. Between there and the entrance Johnny counted seven important looking persons who recognized his host as an acquaintance. He began to wonder at his own presumption in receiving one of Los Angeles' leading citizens as he had received Cliff Lowell. It was with a conscious effort that he maintained his attitude of sturdy independence.

Bland, it transpired, had tired of waiting for Johnny. He was nowhere to be seen, and with a parting salute from the white-gloved doorman they set out briskly for the regular place Cliff Lowell had chosen to honor with his patronage. The regular place was such a very regular place that it had disdained blatant electric signs and portents of its presence. Cliff led Johnny up a flight of narrow stairs and turned sharply to the left through a subdued kind of vestibule that gave no inkling of what lay beyond, except that a chipper young hat boy took their headgear and the cane and gloves before they went on.

B. M. Bower

Johnny Jewel, desert product that he was, nearly stampeded before Cliff had safely seated him, with the help of the head waiter, who spoke with a full French flavor. The table chosen for them stood before a long divan whereon they sat side by side and faced the room filled to overflowing with small groups of diners who seemed very much at home there and very much pleased with life and with one another. Many of them called greetings to Cliff Lowell, who responded with his bored smile, like a matinee idol who feels he needs a vacation.

Girls with improbable complexions and sophisticated eyes sent Johnny curious glances and provocative smiles when their companions were not looking. "Movie queens," Cliff Lowell explained in an under-tone, "coming and going. Some of them dreaming of coronation, others about ready for the axe. It has taken them just about ten seconds to register interest in the strange male person who must be Somebody or he would not be here in high boots and flannel shirt."

Johnny flushed. "You saw the clothes I had on, and you brought me here," he retorted. "The joke's on you."

"No less than seven have given me the high sign to bring you over and introduce you," Cliff Lowell went on imperturbably. "They are frantically searching their memories at the present moment, trying to place you. They are positive that you are some star whom they have not met, and they are trying to remember what picture they ought to mention when the introduction has been successfully accomplished." He paused long enough to murmur an order to a hovering waiter whose English was almost unintelligible to Johnny because of its French.

"Should the crisis have to be met suddenly, do you wish to dodge the publicity that would follow if I told just who you are? There are certain incidents which you do not care to have recalled. I made sure of that at the hotel, you remember."

"I don't want to know anybody. I came here to eat. If I can't do that without being introduced to a lot of folks, I'll beat it and find some lunch counter that will feed me without trying to make a boob outa me. I ain't dressed to meet company, anyway. And I don't want anything from this bunch except to be left alone."

"Fair enough," Cliff sighed contentedly and leaned back at his ease. "You're wiser than you realize. Knowing this bunch wouldn't get you anywhere, except at the bottom of your pile, maybe. What you want is to steer clear of everything that will interfere with what you're after. Here come the eats - you'll know presently why I brought you here."

Waiters came, brought strange preparations of food which were a revelation to Johnny, to whom meat had meant just meat, boiled, roasted or fried, to whom salad meant two or three kinds of vegetables hashed together and served sour. Girls' glances were wasted upon him while he tasted dubiously, succumbed to each new and delicious viand, and explored farther, secretly eager for more wonders.

"I know now why you brought me here," he sighed contentedly after the coffee was served. "It wasn't to see the girls, either. Grub's got possibilities I never dreamed about."

Lowell smiled, sent a negligent nod toward a group

B. M. Bower

that had just come in and recognized him, and tendered Johnny his tooled leather cigarette case.

"I never talk business until after I am fed," he observed. "But now - since you have nothing definite in view except the making of money, suppose you listen to a little proposition I am going to make you. It's rather confidential, however -"

"My ears are open," said Johnny, "and my mouth is shut. I don't have to like your proposition, but in case I don't I can forget things mighty easy."

"Good. I'll make it short, and you can take it or leave it. I am not a reporter; not the kind of reporter you mean. I gather special stuff for a big news syndicate. Big stuff, stuff the little fellows never dream of going after. I get, of course, big returns.

"My real object in seeing you to-night was not exactly the getting of a news item for any paper. I saw your name on the register, found that you had flown over here, and wanted to see you and take your measure for the job I have in mind.

"Briefly, the proposition is this: I need a flyer who can fly, knows a little of the desert, has got some nerve on the ground as well as in the air, and who can keep his mouth shut. It's harder than you may think to find one who measures up, and who is willing to avoid the limelight. They all want publicity, and publicity is what this job must shun. What I am working on now is big stuff across the border. I can get the news, all right - I am in touch with some of the big men over there - but the deuce of it is the going back and forth. This embargo business that has been framed lately is interfering with my work. I could get a passport, yes. Perfectly simple. I could go across, and I could get the news I want. But the bother of it, and the delay here and there is - well, it's a big handicap. You can see that easily.

"My idea, therefore, and I think it's a good one, is to hire you to take me over and back. It might take all your time and it might not - but I should want to have you on call, ready to go anywhere, any time, at a moment's notice. It would make a tremendous difference in the time-saving alone. You would have to - what about your mechanic?"

"What about him? I don't just get you." Johnny looked at him startled.

Lowell sat leaning one elbow lightly on the table, his slim, manicured fingers tapping silently the rhythm of some tune which he was subconsciously following. It was the only sign of nervousness he displayed, save a frequent swift scanning of faces in the room. Any diner there who observed him would have said that Cliff was retailing some current scandal which concerned an acquaintance. Any diner would have said that the good-looking boy in flyer's togs was listening with mental reservations, ready to argue a point, but nevertheless eager to hear the whole story.

"I mean, what about the mechanic? Have you any contract with him, or are you tied up with him in any way? Can you get rid of him, in other words?"

Johnny studied his little cup of coffee, his subconscious mind registering the incongruity of such a skimpy amount of coffee after such an amazingly ample meal. Consciously he was having a hurried. whispered conversation with his native honesty.

"Well - I ain't married to Bland," he stated judicially, meeting candidly the other's intent stare. "I never made any contract with him. He agreed to do certain things for me if I'd bring him here - and I brought him. On top of that, he talked about our doing certain things when we got here - it was exhibition flying and taking up joyriders - and I kinda fell in with the idea. I never said, right out in so many words, that I'd do it. I just kinda let it ride along the way he said. He sure expects me to go ahead, but -"

Lowell exhaled a mouthful of smoke and sipped his coffee as though he was relieved of some doubt. "That's all right, then. You are free to change your mind. And you're lucky that you have something to change to, if I may say what I think. There's nothing in that sort of thing any more. It would scarcely pay for the wear and tear on your machine, I imagine. You certainly could not pull down any real money doing that little stuff. Now let's see -"

He smoked and studied some mental question until Johnny grew restive and finished the demitasse at a gulp. "Let's see. Suppose we say a thousand dollars a week for you and your machine. It will be worth that to me if you make good and take me across where I want to go, whenever I want to go, and fetch me back without bringing all the border patrols buzzing around, asking why and how. That, frankly, is one point that must be taken care of. It is no crime to cross the border without a passport - if you can get across. Technically it is unlawful at the present time, but in reality it is all right, if you can get away with it. We could not walk up boldly and say, 'Listen, we want permission to fly across the line on business of our own.' They'd have to say no. That's their orders, issued to stop a lot of smuggling and that sort of thing. But we are not smugglers - at least," he qualified with a faint smile, "I am not. What I shall bring back will be legitimate news of international importance, gleaned in a legitimate way. In fact it will be of some use to the government, though the government could scarcely authorize me to gather it.

"Now as to credentials, you will do me a favor if you look me up. As to yourself, I know all about you, thanks to that adventurous spirit which brought you into the limelight and is really of tremendous value to me. Seriously now, as a sporting proposition and a chance to make money, how does it strike you?"

"Why - it looks all right, on the face of it." Johnny was trying to be extremely cautious. "I'll have to think it over, though. For one thing, I'll want to do some figuring before I can say whether the price is right. It costs money to keep an airplane in the air, Mr. Lowell. You'd be surprised to see just how much a fellow has to pay out to keep a motor in good mechanical shape. And, of course, I wouldn't look at it at any price unless I was dead sure it was straight. If you'll excuse my saying so, I ain't after dirty money. It's got to be clean."

"That's the stuff! I'm glad to hear you come right out and say so, because that's where I stand. I want you to look me up. Here's the card of the International News Syndicate - they handle nothing but big political stuff, you understand. A sort of secret service of newspaper-dom. Ask them about me and about the proposition. They'll be paying you the money - not me. Ask any

B. M. Bower

one else you like, only don't mention this particular matter we've been discussing. As the lawyers say, secrecy is the essence of this contract." He laughed and crooked a finger at the waiter who had served them so assiduously, got his dinner check and paid it with a banknote that, even deducting the high cost of eating in a regular place, returned him a handful of change. He tipped the waiter generously and rose.

"You'd have to keep under cover as much as possible," he continued planning, when they were again on the street. "How much attention did you attract, Mr. Jewel, when you landed?"

"Why, not any. It was about dark, and we lit in a beanfield over beyond Inglewood. We left the plane there and came in on a street car. I don't guess anybody saw us at all."

"Fine! This is playing our way from the start. If any one notices your name on the hotel register and asks you questions, you came after certain parts for your motor - any errand will do - and you expect to leave again at any time. This does not commit you to the proposition, Mr. Jewel. It is merely keeping our lines straight in case you do accept. I want you to sleep on it - but please don't talk in your sleep!" He laughed, and Johnny laughed with him and promised discretion.

The last he saw of Cliff Lowell that night, Cliff was talking with a group of important-looking men who treated him as though they had known him for a long, long while. Their manifest intimacy struck Johnny as a tacit endorsement of Cliff's character and reputation. It would seem almost an insult to go around quizzing people about a man so popular with the leading citizens, Johnny told himself. He would think the proposition over, certainly. He was not fool enough to jump headfirst into a thing like that at the first crook of a stranger's finger, but -

"Good golly! Talk about luck! Why, at a thousand dollars a week, I can pay old Sudden off in a month, doggone him. And have a thousand to the good. And if the job holds out for another month or two -"

That, if you please, is how Johnny "thought it over and did some figuring!"

CHAPTER FIFTEEN

ONE MORE PLUNGE FOR JOHNNY

The grinding clamor of passing street cars jarring over the Spring Street crossing woke Johnny to what he thought was moonlight, until it occurred to him that the pale glow must come from street lamps. The air was muggy, filled with the odor of damp soot. He sniffed, turned over with the bed covering rolled close around him, snuggled his cheek into a pillow, yawned, rooted deeper, opened his eyes again, and turned on the reading light by his bed. It was five-thirty - red dawn in Arizona where his dreaming had borne him swiftly to his old camp at Sinkhole. Five-thirty would be getting-up time on the range, but in Los Angeles the hour seemed an ungodly time to crawl out of bed. He reached for his "makings" and rolled a cigarette which he smoked with no more than one arm and his head exposed to the clamminess of the atmosphere.

He ought to return to the Thunder Bird by daylight, he mused, but he did not know how to get there. He needed Bland for pilot, but he did not know where to find Bland. Now that he came to consider finding people and places, it occurred to him that neither did he know where to find Cliff Lowell. Thinking of him made Johnny wonder what kind of news gathering it was that could make it worth a thousand dollars a week to a man to have a swift, secret means of locomotion at his command. It had sounded plausible enough last night, but now he was not so sure of it. It might be some graft - it might even be a scheme to rob him of his plane. It would be a good idea to look into matters a little before he went any farther, he decided. When Bland showed up, he'd go out and take a look at the Thunder Bird, and get her in shape to fly. Then they'd get to work. But a thousand dollars a week sure did sound good, and if the proposition was on the square -

He snuggled down and began to build an air castle. Suppose it was straight, and he went into the deal with Lowell; and suppose he worked for two months, say. That would be eight - well, say nine thousand, the way weeks lap over on the calendar. Suppose by Christmas he had eight thousand dollars clear money. (Five hundred a month ought to run the plane, with any kind of luck.) Well, what if he took the Thunder Bird and his eight thousand, and flew back to the Rolling R and lit in the yard just about when they were sitting down to their Christmas dinner. He'd walk in and lay three thousand dollars down on the table by old Sudden, and tell him kind of careless, "I happened to have a little extra cash on hand, so I thought I'd take up that note while I thought of it. No use letting it go on drawing interest."

Say, maybe Sudden's eyes wouldn't stick out! And Mary V would kind of catch her breath and open her eyes wide at him, and say, "Why, Johnny - ?" And say - no, jump up and put her arms around his neck and - slide her lips along his cheek and whisper -

An hour and a half later he awoke, saw with dismay that it was seven o'clock, and piled out of bed as

B. M. Bower

guiltily as though an irate round-up boss stood over him. The Thunder Bird to repair, a big business deal to be accepted or rejected, - whichever his judgment advised and the fates favored, - and he in bed at seven o'clock! He dressed hurriedly, expecting to hear an impatient rapping on the door before he was ready to face a critical business world. If he had time that day, he ought to get himself some clothes. He would not want to eat again in that place where Cliff Lowell took him, dressed as he was now.

He waited an impatient five minutes, went down to the lobby, - after some trouble finding the elevator, - and found himself alone with the onyx pillars and a few porters with brushes and things. A different clerk glanced at him uninterestedly and assured him that no one had called to see Mr. Jewel that morning. He left word that he would be back in half an hour and went out to find breakfast. Luck took him through the side entrance to Spring Street, where eating places were fairly numerous. He discovered what he wanted, ate as fast as he could swallow without choking on his ham and eggs or scalding his throat with the coffee, and returned to the hotel.

No, there had been no call for Mr. Jewel. Johnny bought a morning paper, but could find no mention of his arrival in Los Angeles. Cliff Lowell, he decided, must be playing the secrecy to the limit. It did not please him overmuch, in spite of his revilings of the press that had made a joke of his troubles. Couldn't they do anything but go to extremes, for gosh sake? Here he had made a record night, - he had distinctly told that clerk the time he had made it in, - and Cliff Lowell knew, too. Yet the paper was absolutely dumb. They ignored everything he did that was worth notice, and yawped his private affairs all over their front pages. That man Lowell was taking too much on himself. Johnny hadn't agreed to take the job yet; he very much doubted whether he would take it at all. He would rather be his own boss and fly when he pleased and where he pleased. This flying over into Mexico and back looked pretty fishy, come to think of it. If it was against the law, how did Lowell expect to get away with it? If it wasn't, why be so darned secret about it?

For three quarters of an hour, perhaps longer, Johnny dismissed the thousand-dollar-a-week job from his mind and waited with rising indignation for Bland. What had become of the darned little runt? Here it was nine o'clock, and no sign of him. The lobby was beginning to wear an atmosphere of sedate bustling to and fro. Johnny watched travelers arrive with their luggage, watched other travelers depart. Business men strayed in, seeking acquaintances. The droning chant of pages in tight jackets and little caps perched jauntily askew interested him. Would Bland, when he came, have sense enough to send one around calling out "Mr. Jew-wel - Mr. John-ny Jew-wel"? Johnny knew exactly how it would sound. Cliff Lowell might, but he did not want to see Cliff. The more he thought about him the more he distrusted that proposition. A thousand dollars a week did not sound convincing in the broad light of day. It was altogether too good to be true. Why, good golly! Nobody but a millionaire could afford to pay that much just for riding around; and if they could, they'd buy themselves an airplane. They wouldn't rent one, that was certain.

At ten o'clock Johnny mentally blew up. He had not come to Los Angeles to sit around in any doggone hotel like an old woman waiting for a train, and if Bland or anybody else thought he'd hang around there all day - He went to the desk, left word that he had gone out to Inglewood, watched the clerk scribble the information on a slip of paper and put it in his key box, and went out wondering how he was going to find his way to the Thunder Bird. But his natural initiative came to his aid. He saw an automobile with a FOR HIRE sign on it, held brief conversation with the driver, and was presently leaning back on the cushions watching luckless pedestrians dodge out of the way. The sight, I may add, restored his good humor to the point of forgetting his dignity and crawling over into the front seat where he proceeded to scrape acquaintance with the driver. Los Angeles was a great place, all right - when you can see it from the front seat of an automobile. Johnny began to talk automobiles to the man and managed to extract a good deal of information, that may or may not have been authentic, concerning the various "makes" and their prices and speed. Not that he intended to buy one; but still, with good luck, there was no reason why he should not, when he had that note paid. A car certainly did give class to a man - and according to this fellow it would be a real economy to own one. This man said he looked upon a car as a necessity; and Johnny very quickly adopted his point of view and began to think how extravagant he was not to own one. Why, take this trip, for instance. If he owned the car himself, all it would cost him to go to Inglewood would be the gas he would burn. As it was, it would probably mean ten or fifteen dollars before he was through. An automobile of your own sure did mean a big saving all around - time and money. Take a job like this man Lowell had offered, why, he could very soon own a car. A thousand dollars a week, for a few weeks - it was his to take, if he wanted to do it -

There he went again, playing with the thought until they slid through Inglewood and out on the boulevard that curved flirtatiously close to a railroad track, where he had tramped with Bland - good golly! Was that only last night? Tired and hungry and blue, with a broken plane to think of and Mary V and the Rolling R to forget - last night. And here he was, debating with himself the wisdom of accepting an offer of a thousand dollars a week, thinking seriously of buying himself an automobile! Was it two miles to where they had turned out of the bean field on to the highway? It certainly didn't seem that far today. Except for the curves which he remembered he would have thought the driver had made a mistake when he slowed and swung short into a rough trail that crossed the railroad. But there was the Thunder Bird sitting disconsolately with a broken nose and Lord knew what other disabilities, in the bean field where he had left her. He felt as though he had been away for a month.

With a pencil and paper he was carefully setting down what slight repairs he would need to make, when a big, dark red roadster swung off the boulevard and came chuckling toward them down the rough trail. Cliff Lowell was driving, and he greeted Johnny with a careless assurance of their unity of interest that would make it difficult for Johnny to hold off, if holding off proved to be his ultimate intention.

Cliff climbed out and came up to the Thunder Bird, standing with his feet slightly apart, pulling off his driving gloves that he might light a cigarette.

"They told me at the hotel you were out here, so I

B. M. Bower

came on. Better send that car back to town," he suggested frugally. "I'll take you in. No use wasting money on car hire when you don't have to. I want to talk to you, anyway."

Johnny hesitated, then paid his driver and let him go.

"I've got to go around to a supply house and get me a new propeller," he said afterwards. "And a control wire snapped. We made a bum landing last night - or my mechanic did. He claimed he knew this field, so I let him go ahead."

"Where is he? Did you let him out?"

"I didn't, but I will if he don't show up; pronto." Johnny's tone was the tone of accustomed authority. "He failed to report, this morning."

Cliff reached into an inner pocket and drew out a flat package, which he proceeded to open, using a wing for a table. "I've been busy this morning," he announced, laying his cigarette down on the wing. Johnny promptly swept the cigarette to the ground and crushed it under his heel. Wing coverings are rather inflammable, and he was not taking any chances.

"Pardon the carelessness. I don't know much about airplanes, old man. Well, I went to the boss and had a talk with him, after I left you last night. I put the proposition up to him, and he is rather keen on it. He sees the value of getting news by airplane. The saving of time and the avoidance of publicity will double its value - to say nothing of the chance that we may be able to pick up something of immense importance to the government. Mexican situation, you know - all that sort of thing.

"So he put me in touch with parties that could furnish this." *This* was a large photographic bird's-eye map of a country which looked very much like Arizona, or the wild places anywhere next the Mexican borderline. "Where I got it I am not at liberty to say. It's a practice map - done for the training in aerial photography that is essential nowadays in warfare. The government is going in rather strong on that sort of thing. This is authentic. Take a good look at it through this glass and tell me what you think of it. Can you see any place that would make a possible secret landing for an airplane, for instance?"

"Golly!" Johnny whispered, as Cliff's meaning flashed clean-cut through the last sentence. He studied the photograph with pursed lips, his left eye squinted that his right eye might peer through a small reading glass. "It would depend on the ground," he answered after a minute. "I'd want to fly over it before I could tell exactly. If it was soft sandy for instance -" (Bland would have snickered at that, knowing what reason Johnny had for realizing the disadvantages of soft sand as a landing place.) "But the topography looks very practicable for the purpose." (Nothing like talking up to your audience. Johnny was proud of that sentence.)

"All right. We'll lay that aside for further investigation. I'm glad you have the plane out here away from every one. We'll take a run over to that locality in my car - it's open season for ducks, and there's that lake you see on the map. A couple of shotguns and our hunting licenses will be all the alibi we'll need. You must know how to get about in the open country, living in Arizona as you have, and I'm counting a good deal on that.

That's one reason why I made you the offer, instead of these flyers around here - and by the way, that's one point that made you look like a safe bet to the old man.

"I was talking to him about salary, and he's willing to go stronger than I said, if you make good. He said it would be worth about two hundred a day, which is considerably better than the thousand a week that I named."

Cliff knew when to stop and let the bait dangle. He fussed with a fresh cigarette, paying no apparent attention to Johnny, which gave that young man an idea that he was wholly unobserved while he dizzily made a mental calculation. Fourteen hundred a week - go-od golly! In a month - or would it last for a month?

"How long a job is this?" he demanded so suddenly that the words were out before he knew he was going to ask the question.

"How long? Well - that's hard to say. Until you fail to put me across the line safely, I suppose. There's always something doing or going to be done in Mexico, old man - and it's always worth reporting to the Syndicate. How long will people go on reading their morning paper at breakfast?" He smiled the tolerant, bored smile that Johnny associated with his first sight of Cliff. "I should say the job will last as long as you make good."

"Well, that puts it up to me, then. I'd want an agreement that I'd be paid a week in advance all the time. That's to cover the risk of costly breakage and things like that. At the end of every week I'd be free to quit or go on, and you'd be free to let me out if I didn't suit. With that understanding I'll try her out - for a week, starting to-morrow morning." He added, by way of clinching the matter, "And that goes."

Cliff Lowell blew a thin wreath of smoke and smiled again. "It goes, far as I am concerned. I think the old man will agree to it, providing you take oath you'll keep the whole thing secret. I haven't preached that to you, but the whole scheme blows up the minute it is made public. You understand that, of course, and I'm not afraid of you; but the old man may want some assurance. If he does, you can give it, and if he does not, it will be because he is taking my word that you are all right.

"Now let's get down to business. How long will it take you to get the machine in shape? And can't you make arrangements with the owner of this field to leave it here for the present - and perhaps get him to keep an eye on it? Wait. You leave him to me. I think he's a Jap, and I know Japs pretty well. I'll go hunt him up and talk to him. If we can run it under cover for a couple of days, all the better."

He climbed into his car and went off down the road to where the roofs of several buildings showed just above a ridge. His talk must have been well lubricated with something substantial in the way of legal tender, for presently he returned, and behind him a team came down the road hauling a flat hayrack on which four Japs sat and dangled their legs to the jolting of the wagon.

"He's a good scout, and he will keep the plane under cover for us," Cliff announced in a satisfied tone. "They're going to load it on the wagon and haul it

B. M. Bower

home, where there's a shed I think will hold it. If it won't, we'll buy it and knock out an end or something."

The four Japs, chinning unintelligibly and smiling a good deal, loaded the Thunder Bird to Johnny's satisfaction, hauled it to the buildings over the ridge, and after they had knocked all the boards off one side to admit the wings, ran it under a shed. Afterwards they nailed all the boards on again while Johnny stood around and watched them uneasily, secretly depressed because his Thunder Bird was being penned in by gibbering brown men who might be unwilling to return it to him on demand.

For good or ill, he was committed now to Cliff Lowell's project. Even though he was committed for only a week, qualms of doubt assailed him at intervals during their roaring progress to the city. Cliff drove with an effortless skill which filled Johnny with envy. Some day - well, a car like this wouldn't be so bad. And if the job held out long enough - Why, good golly, think of it! And Mary V thought he couldn't make any money with his airplane. Wanted him to go to work for her dad - think of that!

Thinking of it; he tried to silence the qualms. Tried to reassure himself with Cliff's very evident sincerity, his easy assurance that all would be well. Johnny had been canny enough to make the agreement by the week - surely nothing much could go wrong in that little while, and if he didn't like the look of things after a week's try-out, he could quit, and that would be all there would be of it. It was too good a chance to let slip by without a trial, anyway. A man would be a fool to do that; and Johnny, whatever he thought of himself, did not consider himself a fool.

CHAPTER SIXTEEN

WITH HIS HANDS FULL OF MONEY
AND HIS EYES SHUT

Under Cliff's direction, that afternoon Johnny did what a woman would call shopping. He bought among other things a suit of khaki such as city dwellers wear when they go into the wilds. Cliff had told him that he must not appear among people in the clothes of a flyer, but must be a duck hunter and none other when they left Los Angeles. When that would be, Johnny did not know; nor did he know where they were going. But a duck hunter he faithfully tried to resemble when he let Cliff into his room at five o'clock in the evening, which meant after the lights were on in the quiet hallways of the Alexandria, and the streets were all aglow. Cliff looked, if not like a hunter, at least picturesque in high, laced boots and olive-drab trousers and coat that had a military cut.

"Fine! We'll get under way and eat somewhere along the road, if you don't mind. What about that mechanic? Has he shown up yet?" Cliff's boredom was gone, along with his swagger stick.

"Naw. I guess the little runt went on a spree. I thought he'd be here when I got back, but he wasn't, and the clerk said nobody had called for me except you."

B. M. Bower

"All the better. You won't have to bother explaining to him without telling him anything. If you ever do run across him, give him a temperance talk - and the boot. That will be convincing, without your needing to furnish any other reason for letting him out. By the way," - reaching casually into a pocket, - "here is your first week's salary. The boss made it fifteen hundred a week, straight. And he said to tell you he would add a hundred every week that you deliver the goods. That is giving a tremendously square deal, in my opinion. But it's the boss's way, to make it worth a man's while to do his level best."

Round-eyed, Johnny took the roll of bank notes and flipped the ends with eager fingers. Golly! One with five hundred on it - he had never seen a five-hundred-dollar bill in his life, until this one. And fifties - six or seven of them, and four one-hundreds, and the rest in twenties and three or four tens for easy spending. He had a keen desire to show that roll to Mary V, and ask her whether he could make money flying, or whether she would still advise him to go to work for her dad! Why, right there in his hand was more money than Sudden thought he was worth in a year, and this was just one week's salary! Why, good gosh! In another week he could pay that note, and start right in getting rich. Why, in a month he could own a car like Cliff's. Why -

Cliff, watching him with sophisticated understanding of the dazzling effect of so much money upon a youth who had probably never before seen fifteen hundred dollars in one lump, smiled to himself. Whatever small voice of doubt Johnny had hearkened to, the voice would now be hushed under the soft whisper of the money fluttering in Johnny's fingers.

"Well, I'll call a porter to get these things down so you can settle for the room. You had better just check out without leaving any word of where you're going." Cliff turned to the 'phone.

"That'll be easy, seeing I don't know," Johnny retorted, crowding the money into his old wallet that bulged like the cheeks of a pocket gopher, busy enlarging his house.

"Fine," Cliff flung sardonically over his shoulder. He called for a porter to remove the luggage from room six-seventy-eight, and laid his fingers around the door knob. "I'll be down at the S.P. depot waiting for you, Jewel. There's a train in half an hour going north, so it will be plausible enough for you to take a taxi to the depot. Go inside, just as though you were leaving, see. And when the passengers come off the train, you join the crowd with your gun case and grip, and come on out to where I'll he waiting. Can you do that?"

"I guess I can, unless somebody runs over me on the way."

"Then I'll be going. The point is, we must not leave here together - even on a duck hunt!" He smiled and departed, at least three minutes before the porter tapped for admission.

There was no hitch, although there was a margin of safety narrow enough to set Johnny's blood tingling. He had "checked out" and had called his taxi and watched the porter load in gun case and grip, had tipped him lavishly and had slipped a dollar into the willing palm of the doorman, when he leaned in to get the address to give the driver. And then, just as the taxi was moving on, over the doorman's shoulder Johnny distinctly saw Bland turn in between the rubber plants that guarded the doorway. A pasty-faced, dull-eyed Bland, cheaply resplendent in new tan shoes, a new suit of that pronounced blue loved by Mexican dandies, a new red-and-blue striped tie, and a new soft hat of bottle-green velour.

For ten seconds Johnny was scared, which was a new sensation. For longer than that he had a guilty consciousness of having "double-crossed" a partner. He had a wild impulse to stop the taxi and sprint back to the hotel after Bland, and give him fifty dollars or so as a salve to his conscience, even though he could not take him into this new enterprise or even tell him what it was. Uncomfortably his memory visioned that other day (was it only yesterday morning? It seemed impossible!) when he had wandered forlornly out to the hangar in Tucson and had found Bland true to his trust when he might so easily have been false; when everything would seem to encourage him to be false. How much, after all, did Johnny owe to Bland Halliday? Just then he seemed to owe Bland everything.

It was all well enough for him to argue that his debt to Bland had been paid when he brought him to Los Angeles, and that Bland could have no just complaint if Johnny declined to continue the partnership longer. Bland, he told himself, would have quit him cold any time some other chance looked better. It was Johnny's plane, and Johnny had a right to do as he pleased with it.

For all that, Johnny rode to the S.P. depot feeling like a criminal trying to escape. He took his luggage and sneaked into the waiting room, sought an inconspicuous place and waited, his whole head and shoulders hidden behind a newspaper which he was not reading. Cliff Lowell could have found nothing to criticize in Johnny's manner of screening his presence there; though he would probably have been surprised at Johnny's reason for doing so. Johnny himself was surprised, bewildered even. That he, who had lorded over Bland with such patronizing contempt, should actually be afraid of meeting the little runt!

A stream of hurrying people, distinguished from others by their seeking glances and haste and luggage, warned him presently that he would be expected outside. He picked up his belongings and joined the procession, but he came very near missing Cliff altogether. He was looking for the dark-red roadster that had eaten up distance so greedily between Inglewood and the city, and he did not see it. He was standing dismayed, a slim, perturbed young fellow in khaki, with a grip in one hand and a canvas gun case in the other, when some one touched him on the arm. He needed the second glance to tell him it was Cliff, and even then it was the smooth, bored voice that convinced him. Cliff wore a motor coat that covered him from chin to heels, a leather cap pulled down over his ears, and driving goggles as concealing as a mask. He led the way to a touring car that looked like any other touring car - except to a man who could know the meaning of that high, long, ventilated hood and the heavy axles and wheels, and the general air of power and endurance, that marked it a thoroughbred among cars. The tonneau, Johnny saw as he climbed in, was packed tight with what looked like a camp outfit. His own baggage was crowded in somehow, and the side curtains, buttoned down tight, hid the load from

B. M. Bower

passers-by. Cliff pulled his coat close around his legs, climbed in, set his heel on the starter.

A pulsing beat, smooth, hushed, and powerful, answered. Cliff pulled the gear lever, eased in the clutch, and they slid quietly away down the street for two blocks, swung to the left and began to pick up speed through the thinning business district that dwindled presently to suburban small dwellings.

"Put on that coat and the goggles, old man," Cliff directed, his eyes on the lookback mirror, searching the highway behind them. "We've got an all-night drive, and it will be cold later on, so the coat will serve two purposes. It's hard to identify a man in a passing automobile if he's wearing a motor coat and goggles. You couldn't swear to your twin brother going by."

"This is a bear of a car," Johnny glowed, all atingle now with the adventure and its flavor of mystery. "I didn't know you had two. I was looking for the red one."

"I forgot to tell you." Which Johnny felt was a lie, because Cliff Lowell did not strike him as the kind of man who forgot things. "Yes, I keep two. This is good for long trips when I want to take luggage - and so on." His tone did not invite further conversation. He seemed absorbed now in his driving; and his driving, Johnny decided, was enough to absorb any man. Yard by yard he was sending the big-nosed car faster ahead, until the pointer on the speedometer seemed to want to rest on 35. Still, they did not seem to be going so very fast, except that they overhauled and passed everything else on the road, and not once did a car overhaul and pass them. Cliff glanced often into the mirror, watching the road behind them for the single speeding light of a motor cop - because Los Angeles County, as you are probably aware, does not favor thirty-five miles an hour for automobiles, but has fixed upon twenty-five as a safe and sane speed at which the general public may travel.

But Cliff was wary, chance favored them with fairly clear roads, and the miles slid swiftly behind. They ate at San Juan Capistrano not much past the hour which Johnny had all his life thought of as supper time. Cliff filled the gas tank, gave the motor a pint of oil and the radiator about a quart of water, turned up a few grease cups and applied the nose of the oil can here and there to certain bearings. He did it all with the fastidious air of a prince democratically inclined to look after things himself, the air which permeated his whole personality and made Johnny continue calling him Mr. Lowell, in spite of a life-long habit of applying nicknames even to chance acquaintances.

Cliff climbed in and settled himself. "We want to make it in time to get some hunting at daylight," he observed in a tone which included the fellow at the service station who was just pocketing his money for the gas and oil. "I think we can, with luck."

Luck seemed to mean speed and more speed, The headlights bored a white pathway through the dark, and down that pathway the car hummed at a fifty-mile clip where the road was straight. Johnny got thrills of which his hardy nerves had never dreamed themselves capable. Riding the sky in the Thunder Bird was tame to the point of boredom, compared with riding up and over and down and around a squirmy black line with the pound of the Pacific in his ears and the steady beat of the motor blending somehow with it, and the tingle of uncertainty as to whether they would make the next sharp curve on two wheels as successfully as they had made the last. Mercifully, they met no one on the hills. There were straight level stretches just beyond reach of the tide, and sometimes two eyes would glare at them, growing bigger and bigger. There would be a *swoo - sh* as a dark object shot by with mere inches to spare, and the eyes would glare no longer. By golly, Johnny would have a car or know the reason why! He'd bet he could drive one as well as Cliff Lowell too, once he had the feel of the thing.

"Too fast for you?" Cliff asked once, and Johnny felt the little tolerant smile he could not see.

"Too fast? Say, I'm used to *flying*!" Johnny shouted back, ready to die rather than own the tingling of his scalp for fear. He expected Cliff to let her out still more, after that tacit dare, but Cliff did not for two reasons: he was already going as fast as he could and keep the road, and he was convinced that Johnny Jewel had hardened every nerve in his system with skyriding.

Oceanside was but a sprinkle of lights and a blur of houses when they slipped through at slackened speed, lest their passing be noted curiously and remembered too well. On again, over the upland and down once more to the very sand where the waves rocked and boomed under the stars. Up and around and over and down - Johnny wondered how much farther they would hurl themselves through the night. Straight out along a narrow streak of asphalt toward lights twinkling on a blur of hillside. Up and around with a skidding turn to the right, and Del Mar was behind them. Down and around and along another straight line next the sands, and up a steep grade whose windings slowed even this brute of a car to a saner pace.

"This is Torrey Pine grade," Cliff informed him. "It isn't much farther to the next stop. I've been making time, because from San Diego on we have rougher going. This is not the most direct route we could have taken, but it's the best, seeing I have to stop in San Diego and complete certain arrangements. And then, too, it is not always wise to take a direct route to one's destination. Not - always." He slowed for a rickety bridge and added negligently, "We've made pretty fair time."

"I'd say we have. You've been doing fifty part of the time."

"And part of the time I haven't. From here on it's rough."

From there on it was that, and more. There had been a rain storm which the asphalt had long forgotten but the dirt road recorded with ruts and chuck-holes half filled with mud. The big car weathered it without breaking a spring, and before the tiredest laborer of San Diego had yawned and declared it was bedtime, they chuckled sedately into San Diego and stopped on a side street where a dingy garage stood open to the greasy sidewalk.

Cliff turned in there and whistled. A lean figure in grease-blackened coveralls came out of the shadows, and Cliff climbed down.

"I want to use your 'phone a minute. Go over the car, will you, until I come back. Where can I spot her - out of the way?"

The man waved a hand toward a space at the far end, and Cliff returned to his seat and dexterously placed the car, nose to the wall.

"You may as well stay right here. I'll not be gone long. You might curl down and take a nap."

It was not an order, but Johnny felt that he was expected to keep himself out of sight, and the suggestion to nap appealed to him. He found a robe and covered himself, and went to sleep with the readiness of a cat curled behind a warm stove. He did not know how long it was before Cliff woke him by pulling upon the car door. He did not remember that the garage man had fussed much with the car, though he might have done it so quietly that Johnny would not hear him. The man was standing just outside the door, and presently he signalled to Cliff, and Cliff backed out into the empty street. He nodded to the man and drove on to the corner, turned and went a block, and turned again. The streets seemed very quiet, so Johnny supposed that it was late, though the clock set in the instrument board was not running.

They went on, out of the town and into a road that wound up long hills and down to the foot of others which it straightway climbed. Cliff did not drive so fast now, though their speed was steady. Twice he stopped to walk over to some house near the road and have speech with the owner. He was inquiring the way, he explained to Johnny, who did not believe him; Cliff drove with too much certainty, seemed too familiar with certain unexpected twists in the road, to be a stranger upon it, Johnny thought. But he did not say anything - it was none of his business. Cliff was running this part of the show, and Johnny was merely a passenger. His job was flying, when the time came to fly.

After a while he slid farther down into the seat and slept.

　　　　　B. M. Bower

CHAPTER SEVENTEEN

"MY JOB'S FLYING"

The stopping of the motor wakened him finally, and he sat up, stretching his arms and yawning prodigiously. His legs were cramped, his neck was stiff, he was conscious of great emptiness. By the stars he knew that it was well toward morning. Hills bulked in the distance, with dark blobs here and there which daylight later identified as live oaks. Cliff was climbing out, and at the sound of Johnny's yawn he turned.

"We'll camp here, I think. There's no road from here on, and I rather want daylight. Perhaps then we will decide not to go on. How would a cup of coffee suit you? I can get out enough plunder for a meal."

"I can sure do the rest," Johnny cheerfully declared. "Cook it and eat it too. Where's there any water?"

"There's a creek over here a few yards. I'll get a bucket." With his trouble-light suspended from the top of the car, Cliff moved a roll of blankets and a bag that had jolted out of place. In a moment he had all the necessary implements of an emergency camp, and was pulling out cans and boxes of supplies that opened Johnny's eyes. Evidently Cliff had come prepared to camp for some time.

Over coffee and bacon and bread Johnny learned some things he had wanted to know. They were in the heart of the country which Cliff had shown him on the relief map, miles from the beaten trail of tourists, but within fifteen miles of the border.

"There's a cabin somewhere near here that we can use for headquarters," Cliff further explained. "And to-day a Mexican will come and take charge of camp and look after our interests while we are over the line. I have ordered a quantity of gas that will be brought here and stored in a safe place, and there is a shelter for the plane. I merely want you to look over the ground, make sure of the landing possibilities, and fix certain landmarks in your mind so that you can drop down here without making any mistake as to the spot. When that is done we will return and bring your airplane over. It is only about a hundred and forty miles from Los Angeles, air line. You can make that easily enough, I suppose?"

"I don't see why not. A hundred and forty miles ain't far, when you're lined out and flying straight for where you're going."

"No. Well, one step at a time. We'll just repack this, so that we can move on to the cabin as soon as it's light enough. I don't think it can be far."

Daylight came and showed them that the cabin was no more than a long pistol shot away. Johnny looked at Cliff queerly. City man he might be - city man he certainly looked and acted and talked, but he did not appear to rely altogether upon signposts and street-corner labels to show him his way about. Just who and what was the fellow, anyway? Something more than a high-class newspaper man, Johnny suspected.

That cabin, for instance, might have been built and the surroundings ordered to suit their purpose. It was a commonplace cabin, set against a hill rock-hewn and rugged, with a queer, double-pointed top like twin steeples tumbled by an earthquake; or like two "sheep herders' monuments" built painstakingly by giants. The lower slope of the hill was grassy, with scattered live oaks and here and there a huge bowlder. It was one of these live oaks, the biggest of them all, with wide-spreading branches drooping almost to the ground, that Cliff pointed out as an excellent concealment for an airplane.

"Run it under there, and who would ever suspect? Mateo is there already with his woman and the kiddies. Has it ever occurred to you, old man, how thoroughly disarming a woman and kiddies are in any enterprise that requires secrecy?"

"Can't say it has. It has occurred to me that kids are the limit for blabbing things. And women -"

"Not these," Cliff smiled serenely. "These are trained kiddies. They do their blabbing at home, you'll find. They're better than dogs, to give warning of strangers prowling about."

He must have meant during the day they were better than dogs. They drove up to the cabin, swung around the end and turned under a live oak whose branches scraped the car's top, while four dogs circled the machine, barking and growling. Still no kiddies appeared, but their father came out of a back door and drove the dogs back. He was low-browed, swart and silent, with a heavy black mustache and a mop of hair to match. Cliff left the car and walked away with him, speaking in an undertone what Johnny knew to be Spanish. The low-browed one interpolated an occasional "Si, si, senor!" and gesticulated much.

"All right, Johnny, this is Mateo, who will look after us at this end - providing there's nothing to hinder our using this as headquarters. How about that flat, out in front? Is it big enough for a flying field, do you think? You might walk over it and take a look."

Stiffly, Johnny climbed down and walked obediently out across the open flat. It was fairly smooth, though Mateo's kids might well be set gathering rocks. The hills encircled it, green where the rocks were not piled too ruggedly. He inspected the great oak which Cliff had pointed out as a hiding place for the plane. Truly it was a wonder of an oak tree. Its trunk was gnarled and big as a hogshead, and it leaned away from the steep slope behind it so that its southern branches almost touched the ground. These stretched farther than Johnny had dreamed a tree could stretch its branches, and screened completely the wide space beneath. It was like a great tent, with the back wall lifted; since here the branches inclined upward, scraping the hillside with their tips. The Thunder Bird could be wheeled around behind and under easily enough, and never seen from the front and sides. It was so obviously perfect that Johnny wondered why Cliff should bother to consult him about it. He wondered, too, how Cliff had found the place, how he had completed so quickly his plans to use it for the purpose. It looked almost as though Cliff had expected him and had made ready for him though that could not be so, since not even Johnny himself had known that he was coming to the Coast so soon. But to have the place all ready, with a man to take charge and all in a few hours, was an amazing accomplishment that filled Johnny with awe. Cliff Lowell must be a wizard at news-gathering if his talents were to be measured by this particular achievement.

"Well, do you think it will serve?" Catlike, Cliff had come up behind him.

"Sure it will serve. If you can think up some way to hide the track of the plane when it lands, it wouldn't be found here in a thousand years. But of course the marks will show -"

"Just what kind of marks?"

"Well, the wheels themselves don't leave much of a track, and the wind fills them quick, anyway. But the drag digs in. If you've ever been around a flying field you've noticed what looks like wheel-barrow tracks all over, haven't you? That's something you can't get away from, wherever you land. Though of course some soil holds the mark worse than others."

"That will be attended to. Now I'll show you just where this spot is on the map." He produced the folded map and opened it, kneeling on the ground to spread it flat. "You see those twin peaks up there? They are just here. This is the valley, and right here is the cabin. You might take this map and study it well. You will have to fly high, to avoid observation, and land with as little manoeuvering as possible. For ten or fifteen miles around here there is nothing but wilderness, fortunately. The land is held in an immense tract - and I happen to know the owners so that it will be only chance observers we need to fear. You will need to choose your landing so that you can come down right here, close to the oak, and be able to get the machine under cover at once. I'll mark the spot - just here, you see.

"Now, I shall have Mateo bring the blankets here under the tree. I feel the need of a little sleep, myself. How about you? We start back at dark, by the way."

"How about that duck hunting?"

"Ducks? Oh, Mateo will hunt the ducks!" Cliff permitted himself a superior smile. "We shall have sufficient outlet for any surplus energy without going duck hunting. You had better turn in when I do."

"No, I slept enough to do me, at a pinch. If Mateo can get a horse, I want to ride up on this pinnacle and take a look-see over the country. I can get the lay of things a whole lot better than goggling a month at your doggone maps."

Cliff took a minute to think it over and gave a qualified consent. "Don't go far, and don't talk to any one you may meet - though there is no great chance of meeting any one. I suppose," he added grudgingly, "it will be a good idea for you to get the lay of the country in your mind. Though the map can give you all you need to know, I should think."

On a scrawny little sorrel that Mateo brought up from some hidden pasture where the feed was apparently short, Johnny departed, aware of Mateo's curious, half-suspicious stare. He had a full canteen from the car and a few ragged slices of bread wrapped in paper with a little boiled ham. In spite of the fact that he had lately forsworn so tame a thing as riding, he was glad to be on a horse once more, though be wished it was a better animal.

He climbed the hill, zigzagging back and forth to make easier work for the pony, until he was high above the live-oak belt and coming into shale rock and rubble that made hard going for the horse. He dismounted, led the pony to a shelving, rock-made shade, and tied him there. Then, with canteen and food slung over his shoulder, Johnny climbed to the peak and sat down puffing on the shady side of one of the twin columns.

Seen close, they were huge, steeple-like outcroppings of rock, with soil-filled crevices that gave foothold for bushes. In all the country around Johnny could see no other hilltop that in the least resembled this, so it did not seem to him likely that he would ever miss his way when he travelled the air lanes.

For awhile he sat gazing out over the country, which seemed a succession of green valleys, hidden from one another by high hills or wooded ridges. Mexico lay before him, across the valley and a hill or two - fifteen miles, Cliff Lowell had told him. It would be extremely simple to fly straight toward this particular hill, circle, and land down there in front of the oak. Cliff had spoken of risk, bat Johnny could not see much risk here. It must be across the line, he thought. Still, Cliff had said he had friends there, which did not sound like danger. They had considered it worth fifteen hundred a week, though, to fly across these fifteen miles into Mexico and back again. Johnny shook his head slowly, gave up the puzzle, and took out his wallet to count the money again.

Half an hour he spent, fingering those bank notes, gloating over them, wondering what Mary V would say if she knew he had them, wishing he had another fifteen hundred, so he could pay old Sudden and be done with it. An unpleasant thought came to him and nagged at him, though he tried to push it from him; the thought that it would be Sudden's security that he would be risking - that the Thunder Bird was not really his until he had paid that note.

The thought troubled him. He got up and moved restlessly along the base of the towering rock, when something whined past his ear and spatted against a bowlder beyond. Johnny did not think; he acted instinctively, dropping as though he had been shot and lying there until he had time to plan his next move. He had not been raised in gun smoke, but nevertheless he knew a bullet when he heard it, and he did not think himself conceited when he believed this particular bullet had been presented to him. Why?

On his stomach he inched down out of range unless the shooter moved his position, and then, impelled by a keen desire to know for sure, he adopted the old, old trick of sending his hat scouting for him. A dead bush near by furnished the necessary stick, and the steep slope gave him shelter while he tested the real purpose of the man who had shot. It might be just a hunter, of course - only this was a poor place for hunting anything but one inoffensive young flyer who meant harm to no one. He put his hat on the stick, pushed the stick slowly up past a rock, and tried to make the hat act as though its owner was crawling laboriously to some fancied shelter.

For a minute or two the hat crawled unmolested. Then,

B. M. Bower

pang-g came another bullet and bored a neat, brown-rimmed hole through the uphill side of the hat, and tore a ragged hole on its way out through the downhill side. Johnny let the hat slide down to him, looked at the holes with widening eyes, said "Good gosh!" just under his breath, and hitched himself farther down the slope.

His curiosity was satisfied; he had seen all of the country he needed to see and there was nothing to stay for, anyway. When he reached. the patient sorrel pony a minute or two later (it had taken him half an hour or more to climb from the pony to the peak, but climbing, of course, is much slower than coming down - even without the acceleration of singing rifle bullets) he was perspiring rather freely and puffing a little.

For a time he waited there under the shelf of rock. But he heard no sound from above, and in a little while he led the pony down the other way, which brought him to the valley near a small pasture which was evidently the pony's home, judging from the way he kept pulling in that direction. Johnny turned the horse in and closed the gate, setting the old saddle astride it with the bridle hanging over the horn. He did not care for further exploration, thank you.

What Johnny would like to know was, what had he done that he should be shot at? He was down there by Cliff Lowell's invitation - Straightway he set off angrily, taking long steps to the cabin and the great oak tree beside it. The two dogs and five half-naked Mexican children spied him and scattered, the dogs coming at him full tilt, the children scuttling to the cabin. Johnny swore at the dogs and they did not bite. He followed the children and they did not stop. So he came presently to the oak and roused Cliff, who came promptly to an elbow with a wicked looking automatic pointed straight at Johnny's middle.

"Say, for gosh sake! I been shot at twice already this morning. What's the idea? I never was gunned so much in my life, and I live in Arizona, that's supposed to be bad. What's the matter with this darned place?"

Cliff tucked the gun out of sight under his blanket, yawned, and lay down again. "You caught me asleep, old man. I beg your pardon - but I have learned in Mexico that it's best to get the gun first and see who it is after that. Did you say something about being shot at?"

"I did, but I could say more. Here I am down here without any gun but that cussed shotgun, and I didn't have that, even, when I coulda used it handy. And look what I got, up here on the hill!" He removed his hat and poked two fingers through the two holes in the crown. "Some movie stuff! What's the idea?"

Cliff nearly looked startled. He called, "Oh, Mateo!" And Mateo came in haste, bent down, and the two murmured together in Mexican. Afterwards Cliff turned to Johnny with his little smile.

"It's all right, old man - glad you weren't hurt. It was a mistake, though. You were a stranger, and it was thought, I suppose, that you were spying on this place. While it was a close call for you, it proves that we are being well cared for. Better forget it and turn in."

He yawned again and turned over so that his back was toward Johnny, and that youth took the hint and departed to find blankets to spread for himself. He was tired enough to lie down and sleepy enough to sleep, but he could not blandly forget about those bullets as Cliff advised. There were several things he wanted to know before he would feel perfectly satisfied.

Since the Thunder Bird was not here, why should strangers be shot at? Their only trouble would be with the guards along the boundary, when they tried to cross back from Mexico. But they had not tried it yet. The guards were still happily unaware of how they were going to worry later on, so why the shooting?

"Oh, well, thunder! They didn't hit me - so I should care. If Cliff wants to set guards around this camp before there's anything to guard, that's his business. Like paying me before I fly, I guess. He's got the guards up there practising, maybe. I should worry; my job's flying."

CHAPTER EIGHTEEN

INTO MEXICO AND RETURN

Bright-eyed, eager for the adventure trail, Johnny swung the propeller of the Thunder Bird over three times and turned to Cliff. "Here's where you learn one of the joys of flying. Hold her there while I climb in. When I holler contact, you kick her over - if you're man enough."

Cliff smiled, dropped his cigarette and ground it under his heel, then reached up and grasped the propeller blade. "I never actually did this, but I've watched others do it. I suppose I must learn. Oh, before we go up, I ought to tell you that I'd like to go on over the line this morning if possible. If you can fly very high, and when you near the line just glide as quietly as possible, I think it can be managed without our being seen. And since it is only just daylight now, it should not be late when we arrive."

"It should not," Johnny agreed. "Arriving late ain't what worries a flyer - it's arriving too doggone unexpected. Where do we light, in Mexico? Just any old place?"

"Straight toward Mateo's camp, first - flying very high. From there on I'll direct you. Shall we start?"

B. M. Bower

"You're the doctor," grunted Johnny, not much pleased with Cliff's habit of giving information a bit at a time as it was needed. It seemed to betray a lack of confidence in him, a fear that he might tell too much; though how Johnny could manage to divulge secrets while he was flying a mile above the earth, Cliff had probably not attempted to explain.

Because he was offended, Johnny gave Cliff what thrills he could during that flight. He went as high as he dared, which was very high indeed, and hoped that Cliff's ears roared and that he was thinking pleasant thoughts such as the effect upon himself of dropping suddenly to that sliding relief map away down below. He hoped that Cliff was afraid of being lost, and of landing on some high mountain that stuck up like a little hill above the general assembly of dimpled valleys and spiny ridges and hills. But if Cliff were afraid he did not say so, and when the double-pointed hill that Johnny had reason to remember slid toward them, Cliff pointed ahead to another, turned his head and shouted.

"See that deep notch in the ridge away off there? Fly toward that notch."

Johnny flew. The double-pointed hill drifted behind them, other hills slid up until the two could gaze down upon their highest peaks. Beyond, as Cliff's maps had told him, lay Mexico. At eight thousand feet he shut off the motor and glided for the notched ridge. The patrol who sighted the Thunder Bird at that height, with no motor hum to call his attention upward, must have sharp eyes and a habit of sky-gazing. Cliff, peering down over the edge of the cockpit, must have thought so, for he laughed aloud triumphantly.

"Fine! I think we are putting one over on my friends, the guards," he cried, with more animation than Johnny had yet observed in him. Indeed, it occurred to Johnny quite suddenly that he had never heard Cliff Lowell laugh heartily out loud before. "How far can you keep this up - without the motor?"

"Till we hit the ground," drawled Johnny, who was enjoying his position of captain of this cruise. He had been taking orders from Cliff for about forty-eight hours now without respite save when he slept, and even his sleep had been ordered by Cliff.

"I could make that twelve miles or so from here, though. Why?"

"In the twelve miles you would not be using gas - could you glide to the ridge, circle and fly high again, and back to Mateo's camp without stopping for gas?"

Johnny gave a grunt of surprise. "I guess I could," he said. "Why?"

"Then do it. Just that. On this side of the notch you will see - when you are close enough - a few adobe buildings. I want to pass over those buildings at a height of, say, five hundred feet; or a little lower will be better, if you can make it. Then circle and come back again. And try and make the return trip as high as you did coming down, until you are well past those mountains we passed over, just inside the line. Then come down at camp as inconspicuously as possible. I may add that as we pass over the buildings I mentioned, please start your motor. I am not expected at just this time, and I wish to attract attention."

"Hunh!" grunted Johnny. "You'd sure attract attention if I didn't - because how the deuce would you expect me to climb back from five hundred feet to eight thousand or so, without starting the motor?"

Cliff did not answer. He was busy with something which he had brought with him; a square package to which Johnny had paid very little attention, thinking it some article which Cliff wanted to have in camp.

Evidently this was not to be a news-gathering trip, though Johnny could not see why not, now they were over here. Why just sail over a few houses and fly home? He could see the houses now, huddled against the ridge. A ranch, he guessed it, since half the huddle appeared to be sheds and corrals. A queer place to gather news of international importance, thought Johnny, as he volplaned down toward the spot. He threw in the motor and was buzzing over the buildings when Cliff unstrapped himself, half rose in his seat and lifted something in his arms.

"Steady," he cried. "I want to drop this over." Whereupon he heaved it backward so that it would fall clear of the wing, and peered after it through his goggles for a minute. "You can go home now," he shouted to Johnny, and settled down in his seat with the air of a man who has done his duty and has nothing more on his mind.

Mystified, Johnny spiraled upward until he had his altitude, and started back for the United States. Clouds favored him when he crossed the boundary, hiding him altogether from the earth. Indeed, they caused him to lose himself for a minute, so that when he dropped down below the strata of vapor he was already nearly over the double-pointed hill that was his landmark. But Cliff did not notice, and a little judicious manoeuvering brought him into the little valley and headed straight for the oak, easily identified because Mateo was standing directly in front of it waving a large white cloth.

They landed smoothly and stopped exactly where Johnny had planned to stop. He climbed out, Cliff following more awkwardly, and the three of them wheeled the Thunder Bird under the oak where it was completely hidden.

It was not until he had come out again into the warm sunshine of mid-morning that Johnny observed how the kiddies were playing their part. They had a curious little homemade wheelbarrow rigged, and were trundling it solemnly up and down and over and around the single mark made by the tail drag. A boy of ten or twelve rode the barrow solidly and with dignity, while a thin-legged girl pushed the vehicle. Behind them trotted two smaller ones, gravely bestriding stick horses. Casually it resembled play. It would have been play had not Mateo gone out where they were and inspected the result of stick-dragging and barrow-wheeling, and afterwards, with a wave of his hand and a few swift Mexican words, directed them to play farther out from the oak, where the Thunder Bird had first come to earth. Solemn-eyed, they extended the route of their procession, and Johnny, watching them with a queer grin on his face, knew that when those children stopped "playing" there would be no mark of the Thunder Bird's landing left upon that soil.

"I've sure got to hand it to the kids," he told Cliff, who

merely smiled and pulled out his cigarette case for a smoke.

CHAPTER NINETEEN

BUT JOHNNY WAS NEITHER FOOL
NOR KNAVE

Cliff smiled faintly one morning and handed Johnny a long manila envelope over their breakfast table in Mateo's cabin. "Your third week's salary," he idly explained. "Do you want it?"

"Well, I ain't refusing it," Johnny grinned back. "I guess maybe I'll stick for another week, anyway." He emptied his coffee cup and held it up for Mateo's woman to refill, trying to match Cliff Lowell's careless air of indifference to the presence of seventeen hundred dollars on that table. "That is, if you think I'm making good," he added boyishly, looking for praise.

"Your third week's salary answers that, doesn't it? From now on it may not be quite so easy to make good. Perhaps, since I want to go across this evening as late as you can make a safe landing over there, I ought to tell you that a border patrol saw us yesterday, coming back, and wondered a little at a government plane getting over the line. He did not report it, so far as I know. But he will make a report the next time he sees the same thing happen."

"I wish I didn't have that name painted clear across her

B. M. Bower

belly," Johnny fretted. "But if I went and painted it out it would all be black, and that would be just as bad. And if I took off the letters with something, I'm afraid I'd eat off the sizing too, or weaken the fabric or something. I ought to recover the wings, but that takes time -"

Cliff gave him that tolerant smile which Johnny found so intolerable. "It is not at all necessary. I thought of all possible contingencies when I first saw the Thunder Bird. Across the line the name absolutely identifies it, which is rather important. On this side it is known as a bird fond of doing the unusual. Your reputation, old man, may help you out of a tight place yet. Now we are duck hunters, remember. Hereafter we shall be hunting ducks with an airplane - something new, but not at all improbable, especially when it is the Thunder Bird doing the hunting. We must carry our shotguns along with us, and a few ducks as circumstantial evidence. If we stray across the line accidentally, that will be because you do not always look where you are flying, and watch the landmarks."

"This, of course, in case we are actually caught. Though I do not see why that should happen. They have no anti-aircraft guns to bring us down. It may be a good idea to carry an auxiliary tank of gasoline in case of an emergency."

"I don't see why - not if I fill up over there every time I land. I can stay up three hours - longer, if I can glide a lot. Of course that high altitude takes more, in climbing up, and flying while you're up there, but the distance is short. I'll chance running outa gas. I don't want the extra weight, flying high as we have to. The motor's doing all she wants to do, just carrying us."

Cliff did not argue the point, but went out to his car, fussed with it for a few minutes, and then drove off on one of the mysterious trips that took him away from Mateo's cabin and sometimes kept him away for two days at a time. Johnny did not know where Cliff went; to see the boss, perhaps, and turn in what news he had gleaned - if indeed he had succeeded in gleaning any. Sometimes the long waits were tiresome to a youth who loved action. But Johnny had been schooled to the monotony of a range line-camp, and if he could have ridden over the country while he waited, he would not have minded being left idle most of the time.

But he did not dare leave camp for more than half an hour or so at a time, because he never knew what minute Cliff might return and want him; and when one is being paid something like ten dollars an hour, waking or sleeping, for his time, one feels constrained to keep that precious time absolutely available to his employer. At least, Johnny felt constrained to do so. He could not even go duck hunting. Mateo hunted the ducks, using Johnny's gun or Cliff's, and seldom failing to bring back game. It would be ducks shot by Mateo which would furnish the circumstantial evidence which Cliff mentioned that morning.

Johnny went out to the Thunder Bird, shooed three kids from under the wings, and began to fuss with the motor. One advantage of being idle most of the time was the easy life the Thunder Bird was leading. The motor was not being worn out on this job, at any rate.

So far he had not spent a hundred dollars of his salary on the upkeep of his machine. He was glad of that, because he already had enough to pay old Sudden and have the price of a car left over. With the Thunder Bird clear, and a couple of thousand dollars to the good - why, he would not change places with the owner of the Rolling R himself! He could go back any time and vindicate himself to the whole outfit. He could pick Mary V up and carry her off now, without feeling that he was taking any risk with her future. Poor little girl, she would be wondering what had become of him; he'd write, or send a wire, if Cliff would ever open his heart enough to take a fellow with him to where there was a post-office or something.

He was beginning to feel a deep need of some word from Mary V, was Johnny. He was beginning to worry, to grow restive down here in the wilderness, seeing nothing, doing nothing save kill time between those short, surreptitious flights across to the notched ridge and back again. Two weeks of that was beginning to pall.

But the money he was receiving did not pall. It held him in leash, silenced the doubts that troubled him now and then, kept him temporizing with that uneasy thing we call conscience.

He climbed now into the cockpit, testing the controls absent-mindedly while he pondered certain small incidents that caused him a certain vague discomfort whenever he thought of them. For one thing, why must a gatherer of news carry mysterious packages into Mexico and leave them there, sometimes throwing them overboard with a tiny parachute arrangement, as Cliff had done on the first trip, and flying back without stopping? Why must a newspaper man bring back certain mysterious packages, and straightway disappear with them in the car? That he should confer long and secretly with men of florid complexions and an accent which hardens its g's and sharpens its s's, might very plausibly be a part of his gathering of legitimate news of international import. Though Johnny rather doubted its legitimacy, he had no doubt whatever of its world-wide importance. Certain nations were at war - and he was no fool, once he stopped dreaming long enough to think logically.

Those packages bothered him more than the florid gentlemen, however. At first he suspected smuggling, or something like that. But gun-running, that staple form of border lawbreaking, did not fit into any part of Cliff's activities, though opium might. But when he had made an excuse for handling one or two of the packages, they routed the opium theory. They were flat and loosely solid, as packages of paper would be. Not state documents such as melodramas use to keep the villains sweating - they did not come in reams, so far as Johnny knew. He could think of no other papers that would need smuggling into or out of a country as free as ours where freedom of the press has become a watchword; yet the idea persisted stubbornly that those were packages of paper which he had managed to take in his hands.

As a pleasing relief from useless cogitation on the subject, Johnny took his bank roll from a pocket he had sewed inside his shirt. Like a miser he fingered the magic paper, counting and recounting, spending it over and over in anticipatory daydreams. Thirty-two hundred dollars he counted in bills of large denomination - impressively clean, crisp bills, some of them - and mentally placed that amount to one side. That would pay old Sudden, interest and all. What was left he could do with as he pleased. He counted it again. There were three hundred dollars left from what

B. M. Bower

Bland had earned - Bland - What had become of Bland, anyway? Little runt might be broke again; in fact, it was practically certain that he would be broke again, though he must have had close to a hundred dollars when they landed in Los Angeles. Oh, well - forget Bland!

So there were the three hundred - gee golly, but it had cost, that short stay in the burg of Bland's dreams. A hundred dollars gone like the puff of a cigarette! Well, there were the three hundred left - he'd have been broke, pronto, if he had stayed there much longer. Another hundred he had spent on the Thunder Bird - golly, but propellers do cost a lot! And that shotgun he never had had a chance to shoot - Cliff sure was a queer guy, making him buy all that scenery, and then caching him away so no one ever got a chance to size him up and see whether he looked like a duck hunter or not. Well, anyway, let's see. There were a thousand in big juicy hundreds; and five hundred more in fifties and twenties -

Out beyond the oak's leafy screen the dogs were barking and growling and the children were calling shrilly. Johnny hastily put away his wealth and eased himself up so that he could peer out through the branches. He had not consciously feared the coming of strangers, yet now he felt his heart thumping noisily because of the clamor out in the yard. While he looked, two horsemen rode past and stopped at the cabin.

Now Johnny had been telling himself what a godsend some new face would be to him, yet he did not rush out to welcome the callers and ask the news of the outside world which Cliff was so chary of giving. He did not by any sound or movement declare his presence. He simply craned and listened.

One of the men he could not see because of a great, overhanging limb that barred his vision. The other happened to stop just opposite a very good peephole through the leaves. The kiddies were standing back shyly, patently interrupted in their pretended play of trundling the wheelbarrow and dragging the stick horses over the yard. Rosa, the thin-legged girl, stood shyly back with her finger in her mouth, in plain sight of Johnny, though she could not see him in the deep shadow of the leaves.

It was the man that interested Johnny, however. He was a soldier, probably one of the border patrol. He sat his horse easily, erect in the saddle, straight-limbed and alert, with lean hard jaw and a gray eye that kept glancing here, there, everywhere while the other talked. It was only a profile view that Johnny saw, but he did not need a look at the rest of his face with the other gray eye to be uncomfortably convinced that not much would escape him.

"It circled and seemed to come down somewhere on this side the Potreros and it has not been seen since. Ask the kids if they saw something that looked like a big bird flying." This from the unseen one, who had raised his voice as impatience seized him. These Mexicans were so slow-witted!

Johnny heard Mateo's voice, speaking at length. He saw Rosa take her finger from her mouth, catch up a corner of her ragged, apron and twist it in an agony of confusion, and then as if suddenly comprehending what it was these senores wished to know, she pointed jerkily toward the north. Perhaps the others also pointed to the north, for the lean-jawed soldier tilted his head backward and stared up that way, and Mateo spoke in very fair English.

"The kids, she's see. No, I dunno. I'm busy I don' make attenshions. I'm fine out when -"

"We know when," the efficient looking soldier interrupted. "You keep watch. If you see it fly back, see just where it comes from and where it goes, and ride like hell down to camp and tell us. You will get more money than you can make here in a year. You sabe that?"

"Yo se, senor - me, I'm onderstan'."

"You know where our camp is?"

"Si, senor capitan. Me, I'm go lak hell."

"Well, there's nothing more to be got here. Let's get along." And as they moved off Johnny caught a fragmentary phrase "from Riverside."

The children had taken up their industrious play again, and their mother had turned from the open doorway to hush the crying of Mateo's youngest in the cabin. Mateo called the children to him and patted them on the head, and the senora, their mother, brought candy and gave it to them. They ran off, sucking the sweets, gabbling gleefully to one another. Cliff Lowell had been right, nothing is so disarming as a woman and children about a place where secrets are kept.

There had been no suspicion of Mateo's cabin and the family that lived there in squalid content. The incident was closed.

But Johnny slumped down in the seat again and glowered through the little, curved windshield at the crisply wavering leaves beyond the Thunder Bird's nose. He was not a fool, any more than he was a crook. He was young and too confiding, too apt to take things for granted and let the other fellow do the worrying, so long as things were fairly pleasant for Johnny Jewel. But right now his eyes were open in more senses than one, and they were very wide open at that.

There was something very radically wrong with this job. The fiction of legitimate news gathering in Mexico could no longer give him any feeling save disgust for his own culpability. News gathering did not require armed guards - not in this country, at least - and such mysteries as Cliff Lowell dealt in. The money in his possession ceased to give him any little glow of pleasure. Instead, his face grew all at once hot with shame and humiliation. It was not honest money, although he had earned it honestly enough. If it had been honest money, why should those soldiers go riding through the valleys, looking for him and his plane? It was not for the pleasure of saying howdy, if Johnny might judge from the hard-eyed glances of that one who had stopped in plain view.

It was not honest money that he had been taking. Why, even the kids out there knew it was not honest! Look at Rosa, playing shrewdly her part of dumb shyness in the presence of strangers - and she thinking all the while how best she could lie to them, the little imp! It was not the first time she had shown her shrewdness. Why, nearly every time Cliff wanted to make a trip across the line, those kids climbed the hill to where

B. M. Bower

they could look all over the flat and the near-by hills, and if they saw any one they would yell down to Mateo. If the interloper happened to be close, they had orders to roll small rocks down for a warning, so Cliff one day told Johnny with that insufferably tolerant smile. Cliff brought them candy and petted them, just for what use he could make of them as watchdogs. Would all that be necessary for a legitimate enterprise? Wouldn't the guards have orders to shut their eyes when an airplane flew high, bearing a man who gathered news vital to the government?

Once before Johnny had been made a fool of by horse thieves who plied their trade across the line. They had given him this very same airplane to keep him occupied and tempt him away from his duty while they stole Rolling R horses at their leisure. Wasn't this very money - thirty-two hundred dollars of it - going to pay for that bit of gullibility? Gulled into earning money to pay for an earlier piece of gross stupidity!

"The prize - mark!" he branded himself. "By golly, they've got me helping 'em do worse than steal horses from the Rolling R, this time; putting something over on the government is their little stunt - and by golly, I fell for the bait just like I done the other time! *Huhn*!" Then he added a hopeful threat. "But they had me on the hip, that time - this time it's going to be different!"

For the rest of that day he brooded, waiting for Cliff. What he would do he himself did not know, but he was absolutely determined that he would do something.

CHAPTER TWENTY

MARY V TAKES THE TRAIL

On a Saturday afternoon Spring Street at Sixth is a busy street, as timid pedestrians and the traffic cop stationed there will testify. In times not so far distant the general public howled insistently for a subway, or an elevated railway - anything that would relieve the congestion and make the downtown district of Los Angeles a decently safe place to walk in. But subways and elevated railways cost money, and the money must come from the public which howls for these things. Gradually the public ceased to howl and turned its attention to dodging instead. For that reason Sixth and Spring remains a busy corner, especially at certain hours of the day.

On a certain Saturday, months before the traffic cops grew tired of blowing whistles and took to revolving silently at stated intervals with outspread wings after the manner of certain mechanical toys, Mary V Selmer came from the Western Union's main office, and thanked heaven silently that her new roadster of the type called the Bear Cat was still standing at the curb where she had left it. Just beyond it on the left a stream of automobiles grazed by - but none so new and shiny, so altogether elegantly "sassy" as the Bear Cat. Mary V, when she stepped in and settled herself behind the steering wheel, matched the car, completed its elegant "sassiness," its general air of getting where it wanted to go, let the traffic be what it might and devil-take-the-fenders.

Mary V was unhappy, but her unhappiness was somewhat mitigated by the Bear Cat and her new mole collar that made a soft, fur wall about her slim throat to her very ears and the tip of her saucy chin, and the perky hat - also elegantly "sassy" - turned up in front and down behind, and the new driving gauntlets, and the new coat that had made dad groan until he had seen Mary V inside it and changed the groan to a proud little chuckle of admiration.

Mary V was terribly worried about Johnny Jewel. She had been sure that he had come to Los Angeles, and she had pestered her dad into bringing her here in the firm belief that she would find him at once and "have it out with him" once and for all. (Just as though Mary V could ever settle a quarrel once and for all!) But though she had haunted all the known and some of the unknown flying fields, she had found no trace of Johnny. That messenger boy in Tucson had insisted that the plane climbed high and then flew toward the Coast. And at Yuma she had learned that the Thunder Bird had alighted there for gas and oil and had flown toward Los Angeles. But so far as Mary V could discover, it was still flying.

Hoping to wean her from worrying about Johnny, dad had bought the Bear Cat. Mary V had owned it for ten days now, and its mileage stood at 1400 and was just about ready to slide another "1" into sight. The Bear Cat had proven itself a useful little Cat.

Now she shifted from neutral to second, disdaining low speed altogether, and swung boldly out into the stream of traffic. A Ford shied off with a startled squawk to let the Bear Cat by. A hurrying truck that was thinking of cutting in to get first chance within the safety zone passage thought better of it when Mary V honked her big Klaxon at him, and stopped with a jolt that nearly brought the Ford to grief behind it.

But Mary V ignored these trifles. She was busy wondering where she should go next, and she was scanning swiftly the faces of the passers-by in the hope of glimpsing the one face she wished most of all to see.

She reached the corner just as the frame closed against her, and with one small foot on the clutch pedal and the other on the brake, she leaned back and scanned the crowd. Abruptly she leaned and beckoned, saw that her signal went unregarded, and gave three short but terrific blasts of her Klaxon. Five hundred and forty-nine persons reacted sharply to the sound and sent startled glances her way. The traffic cop whirled and looked, the motorman on the car waiting beside her leaned far out and craned, and the conductor grasped both handrails and took a step down that he might see the better.

Mary V ignored these trifles. Bland, for whom she had meant it, jumped and turned a pale, startled pair of eyes her way, and to him she beckoned imperiously. He hesitated, glanced this way and that, making a quick mental decision. Mary V had once been candidly tempted to shoot him and had dallied with the temptation to the point of cocking her sixshooter and aiming it directly at him. She looked now quite capable of repeating the performance and of completing what

B. M. Bower

she had merely started last summer. He went to the edge of the curb, obeying her expectant stare. The expectant stare continued to transfix him, and he stepped off the curb and close to the Bear Cat that was growling in its throat.

"Bland Halliday, where have you *been*, for gracious sake? And where's Johnny?"

"I ain't been anywhere but here - and I wisht I knowed where Johnny was. I -"

"Bland Halliday, you tell me instantly! Where's Johnny?"

"Honest, I don't know. I been looking for him myself, and -"

"Bland Halliday, do you want to be torn limb from limb, right here on the public street before everybody? I want to know where Johnny is, and I want to know *now*."

"Aw, f'r cat's sake! I ain't saw Johnny f'r three weeks - not since the night we got here. I been looking -"

Behind them sounded a succession of impatient honks that extended almost to Seventh Street. The traffic cop had blown his whistle, the street car had clanged warning and gone on. The truck had shaved past Mary V and the Ford had followed. Other cars coming up behind had mistaken the Bear Cat's inaction for closed traffic and had stopped. Others had stopped behind them; then two other street cars slid up and blocked the way around.

Mary V was quite oblivious to all this. She was glaring at the one link between herself and Johnny Jewel. She was bitterly regretting the fact that she had no gun with which to scare Bland into telling the truth, and she was wondering what other means of coercion would prove effective. Bland knew where Johnny was, of course. He was lying, for some reason - probably because he had the habit and couldn't stop.

Bland kept an eye on Mary V's right hand. He suspected a gun, and when, in involuntary obedience to the frantic honkings behind her, she let her hand drop to the gear lever, Bland turned to flee.

"Bland, you come back here!" Bland came. "What do you mean, trying to avoid answering a perfectly civil question?"

"I did answer it," Bland protested in his whining tone. "I said I didn't know -"

"That's no answer; that's nothing but a plain old lie. You do know perfectly well where he is. You left Tucson with Johnny, and you left Yuma with him. Bland Halliday, what have you done with him?"

Bland's eyes turned slightly glassy. Like a trapped animal, he sent roving glances here and there - and took in the purposeful approach of the traffic cop. He turned again toward the curb.

"Don't you dare attempt to leave before -"

"What's the matter here? What you blocking traffic for? Don't you know I can -"

"Oh! Am I in the way here? I shall move immediately, of course. Thank you so much! It's really no trouble at all, and I'm tremendously sorry if I have inconvenienced you or the general public any. I believe you are really *glad*, down deep in your heart, when somebody gives you an excuse to leave that horrid little square spot for a minute. Don't you nearly go wild, having to - Bland! What are you standing there holding up traffic for? Get in!"

Looking completely dazed and helpless, Bland got in.

"Now we're all ready, Mr. Policeman. Run along back and point the herd again before all the nice little tame Fords get walked on. I hear one squalling now. And thank you so much."

Mary V let in the clutch. The Bear Cat slid out across the street, scattering pedestrians and jeopardizing wheels and fenders as it ducked past them. The traffic cop stood still for a minute, rubbing his chin vaguely and staring after Mary V. Then he went back to his post, grinning and frowning - which gave him a strange, complex expression.

"Aw, say, Miss Selmer -"

"Will you be quiet? Haven't you done harm enough, for gracious sake? Aren't you satisfied with getting me almost put in jail innocently? If you had told me at once where Johnny is, I'd be miles away by now. But no - you hold up traffic trying to deceive me, and I almost get pinched. I should think you'd be ashamed. Where is Johnny? If you have done anything to him, Bland Halliday, I'll - hang you!"

"I been telling yuh all I know about it. I don't know where he is, and I don't know where the plane is. They're both of 'em gone, and that's Gawd's truth, Miss Selmer. Last I seen of Johnny he was goin' in the Alexandria. He said he was going to stop there. He registered all right - I seen his name. He stayed all night, and he was gone the next day when I went after him. And the plane's gone, I been out there, and I can't find so much as a sign of it. And that was three weeks ago. And you kin hang me till I'm dead, but I can't tell nothin' more. Don't yuh spose I want to know where's he at?"

"Well -" Mary V crossed the path of a street car, leaving the motorman shivering while he stood on the bell that clamored wildly. "Maybe you are telling the truth - but I doubt it." They were across Figueroa Street and speeding out toward Westlake. The Bear Cat was breaking the speed law, and Mary V had no time to say more.

"Where you takin' me, f'r cat's sake?"

"Oh - for a ride. Don't you like to ride?" Mary V's voice was filled with amiability; too much so to satisfy Bland, who eyed her with suspicion.

"Aw, a fellow can't never git a square deal no more. Here I been hunting the town over trying to git some line on Skyrider. Went and left me in the lurch after me helping him to a roll of kale that would choke a nelephant! And I never charged him nothin' for flying, except just what we agreed on before he got throwed in jail. Handed him over close to five hundred dollars when he come out - piloted him here, took him into town, and was planning on helping him to make more money, and what does he do? Ducks into the Alexandria, leavin' me waitin' outside, hungry and thirsty and tired as a dog. Him with five hundred, me with seventy-five! And *he* wouldn't a knowed any different if I'd trimmed him! Who was to keep tabs on how many passengers I took up? And what does he do? Gives me the slip right there in the Alexandria, that's what he done. I ain't been able to locate him yet, but if ever I do -"

Mary V swung the Bear Cat out and passed a limousine as though it were standing still - which it emphatically was not. What if Bland were telling the truth? What if Johnny had actually dropped out of sight with five hundred dollars in his possession? That would mean - she refused to consider just what it would mean. She would wait until her dad had gotten the truth out of Bland Halliday. She was taking Bland home, hoping that her dad was there so that she would not be compelled to keep Bland any longer than was necessary. Bland was seedier than he had been in Tucson, if that were possible. Too evidently he had no part of the seventy-five dollars left, if he had ever possessed that much. Mary V would like to disbelieve everything he said, but a troubled doubt of his falsity assailed her.

She drove a little faster and presently brought Bland to the door of a cheerful, wide-porched bungalow patterned somewhat after the Rolling R home. Old Sudden was just pulling on his driving gloves ready to step into his own car when the Bear Cat slid up and stopped. He looked at Bland casually, looked again quickly, pursing his lips. Whereupon his poker face hid what he thought.

"Dad, come back into the house and talk to Bland Halliday. He told me the strangest story about Johnny, and - and I wish you'd just talk to him and see if it's true." Mary V was not altogether without consideration for the feelings of another, but candor was the keynote of her nature, and she was very much perturbed, and she did not really feel that a fellow like Bland Halliday had any feelings to consider.

Sudden smoothed a smile off his mouth. "Well, now, this is very thoughtful of you; very thoughtful. I appreciate your coming to consult me before you have settled the whole thing yourself. Come into the house, young man."

An hour later, Sudden leaned back in his chair and looked at Mary V. Tight-lipped, paler than she had any right to be, Mary V met the look wide-eyed. Bland moved his feet anxiously, watching them both.

"I played square with him," he whined. "Either he didn't, or else -"

Sudden's eyes turned to Bland and settled there meditatively. "Yes, I guess you did," he admitted. "Looks like you had played fair. Where are you stopping? I'll take you back down town. Need money?"

"Dad! Aren't you going to *do* anything? If Bland is telling the truth, don't you see what it means? Something must have happened -"

"Well, now, that will all be attended to, kitten. According to Bland, Johnny checked out before he disappeared. Also his airplane disappeared with him. That doesn't look like he'd been made away with, exactly. He's all right, probably - but we'll find out. I've a right to know what he did with that flying machine; it's security for that note of his!"

Mary V sprang to her feet and faced him. "Dad Selmer, I would never have believed a person on oath if they had said you could be so perfectly mean and mercenary! If that's all you care about, why take the Bear Cat and give me that note! Go on - take it! I guess Johnny has a right to do as he pleases until the note is due, at any rate. You might at least treat Johnny with ordinary business courtesy, I should think. You know perfectly well that you wouldn't dare hound your other creditors like that. But if you are really worried about that note, I shall deem it a pleasure and a privilege to pay it myself, and I'm sure the Bear Cat is good for the amount, or if you prefer you may hold back my allowance, and I shall go without clothes and everything until it is paid. It's a perfect outrage to keep nagging Johnny when he's doing his level best and not asking any help from you or any one else. I'm sure I honor and respect him all the more, and you would too if you had a drop of human blood - now what are you grinning for - and trying to hide it? Dad Selmer, you do make me perfectly furious at times!"

Mary V laid hands upon her father and for his shortcomings she "woolled" him until his grizzled hair stood straight on end. Sudden protested, tried to hold her off at arm's length and found her all claws, like an excited wildcat.

"Now, now -"

"Tell me then what you are going to do. And don't try to make me believe you only care for that horrid note.

Every time I think of you making that poor boy sign over everything he had on earth, except me, of course, and you wouldn't let him have me when he wanted - why, dad, I could shake you till -"

Bland was edging to the door. He had no experience with families and domestic upheavals, and he did not know just how serious this quarrel might prove. He expected Sudden to order Mary V from the house - to disown her, at the very least. He did not want to be a witness when Sudden broke loose. But Sudden called him back and turned to Mary V.

"Here, let me go. You're scaring off the only evidence we've got that Johnny landed here. You stay right here and behave yourself, young lady. I might want to 'phone you, if I get a clue -"

"Oh, dad! Cross your heart you'll 'phone the very instant you find out anything? Here's your hat - do, for gracious sake, hurry!"

B. M. Bower

CHAPTER TWENTY-ONE

JOHNNY IS NOT PAID TO THINK

On that same Saturday afternoon, at about the time when Mary V sighted Bland at the southeast corner of Sixth and Spring, Johnny stood just under the peak behind Mateo's cabin and saw a lone horseman ride across the upper neck of the little valley and disappear into the brush on the side opposite him. He waited impatiently. The rider did not reappear, but presently he saw what looked like a human figure crouched behind a rock well up the slope. Johnny stared until his eyes watered with the strain, but he could not be sure that the object was a man. If it were, the man was without a doubt placed there for purposes of observation. The thought was not a pleasant one.

He waited, himself crouched now behind a jutting fragment of rock, and thought he saw the object move. A little later the sun, sliding farther down the sky, reflected a glittering something just above that rock. A bit of glass would do that - the lenses of a field glass, for instance. Two lenses would shine as one, Johnny believed, and was thankful that his slope was in shadow.

Taking it for granted that some one was watching the valley, he studied the spot where the glitter had already winked out - possibly because the man had moved the field glasses, sweeping the valley. It was a good place for a spy, Johnny admitted. There was a slight ridge just there, so that the view was clear for some distance in either direction; Mateo's cabin was in plain sight, and the surrounding hills. He hoped the fellow would see nothing suspicious and would presently give up that post; in the meantime he was effectually treed. There was no shelter that he dared trust on the first rocky half of the descent, and to climb up and over the peak he would surely reveal himself, unless the fellow's attention happened to be centered on something else.

Johnny studied his predicament. The man could see everything - but could he hear? He was half a mile off, Johnny judged, estimating the distance with an accuracy born of long living in the country of far skylines. The spy would need sharp ears indeed to hear anything less than a shout.

Johnny picked up a pebble, aimed, and threw it at the roof of Mateo's cabin. The pebble landed true and rattled off, hitting the ground with a bounce and rolling away in the grass. The children, playing in the open as they always did, stopped and looked up inquiringly, then went on with their play. Mateo came cautiously from the back door and to him Johnny called, thankful that the observer on the hillside could not see through the cabin to where Mateo stood.

"Stay where you are," he called. "Can you hear me?"

Mateo nodded emphatically.

"All right. Take your gun and start off across the flat,

down the way Cliff will come. Act like you didn't want to be seen. There's somebody across on the hill, up here, and I want to see if he'll follow you. You get me?"

"Si, yes. I'm go."

"After awhile you can come back. If you see Cliff, tell him he's after ducks. Sabe?"

"Yo se. I'm onderstan'."

"All right. Go back in the house and come out the front door and start off."

Mateo waved his hand and disappeared. In five minutes or less Johnny saw him walking away from the cabin and glancing frequently at the hills upon either hand. His manner might have been called stealthy, if one were looking for stealth. Johnny was looking for something else, and presently he gave a grunt of satisfaction. The object behind the rock stood up and levelled his glasses at Mateo. Johnny waited until he was sure and then scrambled down to the protection of another bowlder. He peered from there up the valley and after some searching discovered his man working carefully along a side hill, evidently anxious to keep Mateo in sight. Johnny worked down another rod or two, reconnoitered again, made another sliding run for it, and stopped behind a clump of brush. In that way he reached the shelter of the oak, feeling certain that he had not been seen.

Through the screen of branches he looked out across the little valley, but he could not see any one at all, not even Mateo. So he turned to his one solace, The

Thunder Bird, and dusted it as carefully as a young girl dusts her new piano. With a handful of waste he went over the motor, wiping it until it shone wherever shining was possible, and tried not to think of the man on the hillside. That was Cliff's affair - until Johnny was ready to make the affair his.

"I wish I knew just what he's up to," Johnny fretted. "If I just *knew* something! I'd look like a boob now, wouldn't I, if the guards nabbed us? They might try to pin most anything on me, and I wouldn't have any comeback. It don't look good, if anybody asks me! And if they -"

"Man's come here," Rosa announced close behind him in a tense whisper. "Walking."

Johnny jumped and went on his toes to a spot where he could look through the foliage.

"Walking down," explained Rosa, and waved a skinny hand toward the hill behind them.

"Did you see him?"

"No, senor. I'm seeing rocks falling where somebody walks down."

There was nothing to do but wait. Johnny pushed the girl toward the cabin and saw her scramble under the lowest branches and join the others unconcernedly, tagging the boy Josef, and, then running off into the open - where she could see the hillside - with Josef running after. She did not seem to be watching the hill, while she was apparently absorbed in dodging Josef, but Johnny gathered from her gestures that the man was still coming and that he was making for the cabin. He was wondering what she meant by suddenly sinking to the ground in shrill laughter, when he heard a step behind him. He whirled, startled, his hand jerking back toward the gun he wore.

"I approve your watchfulness, but you happened to be watching in the wrong direction," said Cliff, brushing dirt from his hunting clothes. "Well, they are getting warm, old man. They have eliminated Riverside as a probable hang-out for the mystery plane, and -" He waved a hand significantly while he stood his shotgun against the bole of the tree.

"Some one saw us land in this valley," he added. "Luckily they do not suspect Mateo yet. I saw him going down the flat and sent him on to tell the patrol a lot they already knew. He saw the plane come down, but has not been able to find the exact spot. He thinks it took the air again. His ninos told him of a big bird flying east. Great boy, Mateo. Great kids. Did they see me coming?"

"Sure they did. Rosa's eagle eye spotted a rock or two rolling down and came and told me."

"Good girl, Rosa. The car's over in another valley, parked under a tree very neatly and permanently and in plain sight. Its owner is off hunting somewhere. By its number plates they will never know it. Good old car."

"You seem tickled to think they're after you," Johnny observed, rolling a cigarette by way of manifesting complete unconcern. "What's the next move?"

"Get me across without letting them see where we

come from. Can you fly at night?"

"Sure, I can fly at night. Don't the Germans fly at night all over London? I won't swear I'll light easy, though."

"There'll be a moon," said Cliff. "I've got to get over, and I've got to light, and I've got to get back again. There are no if's this time; it's *got* to be done."

"A plane chased us, day before yesterday," Johnny informed him, fanning the smoke from before his face and squinting one eye while he studied Cliff. "It was a long way off, and I got down before it was close enough to see just where I lit. It came back yesterday and scouted around, flying above five thousand feet up. To-day I saw two of them sailing around, but they didn't fly over this way. They were over behind this hill, and high. We'd better do our flying at night, old-timer."

"You can dodge them. You've got to dodge them," said Cliff.

"If I fly," Johnny qualified dryly.

"You've got to fly. You're in to your neck, old man - and there's a loop ready for that." Then, as though he had caught himself saying more than was prudent, he laughed and amended the statement. "Of course, I'm just kidding, but at that, it's important that you make this flight and as many more as you can get away with. There's something to be brought back to-night - legitimate news, understand, but of tremendous value to the Syndicate." He reached into his pocket and drew out an envelope such as Johnny had learned to associate with money.

"Here's two thousand dollars, old man. The boss knows the risk and added a couple of hundred for good measure, this week. When you land me over there tonight I'll give you this." He smiled disagreeably. "I think you'll fly, all right - for this."

"Sure, I'll fly - for that. I was kidding. For two thousand I'd fly to Berlin and bring back a lock of old Kaiser Bill's hair."

"That's the way to talk, old man! I knew you were game. I told the boss so, when he asked if we could count on you. I said you had nerve, no political prejudices, and - that you need the money."

"That's my number, I guess," Johnny admitted, grinning.

Cliff laughed again, which made three distinct impulses to laughter in one conversation. This was not like Cliff's usual conservatism. As Johnny had known him he laughed seldom, and then only at something disagreeable. He was keyed up for something; a great coup of some sort was in sight, Johnny guessed shrewdly, studying Cliff's face and the sparkle in his eyes. He was like a man who sees success quite suddenly where he has feared to look upon failure. Johnny wondered just what that success might mean - to others.

"I bet you're putting over something big that will tickle Uncle Sam purple," he hazarded, giving Cliff a round-eyed, admiring glance.

"It will tickle him - purple, all right!" Cliff's tone had a slight edge on it. "You're sitting in a big game, my boy, but you aren't paid to ask questions. You go ahead and earn your two thousand. You do the flying, and let some one else do the thinking."

"I get you," said Johnny laconically and took himself and his thinkless brain elsewhere.

B. M. Bower

CHAPTER TWENTY-TWO

JOHNNY MAKES UP HIS MIND

"No political prejudices - hunh!" Johnny was filling the gas tank, and while he did it he was doing a great deal of thinking which he was not paid to do. "This newspaper business - say, she's one great business, all right. It's nice to have a boss that jumps your wages up a couple of hundred at a lick, and tells you you needn't think, and you mustn't have any political prejudices. Fine job, all right. Will I fly by moon-light? Will I? And them government planes riding on my tail like they've been doing the last two trips? Hunh!"

Cliff came then with a bundle under his arm. Johnny cast a suspicious eye down at him, and Cliff held up the package.

"I want to take this along - rockets; to let them know we're coming. Then they'll have flares for us to land by."

"Been planning on some night-riding, hunh?"

"Naturally; I would plan for every contingency that could possibly arise."

"Hunh. That covers them planes that have been

line-riding over this way, too, I reckon." Johnny climbed down and prepared to pump a little more air into one tire.

"Possibly. Don't let those airplanes worry you, old man. They have to catch us, you know."

"No? I ain't worrying about 'em. The one that does the thinking on this job can do the worrying. I'm paid to fly." Johnny laughed sourly as he glanced up from where he squatted beside the wheel.

"Let it go at that. Are you about ready? It will be dark in another half hour - dark enough to fly, at least." Cliff was moving about restlessly in the gloom under the tree. For all his earlier exhilaration he seemed nervous, in haste to be done.

"You said moonlight," Johnny reminded him, putting away the pump.

"I know, but it's best to get out of here and over the line in the dark, I think. The moon will be up in less than an hour. Be ready to leave in half an hour - and don't start the motor until the very last minute. Mateo has not come back yet. If they are holding him -"

"I'm ready to go when you are. Let's run her out before it's plumb dark under here. She can't be seen in this light very far - and if a man comes close enough to see her, he'd get wise anyway. Uh course," he apologized quickly, "that's more thinking than I'm paid to do, but you got to let me think a little bit now and then, or I can't fly no two thousand dollars worth to-night."

"I meant thinking about my part in the game. All right,

I've got her right, on this side. Take up the tail and let's run her out."

In the open the children were running back and forth, playing tag and squealing over the hazards of the game. When the Thunder Bird rolled out with its outspread wings and its head high and haughty, they gave a final dash at one another and rushed off to get wheelbarrow and stick horses. They were well trained - shamefully well trained in the game of cheating.

Johnny looked at them glumly, with an aversion born of their uncanny obedience, their unchildlike shrewdness. Fine conspirators they would make later on, when they grew a few years older and more cunning!

"Head her into the wind so I can take the air right away quick," he ordered Cliff, and helped swing the Thunder Bird round.

Dusk was settling upon the very heels of a sunset that had no clouds to glorify and therefore dulled and darkened quickly into night, as is the way of sunsets in the southern rim of States.

Already the shadows were deep against the hill, and in the deepest stood the Thunder Bird, slim, delicately sturdy, every wire taut, every bit of aluminum in her motor clean and shining, a gracefully potent creature of the air. Across her back her name was lettered crudely, blatantly, with the blobbed period where Johnny had his first mental shock of Sudden's changed attitude toward him.

While he pulled on his leather helmet and tied the flaps under his chin, and buttoned his leather coat and pulled on his gloves, Johnny stood off and eyed the Thunder Bird with wistful affection. She was going into the night for the first time, going into danger, perhaps into annihilation. She might never fly again! He went up and laid a hand caressingly on her slanted propeller, just as he used to stroke the nose of his horse Sandy before a hard ride.

"Good old Thunder Bird! Good old Mile High! You've got your work cut out for yuh to-night, old girl. Go to it - eat it up."

He slid his hand down along the blade's edge and whispered, "It's you and me for it, old girl. You back my play like a good girl, and we'll give 'em hell!"

He stepped back, catching Cliff's eye as Cliff took a last puff at his cigarette before grinding it under his heel.

"Thought I saw a crack in the blade," Johnny gruffly explained his action. "It was the way the light struck. All right; turn her over, and we'll go."

He climbed in while Cliff went to the propeller. Never before had Johnny felt so keenly the profanation of Cliff's immaculate, gloved hands on his beloved Thunder Bird.

"Never mind, old girl. His time's short - or ours is," he muttered while he tested his controls. "All right - contact!" he called afterwards, and Cliff, with a mighty pull, set the propeller whirling and climbed hastily into his place.

The kiddies, grouped close to watch the Thunder Bird's

B. M. Bower

flight, blinked and turned their faces from the dust storm kicked up by the exhaust. The plane shook, ran forward faster and faster, lifted its little wheels off the ground and went whirring away toward the dark blur of the mountains that rimmed the southern edge of the valley.

Johnny circled twice, getting sufficient altitude to clear the hills, then flew straight for the border. In the dark Cliff would not know the difference between one thousand feet and five thousand, and Johnny wanted to save his gas. He even shut off his motor and glided down to one thousand before he had passed the line, and picked up again and held the Thunder Bird steady, regardless of the droning hum, that would shout its passing to those below.

"Isn't this rather low?" Cliff turned his head to shout.

Johnny did not read suspicion in his voice, but vague uneasiness lest the trip be brought to a sudden halt.

"It's all right. They can't do anything but listen to us go past. I've got to keep my landmarks."

Cliff leaned and peered below, evidently satisfied with the explanation. A minute later he was fussing with the flare he meant to set off for a signal, and Johnny was left free to handle the plane and do a little more of that thinking for which he was not paid.

The night sky was wonderful, a deep translucent purple studded with stars that seemed closer, more humanly intimate than when seen from earth even in the higher altitudes. The earth was shadowy, remote, with now a growing brightness as the moon slid up into sight.

Before its light touched the earth the Thunder Bird was bathed in its glow. Cliff's profile emerged clear-cut from the dusk as he gazed toward the east. Johnny, too, glanced that way, but he was not thinking then of the wonderful effect of the rising moon upon the drifting world below. He was wondering just why this trip to-night should be so important to Cliff.

It would not be the first time that Johnny had gone ahead with his eyes shut, but that is not saying he would not have preferred travelling with them open. His lips were set so stubbornly that the three tiny dimples appeared in his chin, - his stubborn-mule chin, Mary V had once called it, - and his eyes were big and round and solemn. Mary V seeing him then would surely have asked herself, "What, for gracious sake, is Johnny up to now?"

But Mary V was not present, and Cliff Lowell was fully absorbed in his own thoughts and purposes; wherefore Johnny's ominous expression went unnoticed.

In the moonlight the notched ridge showed clear, and toward it the Thunder Bird went booming steadily, as ducks fly south with the first storm wind of November. A twinkling light just under the notch showed that Cliff's allies were at home, whether they expected him or not. Johnny veered slightly, pointing the Thunder Bird's nose straight toward the light.

Cliff half turned, handing something back over his shoulder.

"Can you drop this for me, old man, when we are almost over the hacienda? The fuse is lighted, and I'm afraid I might heave it on to the wing and set us afire."

Johnny heard only about half of what Cliff was saying. but he understood what was wanted and took the bomb-like contraption and balanced it in his hand. Cliff had said rockets, but this thing was not like any rocket Johnny had ever seen. Some new aerial signal bomb, he guessed it, and thought how thoroughly up-to-date Cliff was in all his tools of trade.

He poised the thing on the edge of the cockpit, waited until they were rather close, and then gave it a toss overboard. For a few seconds nothing happened. Than, halfway to the ground a great blob of red light burst dazzlingly, lighting the adobe building with a crimson glow that floated gently earthward, suspended from its little parachute.

Cliff handed back another, and Johnny heaved it away from the plane. It flared white; the third one, dropped almost before the door of the main building, revealed three men standing there gazing upward, their faces weird in its bluish glare. Red, white and blue - a signal used sacrilegiously here, he thought.

Johnny circled widely and came back to find the landing place lighted by torches of some kind. He was not interested in details, and what they were he did not know or care. The landing was marked for him plainly, though he scarcely needed it with the moon riding now above the low rim of hills.

He came down gently, and Cliff, remembering to give Johnny his money, climbed out hurriedly to meet the florid gentleman who had never yet failed to appear when the Thunder Bird landed. Johnny did not know his name, for Cliff had never mentioned it. The two never talked together in his presence, but strolled away where even their voices would not reach him, or went inside the adobe house and stayed there until Cliff was ready to return. News gathering, as Johnny saw the news gathered, seemed to be mighty secret business, never to be mentioned save in a whisper.

The florid gentleman came strolling toward them through the moonlight, smoking a big, fat cigar whose aroma reminded Johnny of something disagreeable, like burning rubbish. Tonight the florid gentleman's stroll did not seem to match his face, which betrayed a suppressed excitement in spite of the fat cigar. He reached out, caught Cliff's arm, and turned back toward the house, forgetting all about his stroll as soon as he began to speak. He forgot something else, for Johnny distinctly heard a sentence or two not meant for his ears.

"I've put it through all right. I got them to sign with the understanding that they don't turn a hand till you bring the money. You can take -"

That was all, for even on that still night the florid gentleman's voice receded quickly to an unintelligible mumbling. They went inside, and the door closed. Johnny and the Thunder Bird were once more shut out from their conference.

Johnny spied a Mexican who was leaning against the wall of a smaller building, smoking and staring pensively across the moonlighted plain toward that portion of the United States where the Potreros hunched themselves up against the stars.

"Bring me some gas, you!" he called peremptorily.

The Mexican pulled his gaze away from the vista that had held him hypnotized and straightened his lank form reluctantly. From a bench near by he picked up a square kerosene can of the type made internationally popular by a certain oil trust, inspected it to see if the baling-wire handle would hold the weight of four gallons of gasoline, and sauntered to a shed under which a red-leaded iron drum lay on a low scaffold of poles. A brass faucet was screwed into the hole for a faucet. He turned it listlessly, watched the gasoline run in a sparkling stream the size of his finger, went off into a moon-dream until the oil can was threatening to run over, and then shut off the stream at its source. He picked up the can with the air of one whose mind is far distant, came like a sleepwalker to where Johnny waited, set the can down, and turned apathetically to retrace his steps to where he could lean again.

"That ain't all. Bring me a can of water as fast as you brought the gas. We may want to go back to-night."

"Si," sighed the Mexican and continued to drift away.

"Don't be in a hurry. Come and lift the can up to me."

The Mexican returned as slowly as he had departed, and picked up the can. Johnny dropped a half dollar into it, whereat the Mexican's eyes opened a trifle wider.

"What's the name of that red-faced friend of Cliff's?" Johnny asked, taking the can and beginning to pour gas into the Thunder Bird's tank.

"Quien sabe?" murmured the listless one.

Johnny paused, and another coin slipped tinkling into the can.

"What did you say?"

The Mexican hesitated. He would like very much to see that other coin. It had sounded heavy - almost as heavy as a dollar. He turned his head and looked attentively at the house.

"Quien sabe, senor." The senor he added for sake of the coin he had not seen. "Mucho name, Ah'm theenk."

"Think some more." Johnny poured the last of the gas and caused another clinking sound in the can. The Mexican's eyes were as wide open now as they would ever be, and he even called a faint smile to his countenance.

"Some-*times* - Sawb," he recollected, and reached for the can.

"Sawb - What y'mean, Sawb? That's no name for a man. You mean Schwab?"

"Si, senor - Sawb." He glanced again at the house distrustfully, as if he feared even his murmur might be overheard.

"All right. Get the water now."

"Si, senor." And he went for it at a trot, that he might the sooner investigate the source of those clinking sounds.

"Schwab! Uhm-hm - he looks it, all right." He stepped down to the ground, pulled a handful of silver from his pocket and eyed it speculatively, glancing now and then after the receding Mexican. "He'd tell a lot to get it all," he decided. "He'd tell so much he'd make up about four thirds of it. I guess those birds ain't taking greasers like him into their secrets, and he's spilled all he knows when he spilled the fellow's name. Four bits more will do him fine." Wealth, you will observe, was inclining Johnny toward parsimoniousness.

He got the water from the hopeful Mexican, gave him the half dollar and brief thanks, filled the radiator, and waited for Cliff. And in a very few minutes Cliff came out, walking as though he were in a hurry. The florid gentleman stood framed in the doorway, watching him as friendly hosts are wont to gaze after departing guests, out west where guests are few. Like a departing guest Cliff turned for a last word.

"I'll be back soon as possible," he called to the man Schwab. "A little after sunrise, probably. Better wait here for me."

Schwab nodded and waved his cigar, and Johnny grinned to himself while he straddled into his seat.

Cliff went straight to the propeller. "Take me to Los Angeles, old man. You can light where you did before; there won't be any bean vines in the way this time. I had the Japs clear off and level a strip for a landing. It's marked off with white flags, so you can easily see it in this moonlight. Luck's with us; I was afraid we might have to wait until morning, but this is fine. Several hours will be saved."

"I've got you," Johnny said - and he did not mean what Cliff thought he meant. "All ready? Contact!"

B. M. Bower

CHAPTER TWENTY-THREE

JOHNNY ACTS BOLDLY

Off to the right and flying high, two government planes circled slowly over the boundary line. Long before the Thunder Bird had put the map of Mexico behind her the two planes veered that way, their fishlike fuselages and the finned rudders gleaming like silver in the moonlight. Cliff, happening to glance that way, moved uneasily in his seat and cursed the moon he had so lately blessed.

"Better duck down somewhere; can't you dodge 'em?" he yelled back at Johnny, who was himself eyeing perturbedly the two swift scouts.

"You let me handle this. It's what I'm paid for," he yelled back, and banked the Thunder Bird sharply to the left. He had not yet crossed the border; until he did so those scouting machines dare not do more than keep him in view. But keeping him in view was absurdly simple in that cloudless sky, white-lighted by the moon.

To a person looking up from the earth, the situation would have appeared to be simple - a matter of three planes zooming homeward after a long practice flight. The five-pointed star in the black circle, painted on each wing Of the government planes, would probably have been invisible at that height, and the bold lettering of THE THUNDER BIRD indistinguishable also on the shadowed underside of the outlaw plane. To the government planes she was branded irrevocably as they looked down upon her from their superior height. There was no mistaking her, no hope whatever that the scouts might think her anything but the outlaw plane she was, flying in the face of international law, trafficking in treason, fair game if she once crossed the line.

On she went, boring through the night, heading straight for Tia Juana, which lies just south of the line. Just north of that invisible line her pursuers held doggedly to the course.

"Turn back," Cliff turned to shout to Johnny who was driving big-eyed, his lips pursed with the tense purpose that held him to his work. "Turn back and land at the rancho. We'll never make Los Angeles with those damned buzzards after us. I'll have to notify Sch - somebody."

"Send him a thought message, then."

"Turn back when I tell you!" Cliff twisted around as far as his safety belt would permit, that he might glare at Johnny. His tone was the long of stern authority.

"Can't be done! The Thunder Bird's took the bit in her teeth. I'm just riding' and whippin' down both sides!" Johnny laughed aloud, Cliff's tone releasing within him a sudden, reckless mood that gloried in the sport of the chase and forgot for a moment its grim meaning.

"Whoo-ee! Go to it, old girl! They gotta go some to put salt on *your* tail - whoo-ee!"

"Are you crazy, man? Those are government planes! They're probably armed. They'll get us wherever we cross the line - turn back, I tell you! You're under orders from me, and you'll fly where I tell you! This is no child's play, you fool. If they get me with what papers - it'll be a firing squad for you if they catch you - don't forget that! Damn you, don't you realize -"

"Sit down!" roared Johnny. "And shut up!"

"I won't shut up!" Cliff's eyes, as Johnny saw them facing the moon, looked rather wild. "You're working for me, and I order you to take me back to Schwab's. You better obey - it will go as hard with you as it will with me if those planes get in their work. Why, you fool, they -"

"What the heck do I care about them? I'm working for a bigger man than you are right now. Sit down!"

"Stop at Tia Juana then and let me out. But I warn you -"

"Shut up!"

"I will not! You'll do as I tell you, or I'll -"

"Now will you shut up?" Johnny swung his gun, a heavy, forty-four caliber Colt, of the type beloved of the West. Its barrel came down fairly on the top of Cliff's leathern helmet and all but cracked his skull. Cliff shut up suddenly and completely, sliding limply down into his seat.

"By gosh, you had it coming!" Johnny muttered as he settled back into his seat. He had never knocked a man cold before, and his natural soft-heartedness needed bracing. He had let Cliff rave as long as he dared, dreading the alternative. But now that it was done he felt a certain relief to have it over. He could turn his mind wholly to the accomplishment of another feat which would take all his nerve.

That other thing had looked simple enough in contemplation, but the actual doing of it presented complications. The simplicity of the plan vanished with the sighting of those two scouting planes that persisted in paralleling his course and herding him away from the line he fain would cross.

Tia Juana with its flat-roofed adobes lay ahead of him now, its lights twinkling like fallen stars. Away off to the right he could see the blurred lights of San Diego and the phosphorescent gleam of the bay and ocean beyond. Beautiful beyond words was the broad view he got, but its beauty could only vaguely impress him then, though he might later recall it wistfully.

He looked toward San Diego with longing; looked at the two planes that hounded him, then gazed straight ahead at the ocean. Perhaps they would not follow him beyond their station at North Island. They would maybe circle and come back, watching for his return, or they might keep to the shore line, flying north, and thinking to head him off when he turned inland. At least, he reasoned, that is what he would do if he were following an outlaw plane and saw it head out over the ocean, straight for Honolulu.

So over Tia Juana he flew and made for the sea like a

gull that has flown too far from its nesting place. He watched and saw the two planes spiraling upward, climbing to a higher altitude where it would be easy to dart down at him if he swung north. They suspected that trick, evidently, and were preparing to swoop and follow.

The beach, pale yellow in the moonlight, with a riffle of white at its edge, slid beneath him. The ocean, heaving gently, rolled under, the moon reflected from its depths.

Cliff sat slumped down in his seat, his head tilted upon one shoulder. He had not moved nor made a sound, and his limp silence began to worry Johnny. What if he had struck too hard, had killed the man? A little tremor went over him, a prickling of the scalp. Killing Cliff had no part in his plans, would be too horrid a mischance. He wished now that he had left him alone, had let him bluster and threaten. Perhaps Cliff would not have had presence of mind enough to do what Johnny had feared he would do when he saw capture was inevitable: drop overboard what papers he carried that would incriminate him with the United States Federal officers. With empty pockets Cliff would be as free of suspicion as Johnny himself - a mere passenger in a plane that had flown too far south. He would then be fairly safe in assuming that Johnny would never dare to cross the line with him under the eye of those who watched from the sky. It had been the fear of that ruse that had brought Johnny to the point of violence to Cliff's person, but he was sorry now that he had not risked taking that chance.

Flying has its inconveniences, after all, for Johnny could not stop to investigate the injury he had done to

Cliff. He would have to go on, now that he was started, but the thought that he might be flying with a dead man chilled what enthusiasm he had felt for the adventure.

On over the ocean he flew until he had passed the three-mile limit which he hazily believed would bar the planes of the government unless they had express orders to follow him out. Looking back, he saw that his hunters seemed content to wheel watchfully along the shore line, and presently he banked around and flew north.

From the Mexican line to San Diego is not far - a matter of twenty miles or so. Across the mouth of San Diego bay, on the inner shore of which sits the town, North Island stretches itself like a huge alligator lying with its back above water; a long, low, sandy expanse of barrenness that leaves only a narrow inlet between its westernmost tip and the long rocky finger of Point Loma.

Time was when North Island was given over to the gulls and long-billed pelicans, and San Diego valued it chiefly as a natural bulkhead that made the bay a placid harbor where the great combing rollers could not ride. But other birds came; great, roaring, man-made birds, that rose whirring from its barrenness and startled the gulls until they grew accustomed to the sight and sound of them. Low houses grew in orderly rows. More of the giant birds came. Nowadays the people of San Diego, looking out across the bay, will sometimes look again to make sure whether the sailing object they see is an airplane or only a gull. In time the gull will flap its wings; the airplane never does. All through the day the air is filled with them - gulls and airplanes sharing amicably the island and the air above it.

Up from the south, with her nose pointed determinedly northward and her rudder set steady as the tail of a frozen fish, the Thunder Bird came humming defiantly, flying swift under the moon. Over San Diego bay, watching through night-glasses the outlaw bird, the two scouting planes dipped steeply toward their nesting place on North Island. Three planes were up with students making practice flights and doing acrobatics by moonlight. These saw one scout go down and land, saw the other circle over the field and climb higher, bearing off toward the mainland to see what the outlaw plane would do.

The Thunder Bird swung on over the island, banked and came back over Point Loma, heading straight for the heart of the flying station. She was past the finlike reef where the pelicans foregather, when the search-light brushed its white light over that way, seeking her like a groping finger; found her and transfixed her sternly with its pitiless glare.

There was no hiding from that piercing gaze, no possibility of pretending that she was a government plane and flying lawfully there. For straight across her middle, from wing-tip to wing-tip, still blazoned THE THUNDER BIRD in letters as bold and black as Bland's brush and a quart of carriage paint could make them.

She volplaned, flattened out a thousand feet or so above the island, circled as the searchlight, losing her when she dipped, sought her again with wide sweeping gestures of its accusing white finger.

Blinded by the glare, poor Johnny was banking to find a landing place among that assemblage of tents, low-eaved barracks, hangars, shops - the city built for the purpose of teaching men how to conquer the air. Something spatted close beside him on the edge of the cockpit as he wheeled and left a ragged hole in the leather. Johnny's brain registered automatically the fact that he was being shot at. They probably meant that as a hint that he was to clear out or come down, one or the other. Well, if they'd take that darned searchlight out of his eyes so he could see, he would come down fast enough.

In desperation he slanted down steeply toward an open space, and the open space immediately showed a full border of lights, revealing itself a landing field such as he had read of and dreamed of but had never before seen. It shot up at him swiftly; too swiftly. He came down hard. There was a jolt, a bounce and another jolt that jarred the Thunder Bird from nose to tail.

After a dazed interval much briefer than it seemed, Johnny unstrapped himself and climbed out unsteadily. He looked fearfully at Cliff, but there was no sign of life there. Cliff's head had merely tilted from the right shoulder to the left shoulder, and rested there.

Uniformed young men came trotting up from all sides. Two carried rifles, and their browned faces wore a look of grim eagerness, like men looking forward to a fight. Johnny pushed up his goggles and stared around at them.

"Where's your captain or somebody that's in charge here? I want to see the foreman of this outfit, and I want to see him quick," he demanded, as the two armed young athletes hustled him between them. "Here, lay off that grabbing stuff! Where do you get that? I ain't figuring on any getaway. I'm merely bringing a man into camp that stacks up like a spy or something like that. Better have a doctor come and take a look at him; I had to land him on the bean with my six-gun, and he acts kinda like he's hurt. He ain't moved since."

"Well, will you listen to that!" One of the foremost of the unarmed group grinned. "This here must be Skyrider Jewel, boys, no mistake about that - he's running true to form. 'Nother elopement - only this time he's went and eloped with a spy, he claims."

"Here comes the leatherneck. You'll wish you hadn't of lit, Skyrider. You'll be shot at sunrise for this, sure!"

"You know it! It's a firing squad for yours, allrighty!"

Johnny gave them a round-eyed, disgusted glare. "They can shoot and be darned; but the boss has got to see Cliff Lowell and the papers he's got on him, if I have to wade through the whole hunch of you! Do you fellows think, for gosh sake, I just flew over here to give you guys a treat? Why, good golly! You -"

"Here, you come along with me and do your talking to the commandant," a gruff voice spoke at his shoulder.

"And let these gobblers fool around here and maybe lose the stuff this man's got in his clothes! Oh-h, no! Bring him along, and I'll go. I'd sure like a chance to talk to somebody that can show a few brains on this job. That's what I came over here for. I didn't have to land, recollect."

The petty officer gave an order or two. The guards fell in beside Johnny with a military preciseness that impressed him to silence. From somewhere near two men trotted up with a field stretcher, and upon it Cliff was laid, still unconscious.

"You sure beaned him right," one of them observed, looking up at Johnny with some admiration.

"Yes, and I'd like to bean the whole bunch of you the same way. You fellows ain't making any hit with me at all," Johnny retorted uncivilly as he left under guard for headquarters.

A few minutes later he was standing alone before a man whose clean-cut, military bearing, to say nothing of the insignia of rank on his uniform, awed Johnny to the point of calling him "sir" and of couching his replies in his best, most grammatical English. The guards had been curtly dismissed, for which he was grateful, and he had the satisfaction of stating his case in private. Johnny did not want those fellows out there to hear just how easily he had been fooled. They seemed to know altogether too much about him as it was.

The commandant listened attentively to what John Ivan Jewel had to say. John Ivan Jewel had nearly finished his story when he thought of another phase of the affair, and one that had begun to worry him considerably.

"I forgot to tell you about the money. I've got a good deal from them since I started. They paid me on a sliding scale, beginning with fifteen hundred dollars a week and ending with two thousand that Cliff paid me this evening. I've got it all with me."

Prom his secret pocket Johnny drew all his wealth, counted off four hundred dollars and handed the rest to his inquisitor.

"This four hundred dollars is my own, that I brought from Arizona," he explained, flushing a little under the keen eyes of Captain Riley. "This is honest money; the rest is what they paid me for flying back and forth across the line."

The commandant turned the big roll of bank notes over, looking at it quizzically.

"Who is really entitled to this money?" he asked Johnny crisply.

"Well, I - I don't know, sir. It's what they paid me for flying."

"And did you fly as agreed upon?"

"Yes, sir; I made trips back and forth whenever Cliff wanted me to. That is, up to the time I lit out for here, so you could see for yourself what he's up to. He ordered me to go back to Schwab's place, but I wouldn't. I - I knocked him on the head and came on. But until then I flew as agreed upon."

"Do you feel that you earned this money?"

"Well - taking everything into consideration - yes, sir, I do. I think now I worked for them much cheaper than any other aviator would have done.

"Yes. Well, you spoke of that four hundred being honest money, thus differentiating it from this money. Don't you consider this is honest money? What do you mean by honest?"

Johnny flushed unhappily. "Well, it's kinda hard to explain, but I guess I meant that I wasn't doing the right thing when I was earning that money you've got. I meant it wasn't clean money, the way I look at it now. Because it was crooks I was working for, and I don't know how they got it. I worked honestly for it, for them, but the work wasn't honest with the government. It's kinda hard -"

"I think I'll just give you a receipt for this. How much is it?"

"There ought to be about seventy-two hundred there, all told, sir."

Captain Riley looked at him queerly and proceeded to count the astounding wealth of John Ivan Jewel. Then he very matter-of-factly wrote a receipt, which Johnny accepted with humility, not at all sure of what the captain thought or intended.

"Now, tell me this. Is this young man - the one you brought in - is he the only one you know who has been concerned in this - er - business?

"Yes, sir, on this side he is. Cliff spoke about his boss several times, but he never told me who his boss was. An International News Syndicate, he claimed. But I know now that was just a stall. I don't think there was any such thing. There's a Mexican, Mateo, down where we kept the plane -"

B. M. Bower

"Mateo - yes, we have Mateo." Captain Riley sat drumming his fingers gently on the table, studying Johnny with his chin dropped a little so that he looked up under his eyebrows, which grew long, unruly hairs here and there.

Johnny's eyes rounded with surprise. He wanted to ask how they had come to suspect Mateo when they had seemed so unsuspicious, but he let it go.

"There's another one, named Schwab, over in Mexico where we always went," he divulged. "He's the one Cliff got those papers from - whatever they were. And he's the one that expects to get some money in the morning. I heard that much. I - I could get him, too," he added tentatively.

"Out of Mexico?" Captain Riley stirred slightly in the chair.

"Yes, sir. I'm pretty sure I could. I was planning to nab him, if you'd let me."

"You mean you could bring him - as you brought this man Lowell?"

Johnny's lips tightened. "If I had to - yes, sir. I'd knock him on the head same as I did Cliff. Only I wouldn't hit quite so hard next time."

Captain Riley bit his lip. "Better hit hard if you hit at all," he advised. "That's a very good rule to remember. It applies to a great many things."

Then he straightened his shoulders a bit and called his orderly, who again impressed Johnny with his military preciseness when he stood at attention and saluted. Captain Riley's whole manner seemed to stiffen to that military preciseness, though Johnny had thought him stiff enough before.

"Detain this man," he commanded crisply, "until further orders. If he is hungry, feed him; and see that he has a decent place to sleep. The petty officers' quarters will do."

He watched the perturbed John Ivan Jewel depart under guard, and his eyes were not half so stern as his tone had been. Then he reached for his desk 'phone and called up the repair shop.

"Run that Thunder Bird plane into the shop and repair it to-night," he commanded. "You will probably need to shift motors, but preserve the present appearance of the plane absolutely. It must be ready to fly at sunrise."

Then, being all alone where he could afford to be just a human being, he grinned to himself, "So-ome boy," he chuckled. "Hope he doesn't lose any sleep to-night. So-ome boy."

CHAPTER TWENTY-FOUR

THE THUNDER BIRD'S LAST
FLIGHT FOR JOHNNY

Over North Island the high, clear notes of the bugle sounding reveille woke Johnny. Immediately afterward a guard appeared to take him in charge, from which Johnny gathered that he was still being "detained." He did not want to be detained, and he did not feel that they had any right to detain him. He flopped over and pulled the blankets over his ears.

"Here, you get up. Captain wants you brought before him right after chow, and that's coming along soon as you can get into your pants. You better be steppin'."

"Aw, what's he want to see me for?" Johnny growled. It would be much pleasanter to go back to his dream of Mary V.

"Why, to shoot you, stupid. Whadda yuh think?"

"I'd hate to tell yuh right to your face, but at that I may force myself to it if you hang around long enough," Johnny retorted, getting into his clothes hurriedly, for the morning was chill and bleak. "Where's that chuck you was talking about? Say, good golly, but you're a sorry looking bird. I'm sure glad I ain't a soldier."

"Whadda yuh mean, glad? It takes a man to do man-size work. That's what I mean. Wait till about twelve of us stand before yuh waiting for the word! Lucky for you this sand makes soft digging, or you wouldn't have pep enough left to dig your own grave, see."

"You seem to know. Is yours dug already? They musta had you at it last night."

The guard grinned and suspended hostilities until after Johnny had eaten, when he led him out and across to where Johnny's inquisitor of the night before awaited his coming. Captain Riley was not so terrifying by daylight. For one thing, he betrayed the fact that he wore large, light-tan freckles, and Johnny never did feel much awe of freckles. Captain Riley also wore a smile, and he was smoking a cigar when Johnny went in.

"Good morning, Mr. Jewel. I hope you slept well."

"I guess I did - -I never stayed awake to see," Johnny told him quite boldly for a youth who had blushed and said "sir" to this man last night.

"You landed pretty hard last night, I hear."

"Why - yes, I guess I did. It looked to me around here last night as though I had fallen down bad."

"And what has made you so cheerful this morning?" Captain Riley actually grinned at Johnny. He could afford to, since Johnny was not in service and therefore need not be reminded constantly of the difference between officer and man.

"I dunno - unless maybe it's because the worst is done and can't be helped, so there's no use worrying about it."

"Well, I can't agree with you, young man. You may possibly do worse to-day. Last night, for instance, you brought in a man who has been very much wanted by the government. We did not know that he was the man until you landed with him, but certain papers he carried furnished what proof we needed. You spoke of another - a man named Schwab. Now I am not going to ask you to bring him in. He is in Mexico, and the laws of neutrality must be preserved. I shall have nothing whatever to do with the matter. I wish he were on this side, though. There's quite a good-sized reward offered for his arrest - in case he ever does get back on our side of the line."

"Mhm-hmh - I - see," said Johnny, in his best, round-eyed judicial manner.

"Yes. He's a criminal of several sorts, among them the crime of meddling with the government. He's over there now - where he can do the most harm.

"Y-ess - he's over there - *now*," Johnny agreed guardedly.

"However, I can't send you over after him, I am sorry to say. It is impossible. If ever he comes back, though -"

"He'd be welcome," Johnny finished with a grin.

"We'd never part with him again," the captain agreed cheerfully. "Well, that Thunder Bird plane of yours had quite a jolt, from the report. You cracked the crank-case for one thing, and broke the tail. I had the plane run in and repaired last night, so it's all ready now for you to go up. We really are much in your debt for bringing in this man Lowell; though your manner of doing it was rather unusual, I must admit. Are you - er - ready to fly?"

"Fly where?" Johnny nerved himself to ask, though he knew well enough where he intended to fly.

"Fly away from North Island," smiled Captain Riley, who was not to be caught. "Civilian planes are not permitted here."

"If I come back would I be shot at?"

"Oh, no - I think not, so long as you come peacefully."

"I'll come peacefully all right; what I'm wondering now is, will the other fellow?" Johnny looked toward the door suggestively.

Captain Riley laughed and rose to his feet. "Young man, you seem to know a sure way of making men peaceful! They tell me that Cliff Lowell came to himself about two o'clock this morning. For awhile they thought you had finished him."

"Well, it's time all good flyers were in the air; I'll go with you and see you start. I'm rather curious over that Thunder Bird of yours. I want a look at her."

In his youth and innocence - John Ivan Jewel wondered why it was that the soldiers looked astonished even while they saluted their commanding

B. M. Bower

officer. He did not know that he was being especially honored by Captain Riley, which is perhaps a good thing. It saved him a good deal of embarrassment and left him so much at ease that he could talk to the captain almost as freely as if he had not worn a uniform.

"Good-by - and good luck," said Captain Riley, and shook hands with Johnny. "I'll be glad to see you again - and, by the way, I'm just keeping that money until you call for it."

Johnny climbed in and settled himself, then leaned over the edge where the bullet had nicked so that his words would not carry to the man waiting to crank the motor.

"I'll call for that money in about two hours," he said. "I ain't saying good-by, Captain. I'll see yuh later."

Captain Riley stood smiling to himself while he watched the Thunder Bird take the air. That it took the air smoothly, spiraling upward as gracefully as any of his young flyers could do, did not escape him. Nor did the steadiness with which it finally swung away to the southeast.

"That boy's a born flyer," he observed to his favorite first lieutenant, who just happened to be standing near. "They say he never has had any training under an instructor. He just *flew*. He'll make good - a kid like that is bound to."

Up in the Thunder Bird Johnny was thinking quite different thoughts. "He thinks I won't be able to deliver the goods. He was nice and friendly, all right - good golly, he'd oughta be! He admitted right out plain that they wanted Cliff bad. But he's hanging on to my money so he'll have some hold over me if I don't bring in Schwab for him. And if I don't, and go back for my money, he'll - well, firing squad won't be any kidding, is what I mean.

"O-h-h, no! Captain Riley can't fool me! Wouldn't tell me to get Schwab over here - didn't dare tell me. But he makes it worth a whole lot to me to get him, just the same. He knows darn well if I don't I'll never dare to go back, and he'll be over seven thousand dollars better off." Johnny, you will observe, had quite forgotten that receipt in his pocket, which Captain Riley might find it hard to explain if he attempted to withhold the money.

His doubt of the Captain increased when, looking back, he spied two swift scouting planes scudding along a mile or two behind him. That they might be considered a guard of honor rather than spies sent out to see that he did not play false never occurred to him.

"Aw, you think maybe I won't do it!" he snorted angrily, his young vanity hurt. "All right, tag along and be darned. I'll have Schwab and be flying back again before you can bank around to fly hack and tattle where I went. That's what I mean. I ain't going to be done outa no seven thousand dollars; I'll tell the world I ain't."

Getting Schwab was absurdly simple, just as Johnny had felt sure it would be. He flew to where he would be expected to cross the line had he come from Los Angeles. Schwab would be impatient, anxious to get in his fingers the money Cliff was supposed to bring. He did not wait at the house, but came out to meet the

Thunder Bird. Johnny had been sure that he would do that very thing.

To keep the nose of the Thunder Bird toward Schwab so that he could not see that only one man returned with her was simple. Until he was close Schwab did not suspect that Cliff was not along. Even then he was not suspicious, but came hurrying up to know why Johnny came alone. Schwab wanted that money - they always do.

"Where's my man?" he demanded of Johnny, who had brought the landing gear against an old fence post used to block the wheels, and shut the motor off as much as he could and keep it running.

"Your man is sick." Which was true enough; Cliff was a very sick man that morning. "You'll have to come to him. Get in - it won't take long."

Schwab hung back a little, not from fear of Johnny but because he had no stomach for flying. "Well, but didn't he send -"

"He didn't send a darned thing but me. He wouldn't trust me to bring anything else. Get in. I'm in a hurry."

"What's the matter with him? He was all right last night." Still Schwab hung back. "I'll wait until he can come. I - I can't leave."

Then he found himself looking up into the barrel of Johnny's six-shooter. "I was told to bring you back with me. Get in, I said."

"This is some trick! I -"

"You get - *in*!"

So Schwab climbed in awkwardly, his face mottled and flabby with fear of the Thunder Bird.

"Fasten that strap around you - be sure it's fast. And put on this cap and goggles if you like. And sit still." Then he called to the languid Mexican who was idly watching him from afar. "Hey! Come and pull the block away from the wheels."

The Mexican came trotting, the silver of the night before clinking in his overalls pocket. Grinning hope-fully, he picked up the post and carried it to one side. But Johnny was not thinking then of tips. He let in the motor until the Thunder Bird went teetering around in a wide half circle and scudded down the level stretch, taking the air easily.

"This is an outrage!" Schwab shouted.

"Where are you taking me?"

"Oh, up in the air a ways," Johnny told him, but the roar of the motor so filled Schwab's unaccustomed ears that he could hear nothing else. And presently his mind became engrossed with something more immediately vital than was his destination.

They were getting too high up, he shouted. Johnny must come down at once - or if he would not do that, at least he must fly lower. Did Johnny mean to commit suicide?

For answer Johnny grinned and went higher, and the face of Schwab became not mottled but a sickly white.

B. M. Bower

He sat gripping the edges of the cockpit and gazing fearfully downward, save when he turned to implore, threaten, and command. He would report Johnny to his employers. He could make him sorry for this. He would make it worth his while to land. He would do great things for Johnny - he would make him rich.

From five thousand feet Johnny volplaned steeply to four thousand, and Schwab's sentences became disconnected phrases that ended mostly in exclamation points. So pleased was Johnny with the effect that he flew in scallops from there on - not unmindful of the two scouting planes that picked him up when he recrossed the line and dogged him from there on.

"I suppose," snorted Johnny to the Thunder Bird, "they think they're about the only real flyers in the air this morning. What? Can't you show 'em an Arizona sample of flying? What you loafing for? Think you're heading a funeral? Well, now, this is just about the proudest moment you've spent for quite some time. This man Schwab - he craves excitement. Can't you hear him holler for thrills? And don't you reckon that Captain Riley will be cocking an eye up at the sky about now, looking to see you come back. Come, come - shake a wing, here, and show 'em what you're good for!"

Whether the Thunder Bird heard and actually did shake a wing does not matter. Johnny remembered that he had yet some miles to fly, and proceeded to put those miles behind him in as straight a line as possible. Schwab's voice came back to him in snatches, though the words mostly foreign to Johnny's ears. Schwab seemed to be indulging in expletives of some sort.

"Don't worry, sauerkraut, we'll show you a good time soon as we get along a few miles. There's some birds behind us I'm leading home first."

"My God, don't go straight down again! It makes me sick," wailed Schwab.

"Does? Oh, glory! That ain't nothing when you get used to it, man. Be a regular guy and like it. I'll *make* you like it, by golly. Come on, now - here's San Diego - let's give 'em a treat, sauerkraut. You never knew you'd turn out to be a stunt flyer, hey? Well, now, how's this?"

"Whee-ee! See the town right down there? Head for it and keep a-goin', old girl! *Whee-ee*! Now, here it goes, sliding right up over our heads! Loop 'er, Thunder Bird, loop 'er! You're the little old plane from Arizona that's rode the thunder and made it growl it had enough! In Mexico I got yuh, and to Mexico you went and got me a regular jailbird that Uncle Sammy wants. You're takin' him to camp - whoo-ee! Give your tail a flop and over yuh go like a doggone tumbleweed in the wind!

"Come on, you little ole cop planes that thinks you're campin' on my trail! You'll have to ride and whip 'em, now I'm tellin' yuh, if you want to keep in sight of our dust! Sunfish for 'em, you doggone Thunder Bird! You're the flyin' bronk from Arizona, and it's your day to fly!"

With the first loop Schwab went sick, and after that he had no wish except to die. Whether the Thunder Bird rode head down or tail down he neither knew nor cared. Nor did Johnny. As he yelled he looped and he dived, he did tail spins and every other spin that occurred to him. For the time being he was "riding straight up and fanning her ears," and his aerial bronk was pulling off stunts he would never have attempted in cold blood.

He thought it a shame to have to stop, but North Island was there beneath him, a flock of planes were keeping out of his way and forgetting their own acrobatics while they watched him, and Johnny, with an eye on his gas gauge and his mind recurring to his parting words with Captain Riley, straightened out reluctantly and got his bearings. There was room enough for one more nose dive, and he took it exuberantly, trying to see how many turns he could make before he must quit or smash into a building or something.

There was the field, just ahead of him. He flattened, banked, and came down circumspectly enough, considering how his head was whirling when he finally came to a stand. He crawled out, looking first at Schwab to see what he was doing.

What Schwab was doing has no bearing whatever on this story. Schwab was not feeling well, wherefore he was not showing any interest whatever in his surroundings and probable future. John Ivan Jewel laughed unfeelingly while he beckoned a guard who was coming up at a trot and needed no beckoning.

"Here's another man for your boss to take charge of," Johnny announced. "And lead me to him right now. I've got a date with him."

This guard was a new guard and looked dubious. But presently the captain's orderly appeared and took charge of the situation, so Johnny straight-way found himself standing before Captain Riley "Well, I'm back," he announced cheerfully. "And I've got Schwab out there."

Captain Riley dismissed the orderly before he unbent enough to reply. But then he shook hands with John Ivan Jewel just as though he had not seen him a couple of hours before. He was a very pleased Captain Riley, as he showed by the broad grin he wore on his freckled Irish face.

"Schwab," he said, "will be taken care of. He's a deserter from the army, you know. Held a captaincy and disgraced the uniform in various ways, the crowning infamy being the sale of some important information, a year or so ago when things were at the touchiest point with Mexico. We nearly had him, but he deserted and got across the line, and since then he has been raising all kinds of cain in government affairs. Of course, his capture is a little out of my line, but I don't mind telling you that it's a big thing for me to have both these men turned over to me. I can't go into details, of course - you would not be especially interested in them if I could. But it's a big thing, and I want you to know -"

The telephone interrupted him, and he turned to answer it.

"Yes, yes, this is Captain Riley speaking. Yes, who is this, please? Who? Oh, yes! Yes, indeed, no trouble at all, I assure you. Yes, I will give the message - yes, certainly. I shall send him right over. At your command, believe me. Not at all - I am delighted, yes; just one moment. Would you like to talk with him

B. M. Bower

yourself? Just hold the line, please."

One should not accuse a man like Captain Riley of smirking, but his smile might have been mistaken for a smirk when he turned from the telephone. He straightened it out at once, however, so that he spoke with a mere twinkle to Johnny.

"Some one in San Diego," he said, "would like to speak with you. I judge it's important."

CHAPTER TWENTY-FIVE

OVER THE TELEPHONE

"Hello?" cried Johnny, wondering vaguely who could be calling him from San Diego. "Oh - who? Mary V! Why, good golly, where did you come from? . . . Oh, you did? . . . Say, that was some bronk-riding I did up there among the clouds - what? . . . Oh, yes, I just happened to feel that way."

In the U.S. Grant hotel Mary V was talking excitedly into the 'phone. "I don't know why I happened to drive down here, but I did, and I just got here in time to see you come flying over and then you did all those flip-flops - Johnny Jewel, do you mean to tell me *that's* the way you have been acting all the time?"

"Oh, no - I happened to have a fellow along that I wanted to give him a treat!"

"A *treat*! Do you call that a treat, for gracious sake? What are you doing over there? I want you to come over here just as quick as ever you can, Johnny. Bland is here; I brought him down with me because he's a very good mechanic and besides, he was very much worried and trying to find you, so I thought he could help, and he did. He saw the Thunder Bird come sailing overhead before I noticed it, for I was driving,

B. M. Bower

and a street car was hogging the crossing and trying to head me off, so I didn't happen to look up just then. And when I did - why, Johnny, I thought sure you were coming right down on top of us! Did you do that deliberately just to scare me, you bad boy? Now you come right over here just as quick as ever you can! I am sure I have been kept waiting long enough -"

"You have," Johnny agreed promptly. "I'm coming, Mary V, and when I get there you're going to marry me or I'll turn the town bottom side up. You get that, do you? Your dad ain't going to head us off this time, I've made good, and doggone him, I can pay that note and have enough left over to buy me an airplane, or you an automobile or both, by golly! And tell Bland I'll make it all right with him, too. I kinda left him in the lurch for awhile, but I couldn't help that. I've been thinking, Mary V, what I'll do. I'm going to give Bland the Thunder Bird. Doggone it, he's done a whole lot for me, and I guess he's got it coming. There's planes here that can fly circles around the old Thunder Bird, and I'm going to have one or break a leg. I'll . . . What's that? . . . Oh, all right, I'll come on and do my talking later. Being a government line, I guess maybe I'd better not hold this telephone all day. Sure, I'm crazy to see you! All right, all right, I'm coming right now!"

"With apologies for overhearing a private conversation," said Captain Riley, "speaking of getting a new plane, why don't you enlist as an aviator? I can use you very nicely and would like to have you here. How would a second lieutenancy strike you, Jewel? I can arrange it for you very easily - and let me tell you something: Before many months roll by it will be a matter of patriotism to serve your country. We shall be at war before long, unless I miss my guess. Better come in now. You - your being married will not interfere, I should think - seeing you intend to continue flying, anyway. I wonder, by the way, why I am not invited to be present at that wedding?"

"Well, good golly! You're invited right now, if you mean you'll go. Mary V will be one proud little girl, all right. And say, Captain, of course I'll have to talk it over with Mary V first, but that offer you just made me sure listens good. I tried to enlist - that's what I wanted all along - but I was turned down. But if you'll say a word for me -"

"Your Mary V is wanting," Captain Riley grinned. "And if I may judge from the brief conversation I had with her over the 'phone just now, we had better be on our way!"

B. M. Bower

Choose from Thousands of 1stWorldLibrary Classics By

Adolphus William Ward
Aesop
Agatha Christie
Alexander Aaronsohn
Alexander Kielland
Alexandre Dumas
Alfred Gatty
Alfred Ollivant
Alice Duer Miller
Alice Turner Curtis
Alice Dunbar
Ambrose Bierce
Amelia E. Barr
Andrew Lang
Andrew McFarland Davis
Anna Sewell
Annie Besant
Annie Hamilton Donnell
Annie Payson Call
Anton Chekhov
Arnold Bennett
Arthur Conan Doyle
Arthur Ransome
Atticus
B. M. Bower
Basil King
Bayard Taylor
Ben Macomber
Booth Tarkington
Bram Stoker
C. Collodi
C. E. Orr
C. M. Ingleby
Carolyn Wells
Catherine Parr Traill
Charles A. Eastman
Charles Dickens
Charles Dudley Warner
Charles Farrar Browne
Charles Ives
Charles Kingsley
Charles Lathrop Pack
Charles Whibley
Charles Willing Beale
Charlotte M. Braeme
Charlotte M.Yonge
Clair W. Hayes
Clarence Day Jr.
Clarence E. Mulford

Clemence Housman
Confucius
Cornelis DeWitt Wilcox
Cyril Burleigh
D. H. Lawrence
Daniel Defoe
David Garnett
Don Carlos Janes
Donald Keyhole
Dorothy Kilner
Dougan Clark
E. Nesbit
E.P.Roe
E. Phillips Oppenheim
Edgar Allan Poe
Edgar Rice Burroughs
Edith Wharton
Edward J. O'Biren
John Cournos
Edwin L. Arnold
Eleanor Atkins
Elizabeth Cleghorn
Gaskell
Elizabeth Von Arnim
Ellem Key
Emily Dickinson
Erasmus W. Jones
Ernie Howard Pie
Ethel Turner
Ethel Watts Mumford
Eugenie Foa
Eugene Wood
Evelyn Everett-Green
Everard Cotes
F. J. Cross
Federick Austin Ogg
Ferdinand Ossendowski
Francis Bacon
Francis Darwin
Frances Hodgson Burnett
Frank Gee Patchin
Frank Harris
Frank Jewett Mather
Frank L. Packard
Frederick Trevor Hill
Frederick Winslow Taylor
Friedrich Kerst
Friedrich Nietzsche
Fyodor Dostoyevsky

Gabrielle E. Jackson
Garrett P. Serviss
Gaston Leroux
George Ade
Geroge Bernard Shaw
George Ebers
George Eliot
George MacDonald
George Orwell
George Tucker
George W. Cable
George Wharton James
Gertrude Atherton
Grace E. King
Grant Allen
Guillermo A. Sherwell
Gulielma Zollinger
Gustav Flaubert
H. A. Cody
H. B. Irving
H. G. Wells
H. H. Munro
H. Irving Hancock
H. Rider Haggard
H. W. C. Davis
Hamilton Wright Mabie
Hans Christian Andersen
Harold Avery
Harold McGrath
Harriet Beecher Stowe
Harry Houidini
Helent Hunt Jackson
Helen Nicolay
Hendy David Thoreau
Henrik Ibsen
Henry Adams
Henry Ford
Henry Frost
Henry James
Henry Jones Ford
Henry Seton Merriman
Henry Wadsworth
Longfellow
Henry W Longfellow
Herbert A. Giles
Herbert N. Casson
Herman Hesse
Homer
Honore De Balzac

Horace Walpole
Horatio Alger, Jr.
Howard Pyle
Howard R. Garis
Hugh Lofting
Hugh Walpole
Humphry Ward
Ian Maclaren
Israel Abrahams
J.G.Austin
J. Henri Fabre
J. M. Barrie
J. Macdonald Oxley
J. S. Knowles
J. Storer Clouston
Jack London
Jacob Abbott
James Allen
James Lane Allen
James Andrews
James Baldwin
James DeMille
James Joyce
James Oliver Curwood
James Oppenheim
James Otis
Jane Austen
Jens Peter Jacobsen
Jerome K. Jerome
John Burroughs
John F. Kennedy
John Gay
John Glasworthy
John Habberton
John Joy Bell
John Milton
John Philip Sousa
Jonathan Swift
Joseph Carey
Joseph Conrad
Joseph Jacobs
Julian Hawthrone
Julies Vernes
Justin Huntly McCarthy
Kakuzo Okakura
Kenneth Grahame
Kate Langley Bosher
L. A. Abbot
L. T. Meade
L. Frank Baum
Laura Lee Hope

Laurence Housman
Leo Tolstoy
Leonid Andreyev
Lewis Carroll
Lilian Bell
Lloyd Osbourne
Louis Tracy
Louisa May Alcott
Lucy Fitch Perkins
Lucy Maud Montgomery
Lydia Miller Middleton
Lyndon Orr
M. H. Adams
Margaret E. Sangster
Margaret Vandercook
Maria Edgeworth
Maria Thompson Daviess
Mariano Azuela
Marion Polk Angellotti
Mark Overton
Mark Twain
Mary Austin
Mary Cole
Mary Rowlandson
Mary Wollstonecraft
Shelley
Max Beerbohm
Myra Kelly
Nathaniel Hawthrone
O. F. Walton
Oscar Wilde
Owen Johnson
P.G.Wodehouse
Paul and Mable Thorn
Paul G. Tomlinson
Paul Severing
Peter B. Kyne
Plato
R. Derby Holmes
R. L. Stevenson
Rabindranath Tagore
Rahul Alvares
Ralph Waldo Emmerson
Rene Descartes
Rex E. Beach
Richard Harding Davis
Richard Jefferies
Robert Barr
Robert Frost
Robert Gordon Anderson
Robert L. Drake

Robert Lansing
Robert Michael Ballantyne
Robert W. Chambers
Rosa Nouchette Carey
Ross Kay
Rudyard Kipling
Samuel B. Allison
Samuel Hopkins Adams
Sarah Bernhardt
Selma Lagerlof
Sherwood Anderson
Sigmund Freud
Standish O'Grady
Stanley Weyman
Stella Benson
Stephen Crane
Stewart Edward White
Stijn Streuvels
Swami Abhedananda
Swami Parmananda
T. S. Ackland
The Princess Der Ling
Thomas A. Janvier
Thomas A Kempis
Thomas Anderton
Thomas Bailey Aldrich
Thomas Bulfinch
Thomas De Quincey
Thomas H. Huxley
Thomas Hardy
Thomas More
Thornton W. Burgess
U. S. Grant
Valentine Williams
Victor Appleton
Virginia Woolf
Walter Scott
Washington Irving
Wilbur Lawton
Wilkie Collins
Willa Cather
Willard F. Baker
William Makepeace
Thackeray
William W. Walter
Winston Churchill
Yei Theodora Ozaki
Young E. Allison
Zane Grey

www.ingramcontent.com/pod-product-compliance
Lightning Source LLC
Chambersburg PA
CBHW030122180626
46812CB00002B/525